T0278883

Praise for

How to Get Over Your (Best Friend's) Ex

———————

"Relatable and captivating in all the best ways, *How to Get Over Your (Best Friend's) Ex* is a brilliant coming of age story that explores the complexities of love, friendship, and how to be true to yourself."

—Jessica Cunsolo, author of *She's With Me*

"*How to Get Over Your (Best Friend's) Ex* by Kristi McManus is a funny & heartwarming story that will take you on a rollercoaster ride through the turmoils of high school friendships & off-limits relationships. I would highly recommend!"

—Rachel Meinke, author of *Along for the Ride*

"Perfect for fans of *Mean Girls* and Jenny Han, *How to Get Over Your (Best Friend's) Ex* is a candid and dynamic story of friendship, heartbreak, and being true to yourself. Hannah is relatable and angsty in all the best ways!"

—Hailey Alcaraz, author of *Up in Flames*

HOW TO GET OVER YOUR (BEST FRIEND'S) EX

HOW TO GET OVER YOUR (BEST FRIEND'S) EX

KRISTI McMANUS

CamCat
Books

CamCat Publishing, LLC
Fort Collins, Colorado 80524
camcatpublishing.com

Hardcover ISBN 9780744308570
Paperback ISBN 9780744308587
Large-Print Paperback ISBN 9780744308792
eBook ISBN 9780744308785
Audiobook ISBN 9780744309447

Library of Congress Control Number: 2023948095

Cover and book design by Daniel Cantada
Illustrations by iStock™ Credit: Yugoro

5   3   1   2   4

FOR ALICE

THE RULES

Learn the rules so you know how to break them.

CHAPTER ONE

The honk of a horn alerted me to her arrival long before my mom called up the stairs.

"Brae's here!"

I rolled my eyes, frantically shoving the last of my items into my backpack. "I heard her horn, Mom!"

"No need for attitude, Hannah," she called back, her "mother tone" heavy in her voice.

My only response was another eye roll as I bounded down the stairs and into the kitchen, heading straight for the bowl of fruit on the island. My mothers were buzzing around the kitchen, muttering to each other about who would be late for dinner and who would be responding to the wedding invitation still taped to the fridge. It was all so typical Middle America minus the whole "dad" thing.

Turning to me, my mom lifted her eyes from her phone. "Hannah, I have to stay late at school on Thursday. I've opened extended office hours, which means I can't take your nana to her seniors meeting. Can you take her? I'll be able to pick her up after work."

I silently cringed as my mind traced over my calendar, already knowing what this arrangement would force me to miss. Thursday evening was prep sessions with my calculus study group to review before our next test. My stomach roiled at the idea of missing it. Calculus was my worst subject, and I relied on those study sessions to keep my head above water. But bailing on my nana and forcing her to sit in her apartment to watch *Wheel of Fortune* instead of going to her club meeting was out of the question. The guilt that simmered in my core burned away any residual inclination to say no. I would just have to make up the study time another way.

"Sure, no problem," I replied, tapping the change into my phone hurriedly.

Another honk of Brae's horn sounded, her impatience ringing through.

Plucking a banana from the fruit bowl, I spun on my heels and headed for the door.

"You need more than that for breakfast!" Mom called.

"I'll get something at school. I'm already late!"

I didn't wait for a response before I was out the door and down the steps toward Brae's little, white Jetta. The cool air jolted my senses, Tennessee caught in the clutches of spring as the chill of winter slowly loosened its grip. Sliding into the passenger seat, I threw my bag into the back, launching into apologies before I was even fully seated.

"Sorry, sorry," I said quickly. "I slept in."

"As usual," she teased, raising a perfectly arched brow. A knowing smirk decorated her lips before she reached out her fist. Returning the smile, I met it with my own. We linked our pinkies together and shook our joined hands three times. It had been our official greeting since middle school, made up one afternoon on the playground, and somehow stuck long after things like secret handshakes were considered cool.

"Just shut up and drive." I laughed as I released her hand, leaning my head against the back of the seat. Taking a deep breath, I glanced at her in all her perfect high school queen glory.

She chattered as we pulled out onto the street, the gentle breeze from the open window playing with her blond hair. Perfect beach waves cascaded in a way that made the style look effortless, and instinctively, I began to pull my dark hair through my fingers. I could never pull off Brae's effortless beauty, even though I knew the amount of work it actually took to look as she did. Contouring and sprays and flat irons, all to look like you just rolled out of bed. Whereas I really *had* just rolled out of bed. Granted, she was the first to remind me that the grass wasn't always greener, always telling me she wished she had my pale gray eyes because they were "unique." But in overall comparison to her, I had accepted my aesthetic fate in the "cute girl next door" category long ago.

"So how did the calculus homework go?" Brae asked, glancing at me from the corner of her eye. Her well-manicured fingers stayed wrapped around the steering wheel, easily gliding us through the familiar streets. The momentary ease that descended in her presence evaporated at the mention of calculus.

"About as well as can be expected," I said, turning my head back to stare out the window sullenly. "Pretty sure I got every question wrong, but at least I finished it."

Brae sighed at my self-deprecation. "You're too hard on yourself. Quit putting yourself down or I'm kicking you out of the car and making you walk."

I pursed my lips before the corners of my mouth twitched into a grin. I could always count on Brae to find the sliver of positive in my mathematical wallowing. She may have been right, but that didn't change the fact that I hated every moment of that class, forced into academic purgatory by my moms in the belief that it would look good on my college applications.

"Yeah, well, I'll probably bomb the next test, too, since I have to miss the study session on Thursday to take my nana to her seniors club."

Brae's face scrunched in distaste. "Why would you miss a study session? Hannah, those sessions are keeping you from drowning in a sea of 'numerical dismay.'"

"My mom can't take her anymore, and I didn't want to say no. It's just one session," I explained dismissively, avoiding her judgmental gaze.

"If this was for anyone other than Nana, I would remind you that you need to learn to say 'no' more," she said firmly before pausing.

I turned to give her a glare. "I do say 'no.' Sometimes."

As expected, this earned me a scoff. "No, you don't. You hate letting people down, even if it means putting yourself second. I mean, you took two extra shifts at Alley Scoops last week for that flake Jennie even though she didn't give you a reason. You're too nice sometimes, Hannah."

"I could say 'no' to stuff if I wanted to," I replied with false assertiveness.

"Prove it," she challenged with a smirk.

"Not now," I replied. "It'll be a sneaky ninja attack you never saw coming."

"Sure, sure," she laughed with a shake of her head. "Never saw coming because it's literally never going to happen."

It didn't take long for us to reach the school. Teenage voices riding on the breeze as I waited for the metamorphoses that overtook Braelyn every morning. The moment we were out of the car, her smile was in place, waving at people as they called her name like a swarm of paparazzi and adoring fans. Slipping through the front doors, Brae turned on her "social butterfly"'persona like she was emerging from a cocoon, colorful, brilliant wings spread for all to admire. All eyes turned to her instinctively, and she knew it. She relished her popularity, treating it like a living being that needed constant attention and maintenance.

It was like we were under a spotlight, but the attention wasn't on me. I wasn't the one that people noticed, the one whose name everyone knew. I was *that* girl's best friend; the quiet reclusive bookworm to Brae's glamorous and captivating center of the universe. As opposite as two people could be, and yet neither of us doubted we had found our soul mate in each other at the age of six.

As we turned a corner, a sophomore girl almost collided with us, knocking Brae's phone and notebook to the ground. The girl stumbled back, eyes wide in fear when she realized exactly who she had run in to, before stooping down to collect Brae's fallen items.

"I'm so, so sorry," she stammered, passing the items back to Brae with trembling hands. The girl's dark eyes were alight with fascination and a hint of caution. Students of East River High knew crossing Braelyn Walker could mean social suicide and went to great lengths to avoid finding themselves on her bad side.

Brae always said popularity was about finding a balance and making sure people understood it. That she could be their best ally or biggest threat—which depended on them. But I suspected that distinction was determined by Brae and her whims.

Brae's smile appeared genuine, but I knew better. "No problem, things happen," she said, her blue eyes roaming over the girl's clothing of a fitted vest top and pleated shirt. "Cute outfit."

The girl's mouth fell slack in surprise at the compliment, a pink tinge of happiness coloring her cheeks. "Thank you!"

Her smile widening, Brae waved before steering me around the girl and out of earshot. Leaning closer to me, she whispered, "Ugliest outfit ever."

I sighed, shaking my head. "I thought the top was cute."

She gasped, appalled. "If I ever catch you wearing something like that, I'll disown you."

Stepping up to our side-by-side lockers, we settled in for another school day. Michelle and Erin were already waiting, books in hand, leaning against the neighboring lockers like sentries awaiting their queen. Immediately my eyes fell to Erin's socks . . . rainbow frogs today. They had decided that their new look for junior year would include eccentric sock choices, and it had become habit that each morning I assessed their choice. Catching my look, they lifted the leg of their pants to show them off.

"Going for bright and playful today." They smiled, their short, blond pixie cut styled into gentle spikes.

Michelle snorted, a grin toying with her lips. Bright purple eye shadow swept across her lids, shimmering lightly despite the awful florescent lighting of the school. The cool tone against the warm brown of her skin made her dark eyes pop. "As opposed to grim and threatening like yesterday's skulls?"

Erin narrowed their eyes. "They had bows on their heads . . . still playful."

As they began to chat, I immediately started thinking of all the things I would have to rearrange around taking my nana to her meeting. I was so wrapped up in my thoughts, I didn't sense the figure slide up behind me until strong hands tickled at my waist. I shrieked, jumping away from his grip, earning myself a deep laugh for my reaction. It was clearly the one he wanted, as he beamed down at me before joining Brae's side.

"Morning," Seth said, the corners of his eyes crinkling in a playful and stomach-flipping way before pushing his dark hair back from his forehead in a casual gesture. Even in his black T-shirt and jeans, he looked like he had stepped off the cover of one of those stupid romance novels my moms liked to read, and for once, I didn't snort at the ridiculousness of the idea of someone being this attractive in real life. Tall, dark, and handsome are all painfully stereotypical adjectives, but they all describe Seth Linwood to perfection.

"Quit doing that!" I scolded, the flush of embarrassment coloring my cheeks.

He leaned against the locker beside Brae, gaze still on me, teasing.

"But it's my favorite form of entertainment," he stated matter-of-factly before turning his attention to Brae.

"Hi!" Brae chimed, hopping up on her toes to kiss his lips. The moment she pulled away, his gaze returned to me, my breath knocking from my lungs like it did any time he looked my way. I grinned before looking away, hiding within the confines of my locker, walking my tightrope of politeness so I didn't plummet into the depths of romantic longing and despair.

As Brae launched into a tale of the latest gossip, I foolishly allowed myself to steal a glance in Seth's direction like the masochist I was. His eyes were turned to her, a soft, placating smile on his lips.

That smile was what first captivated me when Seth Linwood entered my life in a flurry of black hair and green eyes, knocking the wind right out of me. Literally, since he knocked me to the floor the first time we met. Colliding into my back as I stopped to pick up the notebook I had dropped, he sent me sprawling onto the floor like hallway roadkill. When I sat up, with every intention to cuss the person out and tell them to watch where they were going, all sass and indignation died off on my lips. The horrible school lighting seemed to glow from behind him like a beam straight from the heavens, his silhouette all sharp jawline and broad shoulders, and I swore I could hear angels beginning to sing in the distance. He reached down and plucked me off the tiles with ease, muttering endless apologies for not paying attention, stammering that he was new to school and was a little distracted. I meekly accepted his apology, captivated by the angles of his face, before escaping to my desk in embarrassment.

The mortification only intensified when he took the seat right next to me, throwing me another megawatt smile just as Mr. Hayes brought the class to order. I spent the next hour stealing glances at him shamelessly, my face flaming every time he would catch me staring. When Mr. Hayes partnered us together for an English assignment on *Wuthering Heights*, I was equal parts thrilled and horrified.

I had hoped, albeit foolishly, that Seth was a depthless hot guy. The type of guy that made you swoon but was as shallow as a puddle. Unfortunately for me, the more I got to know him during that fateful English class, I came to find he was the opposite. He was smart and insightful. Funny and kind.

I relished our time together; the stolen hours in the library, passing notes during class. We would spend hours on the phone at night, squabbling over the merits of hardheaded heroines and their kindred heroes. More than once, he showed up at Alley Scoops, the ice cream parlor where I work, and would lean on the counter and chat as if time had no meaning.

Once, when we were discussing the less than redeeming qualities of Heathcliff and Catherine's relationship, he asked what qualities would endear a hero to me. The question threw me, a wave of nervousness cascading over me while he stared. I brushed him off, spouting out a dismissive comparison to Catherine's toxic tendencies in partners, swearing a lifelong vow of spinsterhood. But that night, I let myself fantasize that he was asking not out of humor or bickering, but out of genuine interest in *me*.

That was when I realized I liked him. I liked him dangerously, because it was clear from that first classroom collision that he was way out of my league. And guys like him didn't date girls like me.

Guys like him dated girls like Braelyn.

When they first crossed paths a few weeks later as Seth and I walked down the hall, I should have known it was inevitable. As she turned on the charm with a confidence that I could never pull off, asking him question after question like a flirtatious form of the Spanish Inquisition, I fell all too easily into the role of quiet sidekick.

That night on the phone, she grilled me for information on him. Was he seeing anyone? What was he like? Why hadn't I told her about him? I answered with monotone despondence, praying her interest would wane.

"Would it be okay if I asked him out?" Her words slammed against me, rattling around in my skull as my stomach dropped to my feet. A voice in the back of my mind began screaming, my stomach twisting as I silently shook my head yes.

I shouldn't have been surprised that she was interested in him. If anything, I should have expected it the moment they met, confirmed the second she started asking me every little detail I knew about him. And yet, her question surprised me, terrified me, frustrated me.

I wanted to tell her yes, that I *did* mind. That I liked him; liked him so much, *too* much, and for the first time in my life, I was going to fight for what I wanted.

But I didn't say that. Because it didn't matter what I wanted. Not when there was no way my feelings would be reciprocated. Not when it meant that doing so would require me to put my heart on the line and risk rejection. So instead, my heart cracked as I choked out the words.

"Yeah. That's fine."

Seth found me the next day, telling me Brae had asked him out. I put on my best mask of excitement, one I had perfected over years of being the sidekick to the most popular girl in school.

"Are you okay with that?" he asked, his dark hair falling into his eyes in a way that made my stomach flip.

My throat ran dry, scorched as the Sahara, but I forced a smile. "Of course!" I squeaked, a little too high pitched to be natural. "Why wouldn't I be?"

Silence descended, each of us staring as if trying to read the other's mind. After a beat, he grinned and nodded. "Okay. Good. I mean, I wouldn't want to make things awkward for you."

I shook my head a little too fast. "Nope, all good. You have my blessing."

He smiled again, offering me thanks before heading down the hall. The moment he disappeared, my heart sank.

Plucking my biology book from the shelf, I silently chastised myself for longing after someone so unattainable even after all these months. But he was my guilty pleasure that I just couldn't seem to give up.

The warning bell for first period trilled through the hall, breaking me from my shameless gawking. Closing the door to my locker, I watched as Brae scrambled to collect her things in the few meager moments we had left.

"Babe, are we still on for the movies on Friday?" she asked, fiddling with the books in a disorganized fashion.

"Yeah, we're good. I just have to help my dad move a couch for my aunt, but I'll pick you up right after."

"Okay, well, just please don't be late," she whined gently. "We're meeting up with Matt and Sarah, and Chase might meet us later at The Diner."

"I won't be late," he said firmly, his charming smile still in place to soften the bite before sighing. "Do we have to meet up with everyone? I mean, we could always spend time just you and me."

Brae's lips pulled down into a pout, looking to Seth. "But we already have the plans, and you like Matt."

Seth shrugged in a noncommittal fashion before letting the topic slide. Of course Brae was oblivious to his gentle irritation as she closed her locker and slipped her arm through his. Turning to me, she tilted her head as if only then remembering my presence.

"Do you wanna come with us?" she asked, her face taking on a pitying expression. "We're seeing that new movie you wanted to see."

"No, that's okay."

"You should come! Seth, you don't mind, do you?" she asked, looking up to him with her big blue eyes. "It would be like a threesome." She laughed innocently with a suggestive raise of her eyebrow.

"Get a room," Erin muttered, rolling their eyes playfully at Brae's display.

My stomach clenched as my eyes flickered to Seth, who was thankfully smiling down at her and oblivious to my embarrassment at my best friend's lack of filter.

"Yeah, that's fine—" Seth started before I cut him off.

"No, seriously, it's okay," I said, hugging my books to my chest. "You guys go have fun."

Brae sighed, her full lips pouting. "We really need to get you a guy," she said, clinging on to Seth. "Then we could double date, and you could have someone to hang out with like we do. It would be great!" Her eyes widened as her excitement rose. "Oh my God, we should totally set you up!" Turning to Seth, she bounced on her toes. "Babe, who do we know that we can set Hannah up with?"

Michelle scoffed gently. "Yeah, because the dating pool at East River High is full of solid options?" Glancing to Seth, she waved a hand toward him. "Present company excluded, of course."

Seth turned his concerned eyes to me, assessing my reaction quietly. I was pretty sure my wide eyes, flushed cheeks, and overall sense of mortification spoke volumes.

"I'm sure Hannah is perfectly capable of finding her own dates, Brae," he finally responded after accurately determining my humiliation.

"Oh, come on," she whined. "If that were true, she would have someone by now."

Her words prickled like a bee sting, but my features remained unaffected.

"Okay, well," I called, giving them a dismissive wave as I broke myself away from the little net of tragic singledom that Brae had thrown over me. "I'm going to take my single, dateless ass to class."

"Aw, Hannah, that's not what I meant," Brae sighed, finally clueing in. "Don't be mad—"

"I'm not mad," I said, throwing her a smile. "I just don't want to be late again."

Reaching up onto her toes, she placed a quick kiss on Seth's lips before turning to me with a regretful pout. "Well, I'm still sorry."

"And it's still fine," I assured her, plastering on a reassuring smile just as Seth stepped up to my side like he did every morning. And just like every morning, a little thrill of excitement sang in my system in his proximity.

"Ready for English?" he asked, tucking his books under his arm as he looked down at me with a heart-stalling smile. Again, a flush of embarrassment crept up the back of my neck as I remembered where my thoughts had taken me only moments before, rendering my voice mute.

Reaching his arm out in a gentlemanly gesture, he guided me down the hall toward our first period English class. As if fate hadn't dealt me enough of a tragic hand last semester, it had somehow brought Seth and I back together in English yet again. Only this time, the stakes were even higher: paired up together the first week to rewrite a classic into a modern-day novella, which would be worth thirty percent of our final grade and due at the end of the semester. The ill-fated love of *Romeo and Juliet* took on a whole new meaning as we deconstructed it side by side.

The moment we were away from my friends, Seth launched into conversation.

"My dad and I went hiking at Hidden Lake this weekend. You were right, it's a great spot."

I smiled, my eyes remaining downcast. "Told ya."

I could hear the faint sound of his light chuckle over the din of chatter around us. A comfortable silence fell between us as we navigated the halls.

"I'm sorry for what Brae said," he said, his deep voice gaining my attention. "You know, single-shaming you."

I snorted a mortified laugh, looking away quickly as we stepped into the English room. It was meant to sound dismissive, like it didn't bother me at all, but came out more like a choke of panic to be discussing my tragic love life with Seth Linwood—the object of my desire and completely-off-limits dreamboat.

"It's fine," I assured him with the same well-practiced control I reserved for Brae. "She didn't mean it like that. Besides, it's not like it isn't true."

Seth frowned as he slid into the chair next to mine, setting his books on the desk.

"Why don't you date?" he asked curiously, turning his long, lean body toward me. The movement was intoxicating in its simplicity, and made my head swim. "I mean, not to be a jerk, but I just realized you haven't dated anyone since I've known you."

I shrugged, my eyes locked on the unicorn-adorned pencil in my hand. A gift from Brae.

"I told you. I took a vow of spinsterhood. And one does not just *break* such a vow."

"Seriously," he chastised. "Spinsterhood and toxic Heathcliff attractions aside."

I pursed my lips, knowing I was not going to be able to avoid answering. But it didn't mean I couldn't lie through my teeth.

"I just haven't met anyone I like that way, I guess. Plus, it's hard to compete when your best friend is Brae Walker."

He rolled his eyes. "It's not a competition, Hannah."

Now it was my turn to emit an indignant scoff. "Isn't everything in high school a competition, though? Sports, grades, popularity? Interest from guys when the girl next to you is nothing short of high school royalty?"

The moment I stopped speaking, I chided myself for my honesty. It sounded like I was whining, when in reality, I was just being honest. Everything in high school *was* a competition, even if it shouldn't be.

Seth was silent for a moment. Pushing my better judgment aside, I looked his way to find him watching me with a frown.

"They're stupid," he said firmly, turning to face forward again.

"Who?"

"The boys who aren't asking you out. They're morons. You're awesome, Hannah. You're like Beth in *Little Women*. Quiet, with a good heart, and everyone loves you. You deserve to be happy."

I couldn't suppress a little snicker as I shook my head. "Sure, compare me to a dead girl."

"Technically, she's a *fictional* dead girl," he corrected firmly. "But it's still true. And you shouldn't compare yourself to Brae."

He didn't look my way again as the teacher called the class to order, successfully ending our conversation. It left me in a myriad of emotions, ranging from guilt, to confliction, to a tiny swell of happiness to know that Seth thought anyone who didn't ask me out was a moron. Granted, he had never asked me out either when he had been free and able to do so. Not that I gave him any sign that I would welcome such an offer, but still.

For the next hour, I all-too-easily fell down the fantasy rabbit hole of *what if.*

What if I had had the courage to tell Seth how I felt all those months ago? Or tell Brae how I felt back then, knowing full well she wouldn't have dated him if she knew. The biggest reason I was watching from the sidelines as the first boy to ever make me feel this way belonged to someone else was me. And because of that choice, he was forever off-limits. Because no matter what happened back then, and regardless of what happened in the future, Seth Linwood would always be tied to Braelyn Walker.

And you never *ever* dated your best friend's ex.

CHAPTER TWO

"So, how's school?" Mom asked as she passed Ma a bowl of pasta. "Any new earth-shattering drama shaking up the halls of East River High?"

I looked up from my plate. "Why do you assume there's drama?"

Mom raised a brow. "It's high school. Isn't there always?"

She wasn't wrong, but I wasn't about to let her know that.

Pushing my noodles around on my plate, I shrugged. "School's fine. No drama."

"Just fine?"

I held back the inclination to roll my eyes. Of course, parents never let the "it's fine" response stand as sufficient. They always wanted the fluffy "school is great" speech that I was never very good at. It was like they forgot that being a teenager and being forced into high school was nothing short of purgatory. Certainly nothing to sing sonnets about over pasta.

"Yeah, it's fine," I answered, plucking a piece of garlic bread from the plate in the middle of the table.

"How is your calculus class?" Ma asked, pushing the subject. "I know you said you struggled with the last test."

Cringing, I muttered, "I still don't understand why you made me take that class."

"Because you need a well-rounded timetable, Hannah," Mom said. "It can't all be English and study hall."

"It will help you get into college," Ma explained before taking a sip of her wine. "And you never know. You might learn that you actually like math."

This caused me to roll my eyes.

My less than receptive responses to their line of questioning ceased the interrogation. Of course I immediately felt bad for not participating. But today I just wasn't up for family small talk around the dinner table. I had spent my free period drowning in my calculus textbook, trying to make up for missing the study session with my group the other day. All I got for my effort was more confused and a massive headache.

As if sensing I wasn't in the mood to take part in casual family chatter and needed an escape route, my phone began to vibrate with a call from Brae. She knew I wasn't allowed to take calls during dinner. For her to be calling now couldn't be good.

"Hannah, no phones at the table," Mom chastised, giving me a gentle glare.

"Sorry, it's Brae. Just a second." Sliding my thumb across the screen. "Hello?"

"He broke up with me!" she wailed, her shrill, sobbing voice stinging my ears. She was so loud, both my moms turned with concerned eyes.

I covered my mouth and the receiver with my hand, ducking my head to hide from their stares. "What?"

"Seth just broke up with me!" she repeated, hyperventilating between words. "Like, he actually ended things."

Oh crap.

"Hang on," I said, turning to my moms. "Sorry, but Brae is having a meltdown, can I be excused?"

Ma frowned with concern. "Is she okay?"

The sound of Brae sobbing through the phone, the indelicate hyperventilation with intermittent hiccups proved that she was bordering on hysterics. "It's boy trouble. Can I go?"

They exchanged a glance before Ma nodded. "Yes, you may be excused."

I was up and out of my seat before the words were completely out of her mouth, my fork clattering against the plate in my haste to escape the dining room. Bounding up the stairs to my room, I closed the door behind me with a soft click before leaning against it.

"Okay, what happened?"

Her hysterical crying made her almost incoherent. "He showed up at my door ten minutes ago. I thought he was surprising me, trying to do something nice since things have been feeling, I don't know, a little off lately. I should have known something was wrong when I opened the door, because he didn't kiss me hello." She paused to blow her nose indelicately. "Anyway, he said that he cared about me but that things just weren't working out. That we were too different, and that he wanted to break up."

I said nothing as she rambled, her words coming out so quickly, they practically blended together. Clearing my throat, I tried to think of what to say. "So, he just said you had nothing in common and that he wanted to break up? He didn't say anything else?"

"No!" she cried. "I mean, we didn't have much in common when we started dating, and he didn't mind it then! God, Hannah, how the hell did this happen? I mean, *he broke up with me*! I was actually *dumped*!"

Closing my eyes, I tried to formulate a response. Most girls would be upset that their boyfriend ended their relationship because they loved them and didn't want to be without them. But for Brae, it was about the reputation. Ever since her parents' divorce and the gossip storm that followed, Brae had an obsession with status and social standing. As much as she loved to hear and spread gossip, it was one of her biggest fears to be the subject of it.

"Maybe he just needs some time?" I offered, trying to ease her upset. "Maybe—"

"No. Screw that. He doesn't get to come in here and breakup with me one minute and have me take him back the next." She paused, her frantic mind running amuck. "Oh God, Hannah, everyone at school will know! Ugh, everyone will know he *dumped* me!"

"Brae, who cares if people know? People break up all the time."

"Yeah, I know, but . . . this time it's *me*!"

I silently thanked God that she couldn't see my eyes roll. "Brae, get a grip, will you? It's not like you've never been in a relationship that ended before."

"But it's always been me ending it," she reminded me. "Usually, I'm the one who gets bored and leaves. Oh God! What if he got bored of me? What if that's the reason? That I'm *boring*!"

"Jesus, Braelyn, you are *not* boring! You're a drama queen, but you are not boring."

She paused, taking in my words. "I don't know if that was an insult or a compliment."

"Both."

She sniffed loudly. "Hannah, what am I going to do? I mean, I've never had this happen before. I don't even know what I feel right now."

"That's okay. You aren't expected to understand it all right away. We'll get through this."

"How do you know?"

"Because I'm your best friend. And rule three says you always have to give your best friend the benefit of the doubt. So, when I said you will get through this, you have to believe me," I said, sliding down to sit on the floor with my back against the door.

"I swear you bring up those rules just to calm me down." She sighed deeply.

She wasn't wrong. Because I knew she held to our rules like commandments, even if they were created in middle school and amended over the years. Created to ensure a long and strong friendship, they were both a blessing and a curse—especially when one of us would use them against the other, like now.

"I do, sort of. But it's still true. So when I tell you that you'll get through this, you're required to give me the benefit of the doubt and believe that I'm right."

I listened as she blew out a long exhale through the phone. "I know I'm a dramatic pain in the butt, but I love you. You're my best friend."

"And you're mine. Even if you make me want to pull my hair out sometimes."

Brae laughed lightly before sighing again through the phone.

"What if he likes someone else?"

"What?" I balked, my entire body tensing at the mere suggestion.

"I mean, he gave me all these stupid reasons for why he wanted to end things. What if the real reason was he's into someone else?"

I couldn't ignore the little flip of my stomach at the possibility that Seth liked someone else and the far-fetched dream that that someone else might be me. Just as quickly, I violently tensed to chase the feeling away. Things like that just didn't happen in real life: the cute boy you liked actually liking you back and ending his mismatched relationship because he realized that you were perfect together.

And besides . . . he was still off-limits because of rule five: never date your best friend's ex.

Pulling myself together, I swallowed back the lump that had formed in my throat.

"I doubt that's it," I said with as much confidence as I could. "You're the most popular girl in our class."

"I know, but what if it is?"

"Brae, stop. You'll drive yourself crazy trying to figure out why he did what he did. Stop worrying about why, because it doesn't matter. Just focus on what to do now."

"And what *do* I do now?"

I pursed my lips, contemplating her question.

Maybe this was a good thing, I thought selfishly. Maybe this way, I wouldn't have to be around him as much. Sure, we had our English project, but there were only a couple months left of the semester, and we only worked on it once a week. Even though I hated the idea of not being around him, I couldn't ignore the fact that this was probably for the best. It would finally allow me to have the space I needed to clear him from my system in an unrequited crush detox.

"What do I do, Hannah?" she repeated, her voice small and lost, reminding me so much of when we were kids. When her father left, when her mother was standing on a ledge of depression, and she didn't know what the future held.

Those first few weeks after her father walked out were some of the most difficult of our friendship. I had never felt so helpless, not knowing how to help her. Her mother swung on extremes, from raging, drunken tirades of smashing dishes and cutting up Mr. Walker's two thousand-dollar Armani suits to spending days in bed at a time staring at the wall. She wouldn't eat, wouldn't drink, and certainly didn't take care of Brae.

Brae didn't handle it much better. While she didn't break things or hide in her room, instead she put on the "everything is fine" mask and wore it like armor. School days were spent with smiles, laughter, and attention, while evenings were spent cleaning up after her mother's latest drunken fit or texting her father incessantly, begging him to come home. I spent almost every night at her house, watching her go from the glittering cover girl to the broken shell over and over again.

Hearing the pain in her voice now caused the memory to flicker in my mind, and I hated that she felt so lost. That she didn't know how to fix what had happened with Seth any more than she knew how to get over the breakup of her family.

But to her question, I actually had an answer. It was the same five words I told myself repeatedly since I first met Seth, like a mantra meant to guide me to the end goal. Clearly, it didn't work too well for me, but I hoped that it would work for her.

"You get over Seth Linwood."

CHAPTER THREE

"Today freaking sucked," Brae groaned for the third time.

I held back the inclination to smack her. "I know."

"I'm freaking exhausted. All the fake smiling and crap. It's like I've just been in battle."

I snorted. "Only *you* would compare a first post-breakup appearance to a battle."

At least this earned me a weak smile.

"Well, it is, isn't it? In a way? Dividing the assets, setting down turf boundaries." She paused, her smile fading quickly. "Kind of like my parents' divorce."

I stole a glance at her from the corner of my eye, preparing to see a new swell of tears.

Instead, she was staring at the ceiling. It was what she did when she wasn't sure what to do or how to feel.

We had taken our places on her bedroom floor not long after returning home from school. Side by side, our backs supported by the plush cream carpet, our hands folded over our stomachs.

It had been our official "heavy subject matter" position for as long as I could remember. The light, pastel colors of her room blended together in the warm afternoon light, accents of pink and peach splashed against the white walls. Everything in this room was soft and feminine and light. So much like Brae. And yet, the air itself was heavy and tinged with her sadness.

"I mean, I'm not stupid. I know this happens to everyone at some point. But I guess I just never actually thought it would happen to *me*, ya know? That probably sounds really rude and arrogant—"

"Yup."

Brae gave me a side-eyed glare before continuing. "Yeah, I know it does. But it's the truth. I've never been dumped before, Hannah. It's a really crappy feeling."

"I know."

"You don't know," she said gently. "You've never been dumped. You've never even really dated anyone."

I glanced at Brae from my place beside her, finding her staring at the ceiling again. She wasn't trying to be harsh with her words, I knew. She was just venting, so I ignored the little twinge of hurt that touched at my chest at the reminder of my spinsterhood. Instead, I kept my focus on the task at hand.

"I know I haven't. But I can understand that it would suck."

She turned to me, her blue eyes swollen from tears desperate to be shed.

"I'm sorry," she sighed, her lips turning down. "I didn't mean to make that sound so—"

"I know. It's fine," I replied. It was almost too easy to brush off the sting of her comments after so many years.

"I still can't stop thinking about today," she murmured, and for a moment I wondered if she was speaking to me or just talking to herself aloud. "I mean, I knew it was going to suck having to explain to everyone that we broke up. All the fake pity and crap." She paused, turning to look at me. "All the stuff they said to me was the same stuff I've said to others a million times over and thought nothing of it. But having it said *to* you really freaking sucks."

I nodded. "Well, at least Seth was at a baseball tournament. You didn't have to face him *and* listen to all the talk about you guys. Which, by the way, wasn't all that bad."

"I know, I know," she muttered with a dismissive wave. She was silent for several moments before gasping, turning her head to me quickly. "Oh my God! You're doing that project with him! You'll see him all the time, and—"

I tried to think of what to say that would ease her concern. "We'll be just working on the project, like we always did, Brae. Yeah, it will probably be awkward, but its only for a couple more months. It's not like I can back out, or—"

"No, no, I know that," she said quickly, waving her hand at me. "And I would never ask you to do that, Hannah. I know you guys are friends and were before I even met him. I'm totally okay with you guys still doing your project and stuff. I'm not going to be *that* crazy ex. I guess I just didn't think about it until now. That you would still be seeing him. I kind of panicked."

A silence fell over the room. But despite it, I could almost hear her mind racing, whirring frantically.

"I know we weren't together for really all that long, but I liked him. I've dated a lot of guys, but he was different. He was . . . I don't even know if this makes sense, but I felt calm around him. Like, if I wanted to, I didn't have to keep up with the act people at school expect, and I could just be me around him. Like I am with you."

I nodded in agreement, my eyes roaming around the room as I considered the thoughts she voiced aloud.

"You know, no one expects you to keep up some persona, Brae. You're the one who feels that you have to be 'that' girl."

I didn't turn to watch her reaction, but I still knew she would be frowning.

"I can't help it," she admitted after a few moments of silent consideration. "I mean, I think it's just habit now. When Dad left that summer before junior high, I kind of vowed to be as perfect as possible. If I was the loud, adventurous, flirtatious person every girl wanted to be and every guy wanted to be with, then I would call the shots, you know?"

My heart ached as she described the act of self-preservation she had adopted. "But, Brae, the you that you are here with me, without all the makeup and flirting, is pretty great. She can call the shots too, if you let her."

She was already shaking her head. "I can't. I know it probably doesn't make sense, Hannah, but I feel like if I am not on top of the world, I will just be crushed under its weight. Lord knows my mom is too wrapped up in her own crap to notice me, and my dad has his girlfriend. At school, people notice me, and I have some sense of power. I'm not willing to let that go when it's the only control I really have."

My heart seized for her. I may not be the popular girl, the one everyone wanted to be or wanted to be with. But at least I knew I could just be *me*, and that would be enough.

For the first time, maybe ever, I didn't feel so envious of Braelyn Walker.

"When I told my mom that Seth broke up with me, she started berating me, asking what I had done wrong," she continued, scowling. "Like it was my fault somehow. I wasn't attentive enough to him, or I didn't support him enough. It was all so stupid because it's all the same stuff she thinks about herself for why my dad left, and she's just putting that same crap on me. I couldn't even really *talk* to her about it because she just made me feel like I had done something to deserve it."

My lips turned down at the picture she painted; of Mrs. Walker standing in her immaculate kitchen, her perfect manicure and styled hair, ignorant to her daughter's pain. I could all too easily remember the days I would be over at Brae's and her mom would be in the living room, torn sweatshirt on and hair uncombed, asking those same questions aloud to herself in the days that followed her husband leaving. No wonder Brae had such a hard time finding her footing post-breakup when her mother was still reeling from her own, even years later. She learned from example.

Brae paused to glance at me, and the vulnerability in her eyes glistened. "I just wish I knew how to get over him."

I turned my gaze away from her, considering Brae's desire. She was right when she said I had never gone through a breakup, but she was wrong when she said I had never suffered heartache. Because my first—and only—heartache had happened at her hands, the day she asked out Seth Linwood. And every day since had been spent trying to stop liking him, stop thinking about him, and finally be able to move on.

It was then that it hit me. My mind latched on to a memory from months before, of searching online for tips and tricks to getting over a breakup, hoping it would help me get over my crush. It was a basic premise that required a strategic plan; getting over a boy in the fewest, most concise steps possible.

Sitting up quickly, my action startled Brae.

"Jesus, you're like a damn groundhog popping up out of a hole," she murmured, her hand resting on her chest. "You scared the hell out of—"

"I know what to do," I said firmly, climbing to my feet.

Brae pushed herself up into a seated position, her blond hair hanging in straggles from the ponytail it was attempting to escape. "You know what to do about what?"

"About Seth," I said as I grabbed a piece of paper and a pen from her desk. Plucking the old lap desk from under her bed, I rejoined Brae on the floor with a new sense of purpose. "You want to get over him, right?"

"Yeah?" she responded with a confused raise of her brow.

"Well, I know how to do that."

"How?"

"The six easy steps to getting over a guy," I said proudly. Bringing my hand to the page, I started to write.

Brae paused before leaning toward me in curiosity.

"Is there such a thing? Or are you high on chocolate and my sorrow?"

"No, smart-ass. It's a thing. There are hundreds of articles online about how to get over someone, and they all basically say the same points. It's just a matter of breaking them down and finding the patterns."

She narrowed her eyes at me. "You searched online for how to get over a guy?"

Her question stayed my hand for a beat, my chest constricting. "Yeah . . . um . . . it was for an AP Psychology paper. Emotional relationships and stuff."

I angled toward her, quick to move on.

"Okay, here they are."

1. *Passing her the page, she looked them over.*
2. *Allow yourself time to grieve*
3. *Get rid of reminders of the relationship*
4. *Focus on yourself*
5. *Get back into your life*
6. *Try dating again*
7. *Accept it's over, plan your future, and don't look back*

Her lips curled downward, brow pinched in doubt, before a curious tilt angled her head. After a few moments, I saw something else flicker across her features before it disappeared.

"I don't know," she said with a shake of her head. "How do you even put stuff like this into action?"

"You break it down into easy-to-follow steps," I said simply. "Just like when we have to write papers for English, you make a plan and execute it."

"My failed relationship isn't an English paper, Hannah." She frowned, pushing the paper back to me defeatedly.

"I know that. But look, outlining stuff makes it easier to do, right? It gives you a clear path to follow to your end goal."

Under the first step, I began to write.

"Most articles say that you should give yourself about half the time of the relationship to get over it. You and Seth dated for about six months, right?"

"Right," she nodded.

"So you should technically be able to successfully get over him by following these steps in three months."

"Three months!" she shrieked. "Hannah—"

"Step one," I said firmly, silencing her argument.

Allow yourself time to grieve

1. *Go for walks, talk to friends, get out of the house*
2. *Don't pretend you don't need to talk about it, don't wallow in self-pity, or call/text when upset*
3. *It's okay to feel sad!*

Brae hung over my side, her eyes following along as I made bullets by the first point.

She bit her lip. "I guess those make sense."

A thrill of hope sung in my veins at her agreement. "Of course it does. *Cosmo* gave those points."

This made her laugh. One of the perks of knowing Brae so well was that I knew what to say to sway her in my favor. She considered *Cosmopolitan* a bible of popularity, relationships, and general female domination. As long as I said these came from *Cosmo*, she would follow them like doctrine.

"Okay, step two."

Get rid of reminders of the relationship

1. *Give away stuffed animals and other items to charity or toy drives*
2. *Erase photos from phone/throw away printed photos*
3. *Remove him from social media, contacts, phone*

"Wait, wait . . . I have to get rid of the stuff he gave me?" she asked, a touch of panic in her eyes.

"Do you really want to sit around and look at them every day and night, thinking about when he gave them to you or what he said or all that sappy shit?"

She pursed her full lips. "No."

"Exactly." I nodded with determination. "Now, step three will be the most fun. It's all about doing things that make you feel like you again."

Focus on yourself

1. *Spoil yourself with girls' nights, shopping, exercise to let off steam*
2. *Have a facial, manicure, or pedicure to make yourself feel pretty*
3. *Find a new hobby that you enjoy, and that will take your mind off of the breakup*

"That step does sound fun." She smiled.

"It will be, but we have to get there first," I promised her. "And by the time you do, you won't hurt as much, so you will actually be able to *have* fun."

Brae nodded in understanding, her veil of skepticism slowly lifting. I quickly continued my list.

Get back into your life

1. *Go to movies, to clubs, shopping*
2. *Meet new people*
3. *Spend time with friends*

"That step sounds okay," she murmured, her gaze eager on the page. "I mean, that's mostly stuff we've always done."

"Exactly. So we can do it again."

"Ugh, but I don't feel like going out—"

I stopped her with a glare. "That's because you haven't even started step one yet. By the time you get to step four, you'll feel like getting out and meeting new people." Pushing back the reaction to reject my next words, I forced them past my lips. "Seth Linwood isn't the only guy in the world. By the time you get to this step, you'll be ready to go out and see who else is out there. And maybe you will meet someone who you will consider step five with."

Try dating again
1. *Go on CASUAL dates, meet new people*
2. *Don't compare them to your ex!*
3. *DON'T jump into a new relationship before the steps are complete! No rebounds!*

"You need to meet new people, experience what else is out there, but don't need to hook up with them to do that. It will help you find out what you really want in a guy, which will help you learn more about yourself, too."

She grinned at me with a soft tilt of her head.

"When did you get so smart with this stuff?"

I met her smile. "I've always been smart. We've just never had to apply it to this before."

Brae laughed, and I breathed a sigh of relief at another successful deflection.

"Which brings us to the final step."

Accept it's over, plan your future, and don't look back

"No sub points for that one?" Brae queried, giving me a teasing smirk.

"Nope. There is no step-by-step guide for planning your future or what you want in a relationship. That is what you will figure out as you go through the steps."

Passing Brae the paper, I let her read it over again. Anxiety knotted in my core as I waited to see what she would say. Getting over Seth was a challenge I had been attempting since the day he knocked me off my feet, and each time, I failed the moment I saw that crooked, dimpled smile. But this time, I felt determined, as if guiding Brae through these steps would somehow force me to commit and get over him once and for all.

I needed this just as much as she did.

"So? What do you say?" I asked, trying to keep the touch of hopeful anticipation out of my voice.

Brae was quiet for a moment, her eyes still on the page. "I'll probably flunk these," she said.

"I'll make sure you don't."

"I'll probably go off the rails," she continued.

"And I'll help keep you on track."

She smiled, shaking her head at me. "Only you would come up with a twelve-step program for getting over a broken heart."

I plastered a smile on my face. "Technically, it's a six-step program, but it does the same thing."

Brae giggled, setting the paper on the floor in front of us. "Do you promise this will work?" she asked, looking up at me from under her lashes.

I couldn't honestly promise that she would succeed at this any more than I could promise myself that I would come out on the other side no longer lusting after a certain green-eyed boy. But I could promise her that I would do everything in my power to help her. I would put her first, determined to do whatever it took to make sure she healed. And if I mended my own heart in the process, then we were both better off for the effort.

"I promise," I replied with as much conviction as I could muster.

Brae considered me for a moment, her eyes falling back to the page between us. "Rule two?"

Rule two: always keep your promises. I was now bound to my friendship code to ensure that Brae succeeded in this mission. And by extent, myself.

"Promise," I repeated more firmly.

She was silent for a moment. "Okay."

"Okay?"

"Okay." She nodded. "I know this is going to suck and that I'll make mistakes. But I don't want to feel this way. I don't want to feel sad and broken or miss him all the time. I want to get over him and do it fast. So, okay. Let's do this."

I reached across and hugged her tightly, rocking back and forth. Pulling away, I held out my fist between us. Brae laughed before bumping her own fist against mine and linking our pinkies. Three shakes of our joined hands later and it was sealed.

"We'll do great," I promised her. "We can totally do this."

Brae snickered, brushing strands of blond hair from her face. "You mean *I* can totally do this."

I cleared my throat and released her. "Yeah, that's what I meant."

"So, when do you want to start?" she asked, suddenly eager.

I was glad she seemed so hopeful for this task. The more positive she felt about it, the more likely it was that we would be successful. And her success meant that I had a better chance of reaching the finish line, too.

"We start tomorrow."

STEP ONE:
ALLOW YOURSELF
TIME TO GRIEVE

I'm acting like I'm okay.
Please don't interrupt my performance.

CHAPTER FOUR

Tossing her backpack onto the floor beside her locker, Brae rubbed her hands over her face.

"Night two of post-breakup hell complete."

A smirk pulled at the corner of my lip as I leaned against my own locker. "And you survived without any casualties."

She snorted as she pulled open the locker door, ducking to hide behind it as she rummaged inside. "Probably because Seth was still away at that tournament. Pretty sure seeing him for the first time will be my undoing."

Mine too, I thought silently. "Or you'll surprise yourself and be perfectly fine," was what I said instead. "Because we have a plan, and we're going to stick to it."

She scoffed as she emerged from the depths of her locker. Immediately, her eyes snagged onto a pair of sophomore girls walking by, heads bowed close together, whispering rapidly. They glanced at Brae, gossip-fueled excitement glinting on their faces.

Brae's face turned red as she slammed her locker door. "Anything you'd like to say?" Her voice was laced with a menacing warning.

The girls paled before scurrying away.

The moment they disappeared Brae blew an exasperated breath through pursed lips.

I smirked. "Okay. Casualties number one and two down."

She frowned. "I've caught a bunch of underclassmen whispering. Some even had the nerve to point, thinking they were being subtle. It's rude. I'm simply reminding them not to mess with me. I'm not going to lose my rule of the junior class because of this."

I couldn't stop the roll of my eyes, but didn't challenge her. While I didn't think her iron fist rule was necessary, she did. And right now, if it helped her cope, fine.

Michelle slipped from the stream of passing students to join us. "So? How did today go?"

Brae huffed. "I haven't burst into tears yet," she replied. "But the day is still young."

I coughed a laugh. "You're doing fine, apart from the few sophomores you probably made cry just now. Besides, now we officially start with step one."

With a nod of reassurance, she gathered her things, and we quickly exited the school, meeting up with Erin in the parking lot. They both had been briefed on the "How to Get Over Your Ex" plan that morning and were ready to help me pull Brae through the steps by force if necessary. In an attempt to clear her head and cheer her up, we agreed that we would start with ice cream at Alley Scoops. In part because Brae loved ice cream, but also because it was something we did regularly after school, and Michelle was determined not to let Brae fall into a pit of despair and hide away from the world. It was a solid plan to kick off our mission.

Once arriving at Alley Scoops, I wasn't sure Brae would get out of the car. The moment she saw the gathering of students in the parking lot, she froze, her flight response kicking in. Alley Scoops was a regular post-school hangout for most of East River, and while Brae would usually thrive in the attention that extended beyond the school's halls, now she was practically hiding.

Finally, after much reassurance, we got her out of the car, got our ice cream, and took shelter under a large oak tree in the small park beside the shop. Normally, she would hold court at the center table near the store, her admirers gathering around.

But today was all about baby steps, hence the respectable distance from prying ears. Curling up in the grass, we formed a small circle of support to begin step one.

"So . . . what do we do first?" she asked, her hands clasped in her lap from her place on the ground. "The sooner we start these steps, the sooner I can stop feeling like the jilted ex."

"This isn't a race, it's a marathon," I reminded her. "We do what we always do, except this time, with purpose. Step one is essentially thinking about the relationship but not dwelling on it."

"Isn't that a contradiction?" Michelle asked.

"No. At least according to the internet."

This caused Erin to laugh. "Because everything we read on the internet is true?"

"You're the one who believes everything you read on that stupid message board from school. That's your gossip fountain, and you don't question its validity," I challenged. They brought their hands up in surrender.

"Fine, okay," they said, admitting defeat.

Our bickering earned us a small smile from Brae, but it was gone in the blink of an eye. She poked at her ice cream, before lifting her attention across the grass to the parking lot, her jaw tensing. The rest of us to looked over to find several of our classmates stealing glances toward us. Like Brae had said earlier, they weren't even being subtle, their curiosity piqued. Having East River's junior class queen finding herself dumped was like fuel to the gossip fire. Brae was certain the social vultures would begin to circle, looking at her downfall as a means to dethrone her. When coupled with the dent to her ego, her temper was sharper than usual.

Brae bristled, tension raising her shoulders and tightening her grip on her spoon. Thankfully, it was Erin who shouted before Brae could unleash her latest eruption.

"I know we're hot, but you don't need to stare!" they called, flipping a middle finger toward the gawkers before turning back to Brae. "I got you."

"Thanks," she replied, a small smile ghosting at the corner of her mouth, her shoulders dropped as the anger deflated from her system like a balloon. Exhaling a long breath, her eyes fell to the slowly melting ice cream. "So, what do I think about? I've been trying *not* to think about it at all, because it just upsets me."

"That's the point of this first step. Let yourself be upset, think about the relationship, the faults in it, and why it might be better this way. But the main purpose is to accept that feeling sad and hurt doesn't mean you're not strong."

Brae nodded, her fingers clenching around the ice cream cup.

Wanting to urge her participation, I poked her with my toe as she leaned against the trunk of the tree. "Everything here is familiar and comforting, Brae. We've done this a million times, exactly like this. It'll help you work through your feelings."

I was pretty proud for how assured I sounded. Because this venture wasn't just for Braelyn's benefit. We both needed to get down to business and get over our feelings. For me, most of the journey would be silent, lived vicariously through Brae since I certainly couldn't admit that I was just as desperate to get over Seth as she was.

"Well?" I said, looking at her expectantly. "Tell me what you're feeling."

Brae laughed, shaking her head. "Are you my shrink now?"

"I've always been your shrink," I pointed out. "This time, we are just doing it a little more obviously." Squaring my shoulders to her, I waited for her response. "Let's talk about it."

Brae smirked, but held her tongue as she considered my question. I watched as her sass faded, slowly replaced with an expression of sadness. The light dimmed in her eyes, her lips turning down as she considered the subject at hand.

"I don't even know what I'm feeling, to be honest," she admitted. "Partly I understand it, because we *didn't* really have anything in common, so it probably wouldn't last, but mainly, I'm angry and frustrated and a little lost."

I nodded, silently comparing her assessment of her newfound relationship status against my own feelings of the situation. Angry, frustrated, lost . . . yup, I had experienced all of those in the first few months that they had been dating. Regretfully, I couldn't even act like I didn't know how I ended up in that position since I dismissed any chance Seth handed me to test the waters of "something more." All those hours alone in the library. The late night phone calls. For weeks, he was my little secret, and I did nothing about it.

Not to mention that I gave them both my blessing.

Brae wouldn't have asked him out if I had told her not to. But I had convinced myself that Seth and I were merely friends, that any stolen glances and lingering looks were meaningless, and that someone like him would never be interested in someone like me.

Just as Seth would never have accepted Brae's offer if I had told him it made me uncomfortable. Regardless of any possible feelings on his end, he would have respected my wishes. My shy demeanor and endless self-doubt were at the helm of my current predicament, no matter how much I wanted to blame everyone else.

I couldn't decide what was worse. That I allowed all of this to happen in the first place or that even now that he was single again, he would perpetually remain off-limits. That even if I got up the confidence to say something to him, to shoot my shot and let the cards fall, I wouldn't be able to see it through. Because pursuing Seth would mean losing Brae, and that was something I was not willing to do.

A fresh new wave of irritation clawed its way up from my core, digging its talons into my throat.

Why couldn't I be more confident? Why did I always let everything happen around me and never take a chance to control my own narrative? I always said it was because I was used to being Brae's best friend, the sidekick to her superhero. But at some point, that would just be an excuse, and I knew it.

Brae continued, ignorant to my inner self-loathing. "I have this overwhelming panic in my chest. Like . . . I'm no longer Seth's girlfriend. That's so weird to say out loud, even though it never bothered me with other guys."

"That's because you broke up with the other guys first," Michelle reminded her gently.

"Yeah, I know. But now, I feel like I don't know who I am if I'm not his girlfriend. I wasn't prepared to be just me again, you know?"

"Brae, you've always been you," Michelle corrected. "Seth or not, he never really changed who you were."

Brae nodded thoughtfully, taking small bites of ice cream.

"Maybe," she replied with a sigh. "I guess it's just hard because I had a routine with him, and that's gone now."

Michelle leaned back on her elbows in the grass, setting her now empty ice cream cup aside. "So you just make a new routine. One that is *yours*, not tied to a guy."

A new routine, I thought to myself as I nodded in agreement. What would my new routine look like? Other than English, I would no longer have to see Seth between classes or after school. No more third wheeling on dates with him and Brae, and no more playing the mediator to their disagreements and differences. After this semester, when I was no longer academically bound to him, there was a good chance I wouldn't cross his path again beyond a casual wave as we passed in the hallway.

My chest twisted at the thought.

She looked to me with a sigh. "You know, when he agreed to go out with me, I almost didn't go through with it."

I startled, turning to her.

She continued, ignorant to my startled thoughts. "You guys always spent so much time together back then, and I saw how well you got on. You have so much in common, with your books and your hiking. I guess I thought that maybe one of you might have felt something for the other. But you had been hanging out together for so long and neither of you made a move, so I figured maybe I was wrong. That maybe you didn't think of him like that."

A soft tingle of anger rippled along my skin, but I brushed it away. "Why didn't you just ask me?" I blurted before I could stop myself.

"I did," she challenged. "I asked you if it was okay, and you said yes."

My mouth fell slack, words balancing on the tip of my tongue, but nothing jumped into the void between us. Because she was right. She had asked, and I gave her permission.

We all sat in silence again for a long while, Brae lost in her thoughts, me lost in my own frustration.

Suddenly, her phone buzzed loudly, her mom's image popping up on the screen. Mrs. Walker was the type of mom always coiffed to flaw-lessness, her blond hair styled in a smooth, sleek cut to her shoulders. Her makeup, while subtle, enhanced every feature. Even in the privacy of her own home, the woman couldn't leave her master suite without being painted to perfection.

Brae groaned, sliding a finger across the screen and putting her mom on speaker. "Hi, Mom."

"Where are you?" Mrs. Walker demanded, her tone sharp. "You were supposed to help me with—"

"I'm out with my friends," Brae interrupted, eyes scanning over us. "And you're on speaker phone."

There was a weighted silence, and I knew Mrs. Walker would be turning red with irritation that someone had overheard her being anything less than perfect. Quickly, her tone changed to a sticky sweet trill.

"Hi, all," she chirped. "Having fun?"

Brae frowned, not giving us a chance to respond. "Mom, we're talking about my breakup. That's hardly what I would call *fun*."

Mrs. Walker seemed undeterred by Brae's snippy tone. "Braelyn, you need to learn to reflect on the things that happen to you without lashing out. You know, at The Sanctuary—"

"God, Mom, please don't start spouting that healing cult crap at me again."

The Sanctuary was the mental health wellness retreat Mrs. Walker spent time at after Mr. Walker ran off with his secretary. Touted as a place of healing and re-centering, it looked more like a fancy day spa than anything else. When Mrs. Walker returned, she had quickly changed from the depressed, sweatpants-wearing woman we had come to know in the days following her husband leaving back to a resemblance of the woman she had been before. At least outwardly. According to her, The Sanctuary was a godsend. Brae called it a mental institution for rich people who didn't want to accept that bad things happen and they may have a role in the blame.

"Maybe you all can help me out here," Mrs. Walker said, exasperated. "Help her make sense of this."

Raising a brow, I glanced at Brae. "Sense about what?"

Brae looked mutinous, glaring at her phone with fire behind her eyes. "My mother seems to think that I should go and apologize to Seth. That I must have done something to upset him if he broke up with me like this, and I should try to fix it." Turning to me, the pain in her expression twisted at my heart. "She doesn't seem to understand that not all decisions people make are based solely on my actions."

Mrs. Walker's voice was apathetic. "Braelyn, you make it sound like I'm blaming you."

"Aren't you?" Brae tsked with a sarcastic tilt of her head.

"No," her mother replied. "I'm merely speaking from experience that relationships are a two-way street, and that if Seth broke up with you, that you must have—"

"That I must have done something to deserve it," Brae snapped, her voice rising. "Right, Mom? Just like you deserved Dad leaving for Marissa?"

"Don't say her name!" her mother spat, her composure slipping.

I could all too easily picture that beneath her expertly applied makeup, Mrs. Walker's face was red with anger. The effort it took for her mom not to lash out seeped through the phone. But I knew she wouldn't. We were on the call, witness to the imperfections of the Walker household. And Mrs. Walker would be damned if she would let someone see her as anything other than perfect.

"Well, I guess I'll leave you to your evening then," she replied with tightly-bound composure. "Braelyn, be sure to be home before curfew."

The phone disconnected before Brae had a chance to reply.

"UGH!" Brae groaned, throwing her phone down to look anxiously around at the other students across the park. "Do you think anyone heard any of that?"

Erin was quick to shake their head. "Definitely not. They're too wrapped up in their own ice cream comas to listen to your mom's crazy rants."

Brae groaned, throwing herself back into the grass. "I swear, it's like Seth breaking up with me is the worst thing to ever happen to *her*!"

"I'm sorry, Brae," Erin said, reaching out to pet Brae's head soothingly. The night had taken a rather drastic turn from step one of our venture to the secrets behind the closed doors of East River's affluent families.

"It's fine," she replied, shaking her head. "I'm used to it. Everything that happens to me is my fault. Which is funny, since Dad leaving is everyone's fault but my mother's. Glass houses and all that crap, you would think."

I nodded as Brae took a deep breath, blowing the air out through pursed lips. "Maybe it's part of the reason I always feel like I have to be in a relationship. Because she's convinced me that it's the only thing that matters."

"You don't always have to be in a relationship, Brae. You're complete without a boy next to you," Michelle reminded her gently.

"I know, but it's hard to actually put that into practice. I guess that's something I need to work on, but I don't know how. I just feel this constant need to be part of something amazing."

"You *are* part of something amazing," I reminded her with a nudge, reaching out to grasp her hand in mine. Thankfully, she laughed.

"I mean other than what I have with you guys. Being alone is scary. I don't like it."

Erin took Brae's other hand with Michelle linking her fingers with Erin's until we were a chain of support.

"You're not alone," Michelle promised as we all squeezed each other tight.

CHAPTER FIVE

An infernal buzzing echoed through the blissful silence of my bedroom, breaking into my subconscious before I was ever really willing to depart from the comfort of my dreams. Groaning, I buried my face deeper into my pillow, as if it held some refuge from the noise determined to wake me from the first decent sleep I had had in days.

Reaching my arm out blindly, my face still hidden in my pillow, I flailed my hand around in the direction of the irritating sound. I expected to find a text from Brae. Instead, I found one from Seth.

Seth: *Hey. I know this is short notice, but any chance we can get together and work on English?*

The surprise of his olive branch caused me to sit up sharply, my tangled hair flying around my face as I clutched my phone in my hands. Brushing away the flutter in my chest, I considered my options. Immediately, a knot formed in my stomach, confliction pulling me in two directions.

We needed to work on the assignment. We were a little more than halfway through breaking down *Romeo and Juliet*, turning Shakespeare's period masterpiece into a modern day rom-com for the ages. But with his baseball practices, my work schedule, and our respective family obligations, we had missed over two whole weeks. We needed to get this assignment done, and putting it off only caused my anxiety to thrum.

But then there was Brae and my loyalty to her. Despite being friends with both of them, I was firmly on Team Walker. It was no question, despite my feelings for the boy at the helm of the discord. But Brae had already said she understood we still had to work on the assignment and that she was okay with it. Surely she meant that, and I shouldn't feel any guilt for following through.

Right?

I sat staring at the phone for a solid ten minutes, weighing my options, before shaking my head at myself.

Hannah: *Sure.*

The moment I hit send, I cringed, my anxiety spiking. Would he think I was mad at him for breaking up with Brae? *Should* I be mad at him? My curt response could be taken several ways, maybe he—

Seth: *Thank you! Meet you at the library in an hour?*

A breath of relief rushed from my lungs as I shook my head at myself. I was going to have to pull myself together if I was going to be meeting with him with any form of regularity.

Scrambling into a pair of jeans and a T-shirt, I prepared to meet Seth face-to-face for the first time since he and Brae called it quits. I knew it would happen eventually, just like I knew I couldn't avoid him forever despite my attempts at convincing myself he wasn't the boy for me. I was just hoping to have a little more time before I was expected to sit across from him and pretend everything was normal.

He was already there when I arrived, walking into the large main hall, walls of warm wood, the scent of books and knowledge heavy in the air. Sliding into the seat across from him, I tried to appear unfazed by our meeting, but an ominous weight settled over me. Like two generals negotiating a truce.

"Thanks for coming," he said, folding his hands on the table between us. The brilliant green of his eyes forced a lump in my throat, the sharp angles of his face familiar and yet somehow foreign in this post-breakup light. It was strange how much had changed in such a short time, and yet his effect on me was painfully unaltered.

"No worries," I replied, my voice cracking, betraying my nerves. Clearing my throat, I pulled myself together. "It's been a crazy couple of weeks, so we should try to catch up."

I kept my eyes averted, too nervous to actually look at him for too long. Like the sun, he was beautiful but dangerous if I lingered in his warmth. A silence fell between us for a few heavy moments before he sighed. With frustration or resignation, I couldn't tell.

An hour passed with forced and intent focus, but we made significant progress on our assignment. Romeo, now the head of the football team, was in the mix of making plans to ask Juliet, head cheerleader from the rival high school, to prom, battling for the upper hand over Paris. The scandal that would follow would rock both schools. Rosaline, the original object of Romeo's desire, was no longer a vacant fixture in the tale. She was now the popular girl in school, who every boy adored. Of course Romeo would be drawn to her. We had carefully turned every character on their head, fitting their original characteristics into roles within the typical high school setting.

As much fun as the assignment was, I was eternally grateful that we wouldn't be forced to act it out in front of the class. Star-crossed lovers and tragic love triangles were already things I was acting out in real life. I had no desire to do so in front of an audience.

"Too bad we didn't go to a high school like this. Exciting and creative," he commented, finger tracing along the lines of script in his copy of *Romeo and Juliet*.

"You say exciting and creative, I say dramatic and feuding. Let's agree to disagree. Although, going to a school in another country would be cool," I replied with a snort, trying to ease the tension.

Seth laughed lightly, eyes still downcast to his book. "You say that now, but school is school no matter where you go. You'd still have to read R&J if you went to school in Paris, you know."

"Don't remind me," I scowled, shooting him a playful glare for ruining my fantasy.

"How is saving for your trip going?" he asked, looking up from his book. Folding his arms across the table top, the muscles in his forearms flexed in an enticing way that made my mouth water. The intensity of his gaze sent a flush through my limbs as my muddled brain tried to follow the change in conversational direction.

"It's going okay. Scraping my pennies together to pay for it."

"Brae said her dad offered to pay for both of you," Seth said, his voice softer, wrapping around Brae's name delicately. It was the first time he'd said her name since we sat down. I couldn't tell if he realized that or not, but I did.

I nodded. "Yeah. He's paying her way and offered to pay mine, but my moms put a stop to that pretty quickly. They figure if I want to take a trip like that, I have to earn it myself. Hence me slinging ice cream to save for my first big adventure."

"If it helps, my parents would probably say the same. They're all about me paying my own way, working for what I want. It may not feel like it now, but I think you'll enjoy it more when you get there knowing you did it all yourself."

A scoff left me as I rolled my eyes. "Now you *definitely* sound like my moms."

Seth laughed, letting the subject die off, turning his attention back to our assignment.

Reworking the iconic balcony scene using modern prose and laces of humor somehow eroded the tension that built around Seth and me. As we fell easily back into our familiar banter, I began to wonder if step one wouldn't be so hard after all.

I had already grieved the romantic loss of him for months. Maybe over time, some semblance of friendship could rise from the remains. Maybe my first step was more about final acceptance than the grief of something that never was?

It didn't take long for us to be laughing and joking, picking apart each other's dialogue with critical humor.

"That's too corny," I challenged, rolling my eyes as he grinned. "Throwing stones at her window?"

"It isn't corny," he replied firmly, pulling my laptop toward him to commandeer it. "It's romantic and adorable. He wants to get her attention, right?"

"Yeah, but it's been done before," I argued. "We should try to think of something more modern."

"Modern is not romantic," he said, shaking his head. "What would you have him do? Text her 'Sup, girl, wanna Netflix and chill?'"

I snorted indelicately and pushed at his arm. The action earned me a deep, heavy laugh that sent a thrill down my spine, his lips curving upward into the lopsided grin that I loved, and that damn dimple making an appearance. It was like the trifecta of hotness. I allowed myself a glance, feeding the demon I was desperate to conquer. The nervous uncertainty that had been written all over his face when I arrived was long gone, replaced with the easy confidence I equated him with. His green eyes crinkled with teasing, the dimple in his cheek on full display as his fingers flew across the keyboard. With a firm tap, he ended the scene before crossing his arms across himself triumphantly.

"There. Masterpiece," Seth said with a nod before turning to me. "I swear, sometimes I think you're Mercutio."

"What!" I exclaimed loudly, earning myself a round of shhs from others in the library. Lowering my voice, I glared at him indignantly. "How do you figure?"

He grinned mercilessly, pleased he was getting a rise out of me. "Well, you can be a hot head, like you just proved." When I frowned, he laughed knowingly. "You hate pretentious crap, have a biting sense of humor, and sometimes I wonder if you even care about love and relationships."

I bristled, squaring myself to him. He was clearly goading me. This was what we did. Compared each other to characters in books, movies, television shows, based on little quirks or observations. It had become a game of ours, but sometimes it was also a challenge of creativity.

"Well, in that case, you're Benvolio," I countered. "Even-tempered, romantic to a fault, and kind of an enigma."

"How am I an enigma?" he asked, genuinely curious.

I hesitated, wondering if I had somehow backed myself into a corner. My little slip was as much about my personal predicament as it was a comment on his personality, and I feared I may have revealed a little too much about how much I noticed him.

Keeping my composure, I chose my words carefully. "I guess because you don't really say what you think very often, unless pressed. I mean, sometimes it feels like you have a lot to say but never *say* it. Maybe people don't always know where they stand with you because of it."

His steely, captivating stare trapped me in his grip, and as much as I wanted to, I couldn't look away. If he was offended, I couldn't tell. If he agreed, I couldn't decipher from his expression. If anything, he was proving me right.

"Do you really not know where you stand with me?" he asked, his voice surprisingly low.

I held his gaze, the look showing a hint of true curiosity. Clearing my throat, I dropped my eyes to break the spell he cast on me.

"I didn't mean me," I lied, reaching out to pull the laptop back toward me as a distraction. "I just mean in general, you're kind of the quiet, sensitive type. You don't really put it all out there like some people, so I guess your actions aren't always clear."

Whether he believed me or not, I couldn't tell. Mainly because I refused to look at him, to let my own anxious eyes betray me. Silence fell between us, as if waiting to be broken by my honesty or his.

"You mean like with Brae?" he said, forcing me to look up to him again. His eyes were forward now, and immediately I felt bad for being baited into an honesty hour session.

I didn't reply at first. Not because he wasn't right but because the weight of guilt swept over me quicker than I expected. Guilt for projecting a bit of my own insecurities on him by pointing out he doesn't always speak up and guilt for bringing up the one thing that was like a grenade between us, waiting to go off at any minute.

He turned to me, eyes softer now, vacant of the taunting humor they held only moments before. He said nothing, waiting for me to confirm what we both already knew.

"I'm sorry," I finally said, shaking my head. "I didn't mean it like that."

He didn't look away for a long while, as if studying me. Finally, when I still refused to engage in this particular topic, he sighed, rubbed his hands over his face, and looked back to the computer.

"I think we should keep most of the dialogue at the balcony the same. Not the iambic pentameter style, but keep it as true as possible. It's our favorite scene, so we don't want to stray too far."

And with that, the bubble was broken, burst with the pinprick of my evasion.

We worked for half an hour longer, the conversation not laced with tension but not nearly as easy as it should have been. The way it used to be, before his breakup with my best friend.

As noon approached, we finished off the act before calling it a day and going our separate ways. After saying goodbye on the steps of the library, I watched him walk to his car from my place on the sidewalk. Head down, books tucked under his arm, dark hair ruffled in the light breeze, he looked as lost in his thoughts as I felt.

Watching him sway back and forth between the confident, relaxed boy I knew and a guarded, uncertain one wearing his face, I couldn't help but wonder if he was battling his own demons just as Brae and I were facing ours. And if so, what they could be.

CHAPTER SIX

Brae and I pulled into the student parking lot on Monday morning, her fingers wrapped so tight around the steering wheel, her knuckles blanched.

"You'll be fine," I said soothingly, hoping that the tone of my voice somehow calmed her.

"Uh-huh."

A long silence fell between us, her panic spiraling into a tornado.

"Brae?"

"What?" she whispered as she slid her sleek little Jetta into a space near the back of the lot.

"You will be fine," I repeated a little firmer. "It's just another day at school."

"No, it isn't," she huffed with a shaky breath. "It is the first actual day of school where I'll see Seth since we broke up."

"And you'll get through it," I promised her, placing a hand gently on her arm. My touch broke her from her panic, her wide eyes turning to me. I had never seen her look so nervous before in all the years I had known her.

Braelyn Walker didn't *do* nervous. At least, not outwardly. She told me as much when we were eleven and I had to do my first ever presentation in front of the whole class.

I was terrified, spending sleepless nights obsessing over my presentation and long, exhausted days begging my moms to write me a note to excuse me from class.

Public speaking had always been, and remained to this day, one of my greatest fears. If it hadn't been for Brae, I probably would have failed.

Because it was her who stayed up with me on the phone during those nights of panic, talking me down and giving me tips for looking and acting confident even when I wasn't. It was her who listened over and over again as I practiced my presentation until she could mouth the words along with me, correcting me when I missed a sentence or slowing me down when panic sped my voice up to racecar speed.

And it was her—I found out months later—who had threatened everyone in class that if they heckled me and if they did anything short of enthusiastic cheering, she would ensure they suffered long and painful deaths.

She had gotten me through one of the most anxiety-ridden experiences of my young life. I was determined to do the same for her.

"Come on," I said with a squeeze of her arm. "Let's just get this over with. It's like ripping off a Band-Aid. Just do it quick, and it won't be so bad."

To this, she actually snorted. "Yeah right, that crap is a lie. It still hurts like hell."

Walking through the parking lot toward the school, I stayed at Brae's side. Like a faithful protector, I tried to ward off any stares, comments, or smirks that may be sent in her direction while simultaneously considering my own fears for the day to come. What it would be like to see Seth again, with Brae at my side? To ignore the plaguing questions that had continued to rattle in my brain since our study session at the library and to make a stand on Team Walker.

"Want to know something stupid?" she asked, her eyes darting across the faces we passed as if expecting someone to jump out at her at any moment.

"Sure?"

"I just keep thinking how Seth is officially single again. He's free to date whoever he wants, and that thought terrifies me. I know it's stupid but . . . my heart hurts when I think about it."

All I could do was nod, swallowing back the lump that formed in my throat as I reached down to take Brae's hand in mine. A bubble of guilt rose in my stomach because that same thought had crossed my mind over the course of the weekend as well.

But as much as he was free to date, I wasn't free to date him.

Brae's breathing came in rapid, shallow breaths, her lips pulled into a tight line. Shaking her head, she paused in the middle of the hall, forcing other students to edge around us like a rock in a stream.

Panic glinted in her eyes. "I need a minute," she told me, turning toward a water fountain, which was blocked by three freshman girls. It only took a moment for them to notice Brae, each of their expressions ranging from surprise to uncertainty to wonder to find junior class royalty in their presence. When they made no attempt to speak or move aside, Brae brought a hand to her hip, expectantly.

"Move!" she barked, causing them to startle and scatter like leaves in the wind.

Tsking, she took a long drink, before straightening and exhaling slowly. "Okay. I think I'm ready."

I snorted. "Making freshmen crap themselves does have a way of brightening your spirit."

Michelle and Erin were already at our side-by-side lockers by the time we arrived. Michelle was glued to her phone, fingers typing frantically, while Erin had a firm look of determination on their face. Bright orange peeked out from the bottom of their pant leg, and I could have sworn I saw tiny cacti wearing sombreros on their socks.

"You got this," Erin said the moment we joined them. "Remember, you got through last week unscathed. Everyone knows you guys broke up now, so the worst is over."

Michelle nodded in agreement before finally looking up from her phone, her hair loose in a full afro around her head. Today's eye shadow was a brilliant yellow, the color cheerful despite the dim hallway lighting. "And if you need to hide in your car to have a meltdown, just text us, and we'll meet you there."

Brae snorted, but a soft smile played at her lips in thanks as she gathered her books. We parted ways, Erin and I escaping to biology while Michelle and Brae went to history. Next to Brae, I was probably closest to Erin in our little group, but still not close enough to dare sharing my deepest and darkest secrets. We both liked hiking and reading and preferred laid-back nights in over parties and social drama. I stole glances at them as they prattled about their bio assignment, wondering if they somehow could see my betrayal scrawled across my face. Like the letter A branded on my chest, did they know I not only shared affection for public enemy number one but also had yet to actually separate him from my life?

Thankfully, we made it through most of the morning without incident. By the time fourth period came around, Brae was actually starting to relax as we met up at our lockers.

"So how's the day going?" I asked, watching her from the corner of my eye as I tried to convince my temperamental lock to allow me access to my books.

"Okay, actually," she replied. "A few people have said stuff to me. Depending on who they were I either said everything was fine and played up the sympathy, or threatened to burn them alive if they ever approached me again. But otherwise, it hasn't been anything too bad."

"That's great!" I offered with a little too much enthusiasm. I cringed at myself. "I mean, other than the burning people alive thing. I've warned you about open threats of bodily harm," I teased.

"Whatever," she replied with a dismissive wave of her hand. "I haven't seen Seth, which is both the best and hardest part," she admitted. "I mean, I'm so used to seeing him between classes and texting him and stuff. It is a hard habit to break, and I feel like I miss those little things I never thought about before." Closing her locker, Brae sighed as she leaned a shoulder against it to face me. "I spent most of last period thinking maybe it was better to just see him and get it over with, you know? Like the Band-Aid bullcrap you said in the car. Maybe if I see him, it won't be as bad as my mind is thinking. And once it's done, then maybe—"

Her rambling cut off short, her voice fading into a squeak. My brows pinched in confusion as her eyes widened, face paling as her gaze fell over my shoulder.

I already knew what I would find before I saw him.

Seth had just come around the far corner, laughing with Jeff Mills from his baseball team. The two were strolling down the hall, so completely casual, as if nothing had changed.

Until he looked up and his eyes met with Brae's. His expression quickly changed to match hers, of wide-eyed uncertainty, the words he spoke to Jeff dying in his throat before his mouth closed and jaw tightened. My gaze flickered between Seth and Brae, waiting to see what would happen. This first encounter was what Brae had feared, and now that it was here, suddenly I felt just as nervous.

I turned to distract her, but the moment I tried, Seth's gaze moved from Brae to me. He stared at me with a quiet intensity I hadn't seen in him before, and it left me befuddled, with adrenaline singing through my veins. It was an intense look, something penetrating that I just couldn't place.

Just as he moved a step past us, he turned back to Jeff, continuing their conversation. Watching him with a clouded mind, I was left bewildered until he disappeared into the fray of students loitering the halls, blocking him from view.

The moment he was out of sight, Brae lost her mind.

"Oh God," she cried, her voice reaching an unnatural octave. "That was worse than I thought it would be! Did you see that? Hannah, he completely ignored me! He barely even looked at me. It was like I wasn't even here!"

She started to hyperventilate, cornering herself against the lockers to hide from curious eyes.

Pulling myself together despite my own flustered state, I moved in close to her. "Brae, it's okay. Look, that was what you were scared of, right? Seeing him again? Well, it's done now! You can stop worrying about how it will go because it's finished."

"But he didn't even say anything, Hannah," she cried, tears slowly sliding down her cheeks. "He just walked right by."

"Braelyn, that's expected," I said calmly. "It's totally normal for you guys not to talk to each other for a little while as you adjust. He's probably just as nervous about all this as you are, so of course he isn't going to come up and chat. What would he say? He can't exactly act like everything is okay and normal, so he probably figured it best to just keep his distance for now."

Like I should have, I thought to myself, guilt coloring my cheeks.

"But, Hannah . . ." her voice trailed off as she gave in to her upset, taking long, strategic breaths to try and calm herself. I placed my hand on her back, rubbing slow circles. It was an action my mom always did when I was upset as a child, but it rarely worked.

The rest of the day passed without incident, without meltdown, and without any more appearances from Seth. Our drive home was quiet and tense, neither of us seeming to know what to say.

My evening passed in uneventful normalcy; a drastic contrast from my dramatic school day. I finished my homework before dinner, listened to my moms discuss their upcoming marathon training, and endured their endless questions about school and how Brae was handling her breakup.

"She's okay," I said as I finished my last bite of meatloaf. "I mean, she's upset and kind of lost it after she saw him at school, but overall, she's doing okay."

Mom nodded. "Breakups are never easy. Especially for a girl like Braelyn."

Raising a brow, I looked at her curiously. "What does that mean?"

"I don't mean it in a negative way, Hannah, so you can stop shooting me daggers. You know we love Brae like she's your sister, but you can't deny that she is used to getting her own way. She always has. For Seth to break up with her is a blow to her ego, and that isn't something she's had to deal with before."

My jaw tightened in annoyance. One of the hardest parts of having a parent who was a psychology professor was the constant analysis, much of which was much too accurate for comfort. "Don't psychoanalyze her, Mom."

Despite my tone, her smile was patient. "I'm not psychoanalyzing her, Hannah. I'm merely pointing out that Brae is used to things going her way and doesn't handle any deviation well." Taking a sip of her wine, she tilted her head at me. "Remember when she lost out on the lead role in *Sleeping Beauty*? She was inconsolable, even though acting is not her strength, and she knew it."

I scowled. "That was the fifth grade!"

Ma stepped in to defuse the situation like she usually did.

"How is Seth handling it?"

I turned to her, my expression of indignation changing to surprise. "I don't know."

"He's your friend, too, isn't he?"

"Yeah . . ."

"Well, don't give up on him just because of this situation, Hannah. I know being stuck in the middle when friends break things off is hard, but don't forget that you were his friend before Brae was his girlfriend. He might be afraid that you'll push him away in a show of solidarity to Brae, which wouldn't be fair. Try to be there for him, too."

I scowled, instantly irritated at Ma's insight into teen friendship. Ma was always the emotional one, the mediator, and the one who always considered how others felt. Mom, on the other hand, was all facts and hard truths. They were complete opposites, much like Brae and I.

Except when they used those traits against me. While I agreed with Ma that cutting Seth out was not fair, that was easier said than done. It was hard to play the devil's advocate between feuding exes when the devil was whispering in your ear, singing sonnets of Seth's perfection.

Once I finally escaped the inquisition at the dinner table, I settled in for a quiet evening of Netflix and solitude. The last few days had been stressful, between handling Brae's meltdowns, picking up extra shifts at Alley Scoops, and my ever-increasing homework loads, I desperately needed a little me time away from responsibility.

Unfortunately, it only lasted about fifteen minutes before my phone chimed. Seth's name appeared on the screen, clenching icy fingers around my heart.

Seth: *Sorry about today :(*

I didn't have to ask to know exactly what he was referring to.

Hannah: *It's okay. I understand.*

Seth: *But does Brae? Her face pretty much screamed mutiny that I didn't speak to her.*

A sad smile curved my lips.

Hannah: *Yeah, she understands, even if she doesn't like it.*

It was a lie, and I had little doubt he knew that.

A long pause passed, and I wondered if our invisible connection had broken, until I saw the tiny dots flickering to life on the screen.

Seth: *I get that talking to Brae may take a while, but not talking to you feels strange.*

My heart began to gallop, a tingle rising in my fingers as I clutched my phone. Immediately, I groaned in frustration with myself. I shouldn't care that he missed coming up and talking to me. Because I shouldn't want to talk to him. I'm supposed to be getting him out of my system, not swooning over emotional breadcrumbs that keep leading me back to him.

I was the literal worst at this.

He continued before I could reply.

Seth: *Is that weird?*

My mind wandered back to Ma's comments at dinner, that Seth and I were friends before Braelyn was in the picture. That our friendship will need to adjust, but shouldn't dismantle because of my loyalty to Brae.

Pulling myself together, I forced my fingers to dance across the screen.

Hannah: *No. It's not weird.*

I stared at the screen, waiting for his next reply, when Brae's name appeared as an incoming call. Panic tightened around my throat, certain that she could somehow see my indiscretion through the invisible tie between our phones. Taking a few deep breaths, I slid my finger across the screen to answer. I had barely said hello when her frantic voice chimed through the phone.

"I want to text him," she blurted, her words jumbling together in their haste to escape.

"What?" I squeaked guiltily.

"I want to text Seth," she said, no slower for the second attempt. "It's driving me crazy, Hannah. He totally ignored me today, and I need to text him and ask him what the hell is up. Is he seriously just going to act like I don't exist anymore? He can't just ignore me like I am nothing to him! He can't—"

"Braelyn, for goodness' sake, breathe!" I groaned, unable to control myself against her dramatics.

Her words cut off, as a quivering breath, then a long exhale sounded through the phone. Neither of us said anything for a long while as she tried to calm herself.

"Better?"

"Not really," she said weakly.

"Brae, I told you this would be hard. I said it would suck for a while, and that things would feel awkward."

"I know, but I didn't know it would feel this bad."

"Well, it does. But remember step one?"

"Yes. Allow yourself to grieve."

"And what was one of the biggest points under step one?"

When she didn't clue in to which one I meant, I answered for her.

"Don't freak out," I said softly. "You'll want to do something stupid and let your emotions rule. But you can't do that, okay? Don't call him, don't text him, don't reach out to him. I promise, no good can come from it, and it will only end up hurting more in the long run. You can't get over someone you keep talking to."

My words echoed in my ears, a twinge of guilt rising in my chest as if to remind me to take my own advice. I was trying to get over Seth just as much as Brae, and yet, I was the one who had met up with him only a few days ago, was texting him just as often as before, and had broken basically every rule of step one.

Not only did I suck as a friend, I was completely failing my own endeavor of crush detox.

Silence greeted me through the line, a sound so loud in its nothingness that I started to wonder if she hung up on me. Finally, I heard her sigh in resignation.

"But what if he's texting someone else?"

Fear wrapped it's hands around my throat, choking me. Silence crashed through the line, loud in the absence of my response, but I couldn't pull myself together quickly enough.

Did she know? Somehow, in all her infinite gossip sleuthing skills, did she find out I had been texting Seth and this was her way of trying to get me to admit it? Did she know we met up the other day and—despite giving me her blessing to keep working on the project—still consider it the ultimate betrayal?

Panic and guilt threatened to pull me under as I swallowed against the lump in my throat to respond.

"I'm sure he's not," I lied, cringing at myself. "But even if he is, it doesn't matter. You have a plan. It's *your* plan, regardless of him."

A long sigh echoed through the line. "Yeah. You're right."

"Do you feel better?" I asked, the adrenaline in my system slowly ebbing.

"No. But I'm better than I was a few minutes ago."

"That's good."

"I'm sorry I freaked out," she huffed. "This is only the first week, and I'm already screwing up the steps."

"They aren't meant to always go forward. You're going to have setbacks, but that's okay. So long as in the long run you keep moving forward, you'll get through it all."

I adjusted the phone against my ear.

"Thank you for talking me off the ledge."

I smiled as though she could see me. "I'm used to it. I've been doing it since we were kids."

Thankfully, she laughed. "I guess I always have been the dramatic one."

"Understatement of the century."

"Are you trying to upset me again?" she asked with her signature sass.

"No, just stating the truth. You've always been the impulsive one. Remember when Sammy Fenwick told me I was weird cause I didn't have a dad? And even though I wanted to walk away and ignore it, you went over and kick him in the nuts."

The memory of my first real encounter with Braelyn Walker forced a smile to my face, the faint picture of Mrs. Nicholson's classroom entering my mind. Despite sitting next to each other for weeks during first grade, Brae and I had never spoken. Even then, I was all knobby knees and awkward glances, preferring to keep to myself than put myself out there. I supposed this made me an easy target for someone like Sammy Fenwick, who took it upon himself to tease me relentlessly about my less than traditional parental situation.

Invisible hands still clenched around my heart at the memory of his words, the insinuation that I was other, that my moms were strange. The burning in my eyes and throat still echoed like fresh wounds, the inclination to run and hide gripping my limbs.

Until Braelyn came stomping up to us at the sandbox. The determination on her face, her tiny hands balled into fists, jolted a new wave of fear through me. Was she going to join in on my torment?

When she tapped Sammy on the shoulder, his face lit up as if she was about to talk to him. That smile only lasted a moment, however, before she pulled back her leg and kicked him square in the groin. I sucked in a sharp breath of surprise, almost as loud as Sammy's groan of pain, as he doubled over into the sand and Brae berated him for being a bully.

I stared at her in awe as she reached out and brought me to my feet, bringing me over to meet her other friends, Erin and Michelle. We never again spoke about that incident, but from that moment on, we became each other's person.

We saw each other through everything. First crushes, first periods. Losing my grandfather, her parent's divorce. No matter the differences between us, she was my one constant, as I was hers. Our lives bound together by fate and a list of rules we scribbled into a notebook in middle school, ensuring no matter what, our friendship would endure.

Finally, a faint giggle slipped through the phone as she finally conceded to being the dramatic one of our duo.

She laughed lightly at the memory. "He was a jerk. He deserved it."

A smile crept across my lips. "Your mom was so mad at you for that."

"And yours thanked me for sticking up for you."

"See. You've always been the drama queen in this relationship. Now is no different."

She was quiet again, trying not to admit that I was right.

"I hate you," she laughed.

"And I love you."

"See you tomorrow?"

"Tomorrow is another day, Brae," I reminded her.

"And one step closer to getting over Seth."

CHAPTER SEVEN

"What did she want us to get again?" I asked, plucking a shopping basket from the front of the store.

Brae rolled her eyes. "I don't know. Some fancy-ass sauce for some stupid thing she's making for some dinner party."

I snorted. "That narrows it down."

My sass earned me a small smile as Brae pulled her phone from her pocket, showing me the name of the item. I nodded, still having no idea exactly what we were looking for, before leading Brae toward the condiment aisle.

Today was supposed to be a relaxing movie night where we did nothing but watch stabby horror shows and eat junk. We were only halfway through the first serial killer documentary when Mrs. Walker asked us to pick up a few things at the grocery store for her. While Brae was ready to refuse out of pure spite, I couldn't help my habit of needing to constantly please people of authority and agreed. It took promising to buy Brae an extra-large bag of Twizzlers for her to participate.

It didn't take long for Brae to lose interest in our mission, instead disappearing to collect random snacks and ice cream, leaving me to search for Mrs. Walker's fancy sauce. While this wasn't exactly how I expected to spend my Friday evening, at least I was able to get Brae out of the house under the guise of junk food and fresh air.

My eyes snagged on the swirling script of a bottle, a thrill of success zipping through me for finally finding the elusive sauce. Tossing it in my basket, I went in search of Brae. Unable to find her in the chip or chocolate aisles, I was shocked to find her hovering by a stack of bananas with a contemplative purse of her lips.

"What are you doing?" I asked as I stepped up to her side.

"Wondering if mixing in a couple bananas will offset the calorie intake of all this," she said, showing me the bags of chips, chocolate, and carton of ice cream in her grasp.

I coughed a laugh. "I don't think that's how calories work, Brae."

Dumping her items into my basket, she lifted a slim shoulder. "Couldn't hurt," she muttered, plucking a couple of bananas from the pile.

I grimaced. "Can we go home now? We have five more episodes of the documentary, and—"

A sharp gasp cut me off, Brae's eyes widening in horror. Her hands splayed in front of her as if warding off an attack, her face paling.

"Brae, what—"

"Shh!" she hissed, glancing around in panic, attempting to hide behind me. "Don't say my name so loud!"

"What? Why?"

"Because!" she replied in a razor-edged whisper. "Don't bring their attention over here!"

I began to look around the store for the source of her freak-out, befuddled. "Who?"

The moment I saw him, everything made sense. Over by the smoothie bar, flanked by two members from his baseball team, was Seth. My stomach plummeted, reminders of our texting and our study session that I still hadn't told Brae about flashing through my mind.

Turning back to Brae, I focused on keeping her calm. "Brae, it's not a big deal. Just—"

"Not a big deal?" she shrieked, gesturing wildly to herself. "You convinced me that I didn't have to change just to go to the store, and now I'm about to run into my ex looking like *this*!"

She held her arms out to me, displaying her wrinkled T-shirt, yoga pants, and messy bun. Face bare of makeup, bra strap showing, her feet clad in flip-flops.

I didn't see anything wrong with how she was dressed, but for Brae, the fact that she let me convince her to go out in flip-flops spoke volumes to her emotional state.

A snicker threatened to bubble up from my core just as Brae grabbed my arm. "Oh God, they're turning this way!"

Before I had a chance to respond, she dropped to her knees and slipped behind the banana stand, leaving me to stare open-mouthed. Tucking herself behind the produce, she reached out and shoved at my legs. "Go! Get rid of them!"

"Brae—"

"GO!"

The force of her shove almost sent me sprawling, but I quickly intercepted Seth and his friends at the bakery section before they could near Brae's hiding place.

"Hey!" I called, my voice high-pitched and awkward. "Fancy seeing you here."

"Hey, Hannah," Seth replied, a brilliant smile taking over his features. It was so genuine, butterflies erupted in my core, my throat turning dry. The dark blue shirt he wore pulled tightly across his chest and shoulders, emphasizing his frame in the most taunting way.

It was like even his clothes were determined for me to fail in getting over him!

"What are you up to?" he continued, oblivious to my motive.

I lifted a shoulder in an attempt to seem casual. "Just getting weekend snacks."

As their attention fell to my overflowing basket, my eyes closed with embarrassment.

"You having a party or something?" his friend, Shawn, teased, tossing me a flirtatious grin. "'Cause if you were, I'd show up."

Seth frowned, slapping his friend on the chest.

I laughed awkwardly, a flush coloring my cheeks. "No, no. Just . . . errands for my moms." Quickly, I tried to think of a way to get him out of the store. "What are you guys doing? Don't you have practice?"

He lifted an eyebrow. "Practice ended over an hour ago," he clarified. "Just here getting smoothies."

"Ah. Right, sure," I stammered, just as a commotion rose from across the store. Seth looked beyond me, and as I turned, I saw several people casting confused and irritated looks toward the produce section.

"What's going on over there?" Seth asked, taking a step closer.

I reached out quickly, placing a hand on his chest. His muscles tightened beneath my palm, as I jerked away quickly. Heat scalded my face, as I tried to redirect their attention. "Oh, I think some kid made a mess in the fruit section. No big deal."

Ugh, this was a disaster. Not only was I making a complete fool of myself in front of Seth and his friends, I was standing here chatting with the boy I was supposed to be getting out of my system! It was like fate was determined for me to fail and spend eternity in unrequited love with my best friend's ex.

The boys each gave me looks of various confusion as I quickly gestured to the drinks in their hands. "Well, I better go. And you probably want to drink those before they get warm."

Seth's brow pinched, his friends exchanging looks that made it clear they thought I was losing it, before they turned toward the exit. Just as I began to exhale a breath of relief, Seth called over his shoulder. "I'll text you to set up our next study session. We still have a lot of work to get through."

"Yup. Sure. Okay." I waved like a lunatic, earning myself more dubious glances, until they finally slipped through the door and out of sight.

The moment they were gone, I rushed back to the banana stand where Brae was already leaping to her feet. Grabbing my wrist, she dragged me through three more aisles of snacks before pulling me toward the check out.

The moment we were back in the safety of her car, she lost it.

"I failed step one!" she sobbed, her beautiful face streaked with tears.

"Brae—"

"Step one, don't freak out, don't do something stupid. Well, I freaking failed it!"

"No, you didn't."

"Hannah! I hid. Behind the banana stand. Literally dropped to my knees like it was a bomb drill and hid under the produce."

A bubble of laughter threatened to erupt, but I held it back. Brae was hanging on by a fraying, thin thread, and one little giggle might push her right over the edge.

Instead, I stared at her, not knowing what to say. I was silently thankful that her eyes were now closed, wallowing in her despair and self-loathing, so she couldn't see me fighting back laughter.

"The whole time you were talking to him, I had to fight the urge to stomp over there and tell him off. But my sense of self-preservation won out, and I tucked under the fruit instead."

This time, I couldn't stop the little snicker that snuck out.

Brae sat up, looking indignant. "You think that's funny? Hannah, I literally just humiliated myself in the grocery store! I hid from my ex behind bananas, for Christ's sake!"

Again, another laugh escaped, and I shook my head. "Brae, come on. Even *you* have to be able to see how that is kind of funny."

She only glared at me in response. "It is *not* funny. I not only embarrassed myself in front of all those people, but I am totally flunking at your stupid steps! We're still only on the first one, and I've already freaked out at school when I saw him, tried to call him in a tizzy, and now did a stop, drop, and roll at the Publix!"

Her frantic references to putting out a burning fire broke the last of my control, and I laughed loudly as I pulled a bag of Twizzlers from our shopping bag and handed it to her. Junk food was like therapy for Brae, and while I knew there was very little I could say to ease the humiliation of the experience, at least I had snacks to distract her.

She shot me an angry glare from her place in the driver's seat, which was surely meant to calm my laughter. But all it did was make me double over, clutching at my stomach as tears flooded my eyes. When I finally pulled myself together, I was pleased to find her cracking a small smile.

"You have to admit it's kind of funny," I said gently.

"No, it isn't," she resisted as she giggled. "It was humiliating!"

"That doesn't mean it can't be funny," I argued. "If that was me . . ."

She pouted in defeat. "I'd probably pee my pants laughing at you."

"See." Controlling myself, I reached out and took her hands. "Brae, it's fine. You aren't failing at the steps."

"But—"

"What is the main point in step one?"

She paused, silently considering the question. "Let myself grieve."

"And has grieving ever been a pretty experience?" I asked. "Has it ever been smooth and followed any rules?"

I wasn't sure if I was preaching to her or myself at this point.

Again, she hesitated. "No."

"Then you aren't failing. You're going to feel emotional and want to reach out to him, just like you're going to want to hide from him and pretend he doesn't exist. But the whole point of this is to accept that it's normal and start to rationalize it all."

"I feel the complete opposite of rational lately."

"You mean, irrational?"

"Stop correcting my grammar when I'm upset," she scolded, slumping dejectedly.

"You're doing good. This step is the hardest, remember? This is where you deal with all the emotional stuff before you can move on to moving on."

"I don't like emotional stuff," she admitted, as if I didn't already know that. "It makes me feel all . . . weepy and weird. One minute I'm fine, the next I'm crying. Or hiding under bananas."

I grinned, trying to infuse more humor into the situation. "I think what you just experienced is called emotional incontinence. All over the produce aisle."

She blew out a long, frustrated breath, her eyes falling to the bags of food around her. "God, I went overboard," she commented, ripping open the Twizzlers. "All of this is emotional purchasing."

Grinning at her, I picked up a bag of chips, reclining the seat to get more comfortable. "You don't hear me complaining. Your emotional purchases mean I get to eat the stuff too."

We sat in silence, binging on the significant supply of junk food Brae had collected before her escape from Publix. Rolling down the window, the cool night air drifted through the car as our emotions began to level out.

"So, you guys had a study session?"

Her words caught me off guard, causing me to choke on my chocolate bar. "What?"

Turning, I expected to find her glaring at me. Instead, she was twirling a Twizzler between her fingers.

"I heard Seth say he would let you know about your next study session. I figured that meant you guys have met up since . . ." She trailed off, but I knew what she meant. That I had seen him since they broke up.

I tried to swallow against the lump forming in my throat as guilt and panic flooded my system. "Brae, I'm sorry. I wanted to tell you, but I didn't want you to get upset."

She nodded but didn't look my way. "When did you guys meet up?"

I hesitated before responding. "The other weekend. Just for a couple hours at the library."

Again, she nodded before blowing a long breath through her lips. "I get it, Hannah. You guys have an assignment to finish. I told you I was okay with it, and while I might have lied a bit, I refuse to put you in the middle of this. It . . . it was just a bit of a punch to the gut to hear that you can still hang out with him . . . that you *are* still hanging out with him. Even if it's just for school."

I opened my mouth to respond, to promise her that she was my best friend and my loyalty was with her. But all I could say was, "I'm sorry."

"I know," she said, shifting to lay her head on my shoulder. I leaned into her, resting my cheek on the top of her head as guilt gnawed at my heart.

CHAPTER EIGHT

"How did you do on that calculus test yesterday?" Mom asked before taking a sip of her water.

I cringed instinctively at the mention of mathematics. "Okay, I think. I should get my grade back next week." Of course I was exaggerating slightly at my optimism with my mark.

"You were pretty stressed out about it," Ma commented. "But every time we gave you practice questions, you got them right. I think you're better at math than you give yourself credit for."

"And I think you guys are just trying to keep me from crying myself to sleep over my textbook," I countered.

They grinned at my sass as the waitress dropped off three glasses of water, and we returned our attention to our menus.

Aptly named "The Diner," it was a perfect match of old and new. Red chairs, metal table tops, and a 1950s vibe matched against quirky recipes, free Wi-Fi, and a take-out window against the far wall made it one of the most popular spots in our neighborhood. It was a comfortable, familiar place that brought back memories from all our Sunday morning gatherings, and of course the food was amazing. The sound of content patrons was an endless white noise in my ears; the smells of syrup, pastries, and bacon making my stomach growl. Scanning over the menu, I set to my ritual of trying to decide between the French toast, Nutella waffles, or waffle sliders.

"Isn't that Seth?" Mom asked, causing Ma to follow her gaze.

Spinning around in my seat at the mention of his name, I found him immediately, lingering at the door flanked by his parents. I was surprised to see just how much he looked like his dad. Tall and dark, with light eyes, I could clearly imagine what Seth would look like at that age. His mother looked tiny beside him, but as she laughed, I could see exactly where he got his smile.

As if sensing someone staring, Seth turned and locked on my gaze. I froze and even considered turning back around or hunching down in the booth to hide. It wouldn't be quite as dramatic as Brae and her banana stand incident, but as the nervous anxiety raced through my veins, the inclination to hide from the boy I was desperately in love with and equally as desperate to get over, I could understand why she resorted to such measures.

"Oh, look, he's coming this way," Mom said brightly as Seth broke away from his parents to head in our direction.

Crap! Crap, crap, crap!

When he reached our table, he dazzled me with one of his dimpled smirks that made my heart flutter like the traitor it was.

"Hey." He grinned, shoving his hands in his pockets. "Fancy seeing you here."

Pushing down my nerves, I tried to keep my face neutral. "We come here every Sunday. Family breakfast kind of thing."

Seth nodded before turning to my moms. "Nice to see you again," Seth said, giving that breathtaking smile to my mothers.

"So good to see you, Seth." With a teasing grin, Ma jerked her chin toward me. "Maybe you could help us settle a debate. Would you please tell Hannah that calculus is not the work of the devil and will in fact be a benefit to her future?"

"Ma!" I shrieked, mortification flooding my veins.

Seth looked down to me, a curious tilt to his head. "You're struggling?"

Burying my face in my hands, I emitted a pitiful groan of confirmation that earned me a laugh from Seth.

His smooth voice floated above the din of the diner. "I can't say I love calculus, but I have a feeling my dad would probably have the same idea about it looking good on my transcript."

Heat flooded my face as he continued to chat with my mom, fear twisting at my gut as I glanced out the window instinctively as if being watched. While Brae acknowledged that I would still have to work with Seth on our English homework, somehow being seen with him out in public felt like crossing enemy lines. Not to mention that I was struggling to claw my way through my first step, and I was pretty sure that consorting at The Diner with him was against the rules.

Every blond that walked by caused my heart rate to spike, fearing that Brae would catch me in his orbit and brand me a traitor.

"Hey, Hannah." His voice pulled me from my thoughts. "Can I steal you for a second?"

As I rose to my feet to stand closer to him, a pull tugged at my heart as though he were gravity to my soul. I knew that despite all my good intentions, all my rules and all my steps, my body was betraying me to him just like my heart. We moved away from the booth, choosing to lean against the counter in one of the limited vacancies.

Seth lowered his head discretely, dropping his voice.

"So . . . how are you?" he asked. "You sounded . . . a little weird at the store the other day."

"Great!" I said with a little too much enthusiasm. Closing my eyes at my stupidity, I tried to rein myself in. Clearing my throat, I regained my thrown composure. "I'm good. How are you?"

He pursed his lips, as if considering exactly how to answer my innocent question. "Good." A silence overtook us, as if both of us were expecting the other to say something more. He finally said the one thing that we had yet to discuss. "How's Brae?"

"She's great!" I said, again with cringe-worthy, false enthusiasm. "She's doing really well."

He waited a moment. "Is that so?"

"Yup." I nodded eagerly. "She was a little thrown when you guys broke up, but I think she's doing really good now."

He raised an eyebrow, a hint of his sexy, lopsided smirk breaking through.

"So, that's why she hid behind the banana stand at the grocery the other day?" he asked innocently, causing my face to fall.

I stared at him with wide-eyed panic, my mind racing on how to salvage my best friend's reputation. I opened my mouth a few times, determined to say something witty and brilliant on her behalf, but nothing came out. All I could do was stare at his sea-foam green eyes, that stupid dimple, and panic silently.

"You saw her?"

He nodded. "Well, she did kind of drop to the floor like she triggered a trap door, then crawled under a shelf of fruit."

"Ugh."

"Don't worry," he said with a dismissive wave of his hand. "I would never say anything to her about it. My friends didn't even notice. But I figured that was why you rushed over to us, acting all weird. Creating a diversion and all."

I groaned, burying my face in my hands. "I hoped you hadn't noticed."

"It's not a big deal." Seth let a single laugh escape. I sighed, shaking my head at myself for making Brae sound like an unstable mess, even if it was sort of true.

"Does she know we're still seeing each other?"

My eyes shot to his, wide and incredulous. "What?"

"For English," he clarified. "You know? *Romeo and Juliet?*"

"Oh," I said, heat rising along the back of my neck. "Yeah. Sure. She's totally fine with it."

Not exactly a lie . . . more of an embellishment, I told myself.

Again, I opened my mouth to say something more to make Brae sound unfazed by his absence, but the words that came out were not the face-saving comments in favor of Brae, but a question of my own that I had been pondering for some time.

"Why did you break up with her?" I asked bluntly.

The moment the words were out of my mouth, I blanched, taking a step back from him.

"I'm sorry. I shouldn't have asked. Don't answer that."

"No, no. It's fine." Swallowing hard, he dropped his eyes. "I think I just realized that the longer I stayed with Brae, the more likely I was to miss out on something that really fit."

"Like what?" I blurted, no longer hesitant in questioning him.

He stared at me, the electricity between us heightening to become almost audible. I silently urged him to answer me as a figure slid up beside us.

"Seth," his father called, his mother at his flank, breaking our moment like bursting a bubble. "Our table is ready."

"Okay," Seth replied, looking between me and his parents with hesitation. "Mom, Dad, this is Hannah."

His mother was the first to reach out to me, taking my hand. She was smiling so warmly, I couldn't help but return the gesture. "So nice to meet you, Hannah. Do you go to school with Seth?"

"Yes, ma'am," I replied with a nod. "We have English together."

"Oh! You're the young lady he's rewriting *Romeo and Juliet* with, aren't you?" she continued, surprising me with the memory.

I nodded, and Seth's father joined in the conversation. "Hannah," he said thoughtfully, as if trying to place my name. "Are you friends with Braelyn Walker?"

At the mention of Brae's name, Seth tensed noticeably, throwing his father a warning glance the older man ignored.

"Yes," I answered softly, unsure where the direction of the conversation was headed.

Mr. Linwood pursed his lips. "Braelyn mentioned you a couple of times. You two have been friends a long time, if I remember correctly."

"Since we were kids," I confirmed.

"She's such a nice girl," he continued with a wistful tone.

Seth's jaw tensed as he stared at his father. His mother reached out and took her husband's hand. Gently, she pulled him back toward the hostess stand before turning to me. "It was very nice to finally meet you, Hannah."

"You too."

The moment his parents walked away, leaving me alone again with Seth, it was like a vortex had split open, draining all the tension that had built during the short conversation. It was clear that Seth's dad wasn't too happy with his son's decision to break things off with the queen of East River High.

"Sorry about that," Seth said softly, obviously embarrassed. "He was always pretty enchanted by Brae."

I nodded, not knowing what else to say. Or, if there was even anything *to* say. My feet felt nailed to the linoleum tiles, rooted in place with yet another reminder of why I would never compare to Brae. To be the girl to follow her in any boy's life, especially Seth's, would be daunting. Now knowing that his father thought so highly of her made me want to give up on my foolish crush entirely. Like a bucket of cold water forcing me out of step one and on to step two.

Glancing to his parents, he sighed. "I better go. If my dad doesn't get bacon in his stomach before eleven, he gets cranky."

I laughed at his change of topic, and he gave my moms a wave goodbye.

"I'll talk to you later," he said, offering me a wave before following his parents toward a booth at the opposite end of the diner.

Sliding back into my seat, exhaustion enveloped my body despite the fact that all I had done was have a short, tension-filled conversation with Seth and his parents. My moms' eyes were on me, but I refused to look their way. Instead, I turned my own back to the menu, trying to decide which breakfast to order. Although, now my stomach was filled with butterflies, leaving not much room left for waffles.

STEP TWO:
GET RID OF REMINDERS OF THE RELATIONSHIP

Out with the old, in with the anything but you.

CHAPTER NINE

"Ugh!" I groaned, giving my locker a weak punch for good measure. Scowling, I set to work twirling the lock between my fingers for the third time, pausing a little longer than necessary on each number of my combination to show the stubborn device that I was, in fact, choosing the correct digits. Reaching the final number, I was confident that this time I would be victorious. But with a pull of the lock, it held its ground, refusing to open.

I glared at it with vengeful spite. "I hate you."

"Still having bitter conversations with your locker, huh?" His voice caused me to startle, spinning to face him. Seth stood only a foot from me, wearing a black Henley that hugged along the breadth of his chest, clinging to his arms in a taunting way. The color made his black hair seem even darker, his green eyes lighter, and my knees gave a little wobble at the sight.

He smiled at me teasingly, that damn dimple appearing, before he gently pushed me out of the way.

"Here," he said, setting to work on the lock. His deft fingers expertly spun the combination, barely pausing on the numbers, before giving it a successful pull. On the first try, it sprung open, obeying his command.

My locker was just as much of a traitor to him as my heart.

"Show off," I muttered, trying to appear unaffected by his presence, even though I was affected as hell. He laughed.

"It was good to see you the other day," he said, resting a shoulder against the lockers as I fiddled through my books.

"Yeah, you too."

"I think that's the first time we've actually seen each other outside of school without Brae. At least, other than English homework."

I paused, my fingers barely clasped around my history textbook, turning to him.

"Yeah . . ."

He was staring at me with that look again; the one that caused a nauseating feeling in my stomach, goose bumps to rise on my skin, and my mouth to run dry. I couldn't tell he if was doing it on purpose or if he even realized his affect at all, but it was sending me into a tizzy.

"It got me to thinking about how much fun we have, just you and me."

"You mean when we bicker over Shakespeare and the awesomeness that are his tragic love stories."

"We aren't getting into that fight again, Hannah," he chuckled, giving me a playful glare. "I know you love them, but those stories are nothing more than literary clickbait. The entire concept of real-life love tragedy is pointless."

I was already rolling my eyes, mocking him as he spouted out the same reasons he gave me every time this particular argument rose its challenging head. I still didn't agree, even despite my own current love tragedy.

"I thought you said you weren't getting into this fight again?" I teased. "You sure seem to have strong opinions on something you don't want to fight about."

Seth chuckled, raising his hands. "I'm not getting into it."

"That's just because you know I'm right. You've had plenty of time to consider it now that we are knee deep in our assignment, and now you can see that situations like *Romeo and Juliet* are actually possible and that their story is as beautiful as it is tragic."

His smile faded. "I guess I can see how two people who really like each other might not be able to come together," he admitted. "That stuff can get in the way, and somehow, things get messed up. But it isn't the tragedy of their story that's the beautiful part."

I stared at him as I absorbed his words. Again, I couldn't tell if they were purposeful, chosen specifically to convey a particular message or connection between the story and my feelings or if it was simply me trying to find commonality and justify my desire wherever possible.

"What's the beautiful part then?" I asked, trying to keep my voice even.

He grinned at me. "That they ended up together despite it all."

"They killed themselves," I argued, laughing at his logic.

"But before that, they did end up together despite their circumstances. Their hasty decisions and miscommunication led to their death. Not their love."

"What are you trying to say? That the entire story of *Romeo and Juliet* is based solely on a lack of appropriate communication?" I challenged, raising a brow. "Maybe they should have just texted each other their plans, then."

Again, he laughed as our argument escalated. "It would have made things a lot simpler."

I pulled the last of my books from my locker, closing it lightly before turning back to him. We watched each other for a moment, seemingly waiting for the other to say something more.

"Want company on the walk to your next class?" he offered, gesturing a hand along the hall.

A thrill slipped along my spine, followed quickly by the inclination to assess the attention of those around us, then immediately by inner loathing.

If Brae found us chitchatting in the hall, she would probably freak. Required academic partnerships aside, I wasn't about to be caught red-handed if I could help it.

But what was more frustrating was how much I *liked* talking to him. The easy, casual banter, the sarcasm and classic references that only he seemed to understand. I didn't have this with many people and hated that the one person I did have it with was essentially forbidden fruit.

Before I knew it, I was nodding, allowing him to guide me down the hall while simultaneously reminding myself I was supposed to be moving on to step two of my stupid plan. And I was pretty sure purging reminders of him didn't include hallway interludes.

Seth was the one to break the silence.

"So," he finally said. "Still hating calculus?"

I blew out a breath. "You mean mathematical purgatory? Definitely."

Seth snickered. "I still can't believe they made you take that class."

"Yeah, it pretty much sucks. I spend more time trying to figure out the basics of the equations than actually understanding any of it. It's so frustrating. I just couldn't say no when they went on and on about why I should take it and that it would be good for me."

He was quiet for a moment before his next words tumbled quickly from his mouth. "I could help you."

I stumbled at his offer, his strong hand shooting out, catching my arm gently. Immediately, I recalled a fantasy during one of my travel planning sessions with Brae of Parisian streets and handsome strangers rescuing me from my own clumsiness. Only, this wasn't Paris. And this handsome boy was definitely no stranger.

"You okay?"

"Yeah, yeah," I muttered, a flush of embarrassment coloring my cheeks. Clearing my throat as we returned to our walk, I cast my eyes down to the tiled floor. "What do you mean you can help me?"

Seth shrugged casually. "I'm pretty good at math," he said. My brows raised, mouth falling slack in indignation at his sudden admission. Apparently, my surprise was humorous to him as he laughed lightly. "What? I don't strike you as the numerically inclined type?"

"No." I shook my head before realizing how insulting my statement was. "No, no! That's not what I meant. I guess I just didn't *know* you were good at math."

Again, he gave a little shrug. "I've always kind of been good at it. You just never asked."

"And you never offered," I challenged. "All this time you've listened to me whine about calculus, and you're some kind of number whiz?"

"Not a whiz," he snorted. "Math just makes sense to me."

My throat turned dry as we arrived at my classroom. We hovered by the door, neither sure what to say next but seemingly just as unwilling to break this moment like the fragile bubble it was.

Confliction pulled me in two opposing directions, threatening to tear me apart. I was drowning in this freaking calculus class, and no matter how many study sessions or extra hours hunched over my desk I spent, it still never made sense. I was barely scraping by with a C, and it was totally tanking my average. It was too late to drop the class, and I was running out of options to survive with a suitable grade. Seth was offering me a lifeline, and my desperation was already reaching toward it.

But I couldn't ignore the guilt that swam in the pit of my stomach at the idea of accepting his offer. Brae knew about our English project. That was set up months ago at the start of the semester by our teacher. She said she understood, and it wasn't a problem. But this was different. This would be me accepting his help after everything he put her through and making the choice to spend the extra time with him. Knowing my mathematical struggles or not, I couldn't be sure that Brae would understand.

Gnawing on my lower lip, the words slipped out before I could stop them. "Would you really be willing to tutor me in calculus?"

My mouth fell slack the moment the question escaped like a prisoner from a jail. I frantically tried to claw it back, beginning to shake my head and tell him never mind, when he smiled.

"Of course," he said, flashing that dimple to disarm me. "Any time you're free, just text me and we can set it up." Glancing at his watch, he huffed. "I should probably head to class. Just let me know when you want to get together."

Before I had a chance to rescind my request, he merged with the flow of students and disappeared.

The rest of my day passed in a constant state of a Seth-induced haze. Rather than listening to my lectures or taking in any of the readings we were expected to do, my mind was instead rapt in reviewing every moment of our strange and unexpected run in. Somehow, I had gone from plotting my success in step two and preparing to purge Seth Linwood from my heart to finding myself a new calculus tutor.

I was literally the worst at this whole "getting over a crush" thing.

Coming to my locker before my last class of the day, I was still in a distracted state as Erin approached. I didn't feel them at my side, my mind wrapped up in Seth, until they placed a hand on my arm. I held back a shriek that made them laugh out loud.

"Jumpy much?" The teasing smirk crinkled their nose, a scattering of freckles across their cheeks giving them an eternally youthful look. They waggled a finger at me, their nails painted a bright green to match their socks . . . green with pink smiling hearts.

Blowing a breath through my lips, I shook my head. "Just distracted."

I could see them nod from the corner of my eye as I swapped out my books.

"Hey," Erin said, voice dipping low. "Was that Seth I saw you with earlier?"

Spinning to face them, I couldn't stop my eyes from popping wide. "What?"

A small pinch formed between their brows. "Third period," they clarified. "I was headed to art class and saw you talking to Seth. Or, at least it looked like him. I only saw the back of his head."

Panic wrapped around my throat, choking me into silence. Crap. How could I have been so careless? It was bad enough random students saw us, but now Erin? Were they going to tell Brae? Did they think something was going on?

Swallowing down my anxiety, I tried to appear casual.

"Yeah," I said, shrugging indifferently. "He was asking about English."

Erin's brows pinched further, their head tilting. "Huh. Okay."

Disbelief rang in their tone. "Why?" I pressed, immediately trying to run damage control.

It was their turn to shrug. "I don't know. You guys just looked kind of . . . intense. All huddled together and stuff. You were all shifty eyed, him all broody."

"I was not shifty eyed," I countered with a pout. "And Seth isn't . . . broody."

"Oh, yes he is." They nodded firmly. "I don't blame him. He probably can't even help it. Hot guys just brood naturally, like us mere mortals breathe." Lowering their voice, they leaned a little closer. "He was just looking at you all intense. I wondered if I had to come over and tell him to aim that jawline somewhere else or something."

I couldn't hold back my snort, but it sounded more like panic than humor. "It was nothing," I reiterated, hugging my books close to my chest like armor. "Just English talk."

Before Erin had a chance to press further, Brae jogged up to my side.

"Hey," she said, a touch of her old, chipper self finally coming back into her voice. "I feel like I've barely seen you today."

I nodded, forcing a grin as I turned away from Erin. "Yeah, it's been kind of a crazy day."

"Did you get your calculus test back?"

I nodded, rolling my eyes. "Yeah. I got a C-."

"Better than a D," she pointed out as she shoved her books into her bag. "I told you not to worry so much. You always think you're going to fail, then you do just fine. You need to quit doubting yourself so much."

"I guess."

"That's the spirit!" she cheered mockingly before pinching my arm lightly. "Stop being down on yourself with this stuff. Or anything, for that matter. You know it drives me crazy when you do that."

"And you know it drives me crazy when you point it out," I countered with a half smile, expertly avoiding her gaze.

We stood in silence; me slowly gathering my items, Brae watching me curiously. She glanced at Erin, who quickly dropped their gaze to their phone.

"What's up with you?" she asked, waving a hand in front of my face. "You're acting all weird."

Immediately, I tried to pull myself together. "No, I'm not."

"Yes, you are," she countered. "You're usually chattier than this, especially if we haven't seen each other all day. Now, you're so . . . distracted?"

My face flushed with the embarrassment of being cornered, knowing that I certainly couldn't tell her the truth.

Yeah, Brae, I am a little distracted. Because Seth approached me several classes before, chatting me up like old times and like you weren't even a consideration. That while I am supposed to be getting over him, and solidifying my position on Team Brae, I somehow ended up with him as a calculus tutor. Oh, and even though I know I shouldn't, and despite the fact that I am fully aware that he is off-limits in accordance with one of the most important rules in all friendship agreements, I am ass over teakettle in love with him. I thought sardonically to myself.

Yup. None of that was what was going to come out of my mouth, so instead, I just shrugged and made up a lie.

"Just frustrated with calculus, I guess."

Her face turned downward, pouting in sympathy.

"I'm sorry," she said, reaching out to hug me. "I know you hate that class. But hey, we're already more than halfway done the semester. Pretty soon, no more numbers for you! Soon it will be summer, then senior year, then graduation. And then . . . Paris!"

Hugging her back, a nervous, guilty chuckle rose in my throat. It didn't take long for my shame to overtake my confusion about Seth, even as I relaxed against the familiarity of her hold. The rest of the student population buzzed around us; happy chatter, loud laughter, and the overwhelming scent of cologne and perfume mingled together, all of them oblivious to the scarlet letter branded on my skin.

It was stupid to think about our recent encounters so much, especially when it wasn't something I should be thinking about at all. Things between Seth and I were still in a strange, post-best-friend-breakup state, and I needed to stop dissecting every meeting, word, and look so intensely.

Maybe my moms were right, and Seth and I could find some new semblance of friendship that could satisfy both my need to support Brae, and my inability to detox him from my system completely. That was possible, wasn't it? Having a crush on someone, then getting over it and still being able to be . . . friends?

Because it was clear where my loyalty lay, and it was with Brae.

Not with my backstabbing heart.

CHAPTER TEN

Rain drummed against my bedroom window in a steady beat, adding percussion to the music pounding in my ears. The dark sky was menacing, trees waving under the influence of the storm raging outside, cleansing away the world beyond.

It didn't take long for my mind to empty and the nerves that had twisted in my gut since I woke that morning to loosen their hold. I finally cleared my mind, determined to purge myself of Seth Linwood, and take step two by the throat.

Opening my eyes, resolve flooded my system like adrenaline just as a flash of lightening lit up the sky. A cool, eager prickle lifted the hairs on my arm, ready to attack my latest challenge.

Step two: get rid of reminders of the relationship.

While I had no relationship with Seth in the romantic sense, that didn't mean I didn't have things that reminded me of him. Like the masochist I was, I kept every little thing that he gave me, no matter how meaningless. To outside observers, they would probably be random rubbish littered around my room. But to me, they were a link to Seth, no matter how weak, and it was time to break that chain.

Pulling my long, brown hair back into a ponytail, I locked eyes with my first victim. An unassuming scrap of paper hidden in the depths of my desk drawer. Unfolding it slowly, I scanned the words I already had memorized.

Seth's easy scrawl caused a flutter in my chest.

I got it! You're Anne Elliot.

My own handwriting curved below his in reply.

From Persuasion??

Yup. Totally Anne.

Why???

You're self-sacrificing, no matter what. You just offered to let Jake, the laziest person in class use your notes. See. Totally Anne.

My lips curved into a traitorous grin at the memory of us in those early weeks of our friendship, passing this note back and forth during class while trying to escape detection from Mrs. Anderson. The thrill of getting away with it in front of the harshest teacher was exciting, but even more so was passing notes with *Seth Linwood*.

I had kept that note hidden in my drawer for months. Since before he met Brae, before our friendship changed to something more subdued. It was the first relic of my crush that I ever saved, and unfortunately, had to be the first to go.

Swallowing against the inclination to keep just this one little piece of him for myself, I tossed it into the garbage bag on the floor and continued on my mission.

I didn't have gifts, photos or flowers to rid myself of in the hopes of cleansing Seth from my system. But I did have the pencil that I borrowed last semester, still tucked away in my desk. Or the random leaf he gave me as we were walking through the parking lot, saying it was the most symmetrical leaf he had ever seen. I knew he was just being silly, but I still kept it pressed between the pages of my copy of *Pride and Prejudice*.

One by one, piece by piece, I reaffirmed my goal and grabbed hold of step two in a death grip. Tossing the bag of items into the bin at the side of the house, I curled up on the porch swing and turned my attention to my phone.

This part was going to be more difficult. Not the action itself, but the message. Because removing Seth from my social media meant he could see that I had. He would know I was severing a tie between us, and the idea of the questions that would fill his mind or the hurt it may cause stilled my hand.

Seth only had Instagram. He wasn't into social media like the rest of the class and only posted on rare occasions. But somehow, this step felt . . . personal.

My finger hovered over the 'unfollow' button, my teeth wreaking havoc on my lower lip, as a text pinged overtop the Instagram screen.

Seth: *Hey! Baseball practice got canceled because of the rain. Do you want to get together and work on calculus a bit?*

My heart rate spiked, cold slipping over my skin. I couldn't help the irrational fear that he somehow could see me about to erase him from my life, and that was why fate had directed him to reach out at this pinnacle moment. I almost groaned aloud.

Bringing my thumb nail to my teeth, I chewed as I considered my response.

The logical response would be thanks but no thanks. Some excuse why getting together wasn't possible. I was finally finding my way back onto my Linwood detox path and was pretty sure setting up even more study sessions than were already academically required would throw me right off the proverbial wagon.

But at the same time, I couldn't help but think back to the night before: my forehead mashed into my textbook, my eyes burning from exhaustion and frustration as I tried to make sense of the equations on the page. I had a big test coming up on Tuesday and could really use the help to not fail and destroy my entire GPA.

My moms were already berating me about studying any time I dared to venture into the living room to watch TV or say I was going out with friends.

This won't change anything, I assured myself. Just because we would have twice as many run-ins, between English and now calculus, didn't mean I couldn't still find my way through these steps and place Seth firmly in the friend zone where he belonged. If anything, this was like a weird form of exposure therapy. Force myself to face my fears, and steel myself against their influence. Even if that influence was eyes as green as a field and a dimple deep enough to fall into and never get back out.

And surely Brae would understand that while letting Seth tutor me may look bad, it was actually a good thing. She didn't want me to fail either, and this was the most practical way to ensure my success. She couldn't be mad at me for that, could she?

This time, I let my groan escape, echoing above the rain still pounding against the porch roof.

Hannah: *Sure. Library?*

His response came almost immediately.

Seth: *See you in an hour :)*

Rushing through the front doors, I almost collided with an older couple opening an umbrella in the foyer. Rain drops dripped from my hair to my eyelashes, sticking my clothes to my skin beneath my raincoat as I muttered an apology against their looks of disdain. Adjusting my bag over my shoulder, I tried to pull myself together.

Why, oh why did it have to be pouring rain? Why, oh why was the only available parking spot at the very last row of the lot? And why, oh why was I having to show up to see Seth Linwood resembling a drowned opossum?

Maybe fate knew I was going to fail these steps and decided to make me as unattractive as possible to ensure no romantic interludes would occur between the stacks?

Ugh!

Lifting my chin, I tried to appear unfazed as I brushed my wet hair from my face and entered the main study hall. The library was usually a place of calm and solace for me. But the moment I noticed Seth stand from a table halfway down the room, waving a hand to gain my attention, calm was the last thing I felt.

Unlike me, he was perfectly dry and devastatingly attractive. Fate was a wicked, vengeful soul.

Plastering on a smile, I tossed my water-logged bag onto the table.

"Hey," I said, thankful that my voice remained even despite my completely uneven heart rate.

"Hey," he replied, his smile so genuine, guilt swam in my chest at the reminder that I had spent the morning throwing away every reminder of his existence. "Sorry for the late notice, but I know you have a test on Tuesday and when practice got canceled, I figured you might want a bit of help."

"No, yeah, it's great. Thanks."

Ugh. I was a babbling idiot.

Seth held back a laugh, probably choosing not to comment on my flustered state. Taking his seat, he watched as I shed my jacket and spread out my books. Trying to appear normal and at ease under his stare should have been an Olympic sport, because I had never experienced such stress in my life. So much so, I spent a little more time than was probably necessary setting myself up, simply to avoid having to look at him.

When I was finally ready, I swallowed deeply and met his eyes.

He was still grinning. "Ready to get started?"

Over the next two hours, I endured easily one of the best, and worst, calculus lessons of my life. Best, because despite the subject matter, Seth was a great teacher. He explained things in a way that made sense to my numerically-addled brain, and while it wasn't easy by any means, I at least wasn't sobbing over my textbook anymore.

It was the worst, however, because within the first half hour, he had moved to my side of the table to help better explain the information. Sitting this close to him, the smell of his cologne and the heat of his body jumbled my mind like nothing I had ever experienced. And no matter how many times my brain screamed at me to put some space between us, my body adamantly refused like a petulant child.

Shaking my head to clear my lust-ridden thoughts, I tried to focus on Seth's explanation of plane geometry.

"Remember, geometry is about properties of points, lines, and figures in a plane. Two lines are parallel if they never meet. Every pair of lines that are not parallel have a unique point of intersection."

His voice was smooth, hypnotic, and I let myself sigh as I followed his finger along the diagram on the page.

"If you cut a line in two at point C, here, each half is called a ray. Each ray, A and B, start at C and only meet at C."

My brain began to turn to mush. "But how do you describe angles, then, if the lines aren't parallel?"

He smiled, patiently, as he moved a little closer to me to point to the farthest page of the book. My heart stumbled over itself at his proximity. "You can declare any angle to be a unit angle and associate the size of that angle to be whatever multiple of that unit angle is. One option is to look at it in a 360-degree view."

A light clicked on in my brain. "Because it's easier to divide 360 by small numbers?"

His smile widened. "Yes. Exactly."

The enthusiastic praise for my tiny accomplishment felt undeserved, but I took it, anyway.

Leaning back in my chair, I exhaled an exhausted breath. "I won't say this stuff makes sense, because it doesn't. But it isn't as confusing as it was last night."

He snorted. "Crying over equations again, were you?"

"Sobbing," I confirmed, rubbing my tired eyes. "Why can't Mrs. Roache explain things like you do?"

Seth lifted a shoulder. "I don't know. Everyone learns differently. Sometimes it's about figuring out how to explain it in a way that a person understands. I'd probably suck if I had to explain this stuff to a class."

"I have a hard time believing you would suck at anything."

He snorted. "Yeah, right. Remember that assignment last year where we had to turn a scene from *Jane Eyre* into a comic strip?"

The memory made me cough on a laugh. "Oh yeah. Your stick people were so bad, Mr. Simmonds just patted your shoulder and said 'well, you tried.'"

He shook his head at himself. "See. I definitely have my faults. Drawing, in particular."

I conceded with a nod before challenging him. "Fine. But that's just one thing. There isn't much else I've seen you struggle with."

He stilled beside me, a charge shifting between us. Steeling myself, I looked over to find him smiling contemplatively to himself.

"You'd be surprised," he muttered, more to himself than to me. After several heavy moments, he straightened, pushing that distant look from his eyes. I stared at him for several long moments, the look on his face like a riddle begging to be solved. He glanced over at me, his eyes hypnotic, trapping me like a moth to a flame. Without a word, he reached out, tucking a wayward lock of hair behind my ear. It was a simple, gentle gesture that sent my heart racing and turned my mouth dry.

I couldn't look away from him, and he didn't seem willing to release me from the snare he had me trapped in. A hum filled my ears, drowning out the gentle white noise of the library, the movement and presence of other patrons blurring as if we were trapped in a bubble of our own making.

It was Seth who popped the bubble first, retracting his hand with a jolt. His cheeks flushed as though he couldn't believe he had done something so intimate.

After several moments, he cleared his throat.

"Ready to keep going?"

I blew a breath through my clenched teeth. I should probably leave. I was supposed to be ridding my system of him, and instead, I spent the whole afternoon basking in his warmth and losing myself in tense little moments. I couldn't help but feel every time I took one step forward, I was shoved two steps back.

But looking down at my textbook and the diagrams that may as well have been written in Latin, I conceded under the guise of academic survival over my stupid heart.

CHAPTER ELEVEN

"This is it. You ready?"

Brae looked around her opulent bedroom with obvious uncertainty before turning her blue eyes to me.

"Not in the least."

"Ugh. Brae, come on. We've been over this all week. You're doing a lot better than you were. You're now able to pass by Seth in the hall at school without hiding, crying, or freaking out. There have been no more produce aisle incidents, and you've started to act somewhat normal again the last couple of days."

"I know, I know," she groaned, flopping down onto her bed. "My emotional incontinence has been at a minimum."

"Then you've officially completed step one," I said happily, hopping over to her. She eyed me with thinly-veiled irritation. "Honestly though, you really have gotten a lot better. You aren't texting me in complete tizzies over Seth or his general existence in the universe anymore. I say that's proof you're ready for step two."

And I need you to drag me along with you, I thought to myself.

My own recent failures in ridding Seth from my heart tugged at my mind. We were only on step two, and instead of grieving the loss and ridding myself of reminders of him, all I'd accomplished was setting up *more* time together. Ugh. Which was why, as I stood with my arms wide in Brae's opulent bedroom, I was determined to power through, even if that meant dragging her kicking and screaming every step of the way.

Leaning down, I picked up the cardboard box at my feet and set it on the bed beside Brae.

"Get up," I said firmly, reaching down to pull her upright. She groaned, letting herself go limp.

"I don't wanna," she whined, slumping in a pitiful form.

"Brae. Do you trust me?" I said sternly, giving her a harsh look.

Finally, she sighed. "Yes."

"Do you believe in our rules?"

To this, she nodded. "Of course."

"So, rule one. Always have your best friend's back. I've got your back in this and will help you get through it. Okay?"

Her eyes touched on several of the items in question, her lips turning down. "It feels weird getting rid of them."

"I know. But would you rather sit in here and look at them all the time?" I challenged, bringing my hands to my hips. "To always have the reminder of him sitting right next to you?"

Her pout deepened before she sighed with defeat. "No."

"Then get up," I repeated, grabbing her again and pulling her to her feet. "We'll start with the stuffies."

Cringing at myself, I turned my back to her, surveying her room. My overenthusiastic, chipper voice and high-strung behavior felt like a dead giveaway that something was wrong, but maybe it was just me fearing that she could see right through my efforts to the true catalyst.

That I was dragging myself through these steps with her, and while I felt like I was trudging through quicksand, I was determined to keep her moving . . . because her movement meant I could follow in her wake and hopefully find my way out on the other side by sheer will.

Brae's bedroom was littered with little reminders of her relationship. Dried roses, stuffed animals, photos on her corkboard above her desk. It was like he was everywhere, subtle, hidden hints at every corner.

Before she could stop me, I plucked the little stuffed duck from her bed and dangled him over the box.

"No!" she squealed, ripping him from my hands. "Not Quackers!"

I glared at her as she cuddled the little yellow animal. "Brae . . ."

"This was the first thing Seth ever gave me." She frowned, her eyes falling to the little stuffed creature. "It was the school carnival, remember?"

I did remember, in fact. All too well. As the memories began to flood my mind, I tried to keep my expression even.

"Of course I remember," I said, my tone softer. "I was the most awkward third wheel in history."

She tsked in annoyance at me. "You were not."

"I was so," I corrected. "You two, with your new relationship cuteness. Seth and his determination to show us how Skee-Ball was supposed to be played. And me with my singledom written across my forehead."

This only served to increase her pout.

"You don't want to think about him anymore, right?" I urged, trying to sound supportive rather than pushy.

She hesitated for a moment before finally nodding. "Yeah."

"And you want to start feeling like yourself again, right?"

"Yeah."

"Then, as cute as he is, Quackers has to go."

My words only served to make her hands clench around the poor little duck's neck.

"Brae, you know you need to do this," I said firmly, trying to persuade her to see reason. "You can't get over him if you see reminders of him everywhere you look."

She began to touch the soft fluffy hairs on top of the stuffed duck's head, pretending to ignore me.

"And Quackers is going to a children's hospital," I added, using a little guilt in my favor. "Some little kid will absolutely love him."

Her eyes flickered between me and the little duck before she groaned in defeat. "Ugh, fine." I watched as she gently set Quackers in the box before crossing her arms over her chest.

The next hour was much harder than I expected, for the both of us. With each item she pulled from her room, she insisted on telling me the story behind it. Each stuffie, each note, each rose or flower all had a tale of Seth's romantic and caring nature. And while I could see remembering these moments was actually cathartic to Brae, all it did for me was make me long for him more.

For crap's sake.

Once all the toys were in a box to go to the children's hospital and all the flowers and notes were in the trash bag at the door, we sat side by side on her bed, staring at her phone.

"You're almost there," I said, placing my hand on her shoulder.

"I think this is the hardest part for me," she admitted, staring at the device in her hand. "I know it's stupid, but this is how I keep tabs on everyone. All I could ever want to know, I find on social media. And all the pictures on my phone? They're memories, and now I'm just going to delete him? It feels so . . . mean."

I didn't say aloud that I had had the same consideration just the morning before. Instead, I gave her the middle ground to the step that I had ultimately employed myself. Mute, not delete.

"It isn't mean, Brae. It isn't because you hate him, it's because it's what you need right now. You said so yourself that you stalk his socials when you can't sleep. Maybe this will cut that tie and help you quit the habit? You're not deleting him, just muting until you're in a better place. This kind of stuff is never permanent."

She only nodded in response, casting me a glance. "Would you remove him if you were me?"

I startled, leaning back. "What?"

She huffed, shaking her head at herself. "I mean, if you were trying to get a guy out of your system and move on and all that stuff, do you think you would have as much of a hard time as I am?"

My heart fluttered with nerves, my face heating. I couldn't tell her the truth; that yes, I definitely would be having a hard time, because I *was* having a hard time. Having to lie to Brae with each passing day, with each inch we gained through this process, was like a lashing to my heart.

But I had no choice if I wanted to keep my friendship intact.

"I think I would." Not a lie, but an evasive truth.

She blew a long breath, her gaze locked on her phone. Her expression was so sad, guilt swarmed my system and coiled in my gut.

Leaning my head against her shoulder, I followed along as she scrolled through the endless photos she kept on her phone. Every once in a while, she would pause at one of Seth and stare at it. I would follow suit, but while she was looking at it with confliction, I felt only guilt, longing, and jealousy. Guilt for not telling her how I felt and for keeping so many secrets from her. Longing for the boy on her screen, beautiful and oblivious to the whirlwind he had created. And jealousy because even if it was over, Brae still got to experience a side of Seth that I never would. And as much as it shouldn't, I couldn't help but see everything through green-tinted envy.

I was the worst best friend in history.

"This is the last part," I said gently, trying to give her a nudge forward.

"I know."

"Was it really so bad? Getting rid of it all?"

Surprisingly, she shook her head. "Not really. I mean, it sucks, and I feel a little bad, but when I think about having to look at it all, it just makes me sad. I know I need to do this to move on."

I wrapped my arms around her waist in a supportive hug. It was the most insightful thing Brae had said about this whole process so far.

"Start with social. It might be easier," I suggested.

She navigated through her social profiles, and each time, she hesitated over the "mute" option. And each time, my own guilt rose. Until she gasped loudly, her body turning rigid.

"What?"

Her response was only a growl, her knuckles blanching as she gripped her phone.

"Brae, what—"

"That witch!" she shouted, teeth grinding together.

"Who? Brae, what's going on?"

Shoving the phone toward my face, fury lined her expression. "Sarah MacInnes!"

Taking her phone, my brow pinched. "The girl in your Spanish class?"

She stood abruptly and began pacing. "Yes! That social wannabe who is always copying me. If I wear something new and trendy, the next day she does the same. If I talk about my trip to California with my cousins over the summer, she brags about her trip to New York. She's just a cheap knockoff version of me and has been trying to climb the ladder since freshman year."

"So what?" I asked, staring at Seth's Instagram profile in confusion. The photo on the screen was one of him hiking, standing on a hilltop, arms wide in victory. I didn't have a chance to swoon and pine for him before Brae pointed at a comment below the picture.

"This is what!" she screeched.

SarahActually: Looking hot as ever! I should come with you next time. I know some great "secret" spots. ;)

Oh, no.

Snatching the phone away, Brae's fingers began to dance across the screen. "What loser thinks she can hit on my ex publicly like that? She has to know I would see it. Does she really think she can start dating Seth and it will somehow make her popular?"

I shook my head. "She could actually like him—"

My attempt at being rational was interrupted with a hush and a flick of her hand. "Screw that. She just wants what was mine. Trying to overthrow me when she thinks I'm weakened. Not likely."

I watched in horror as Brae switched to her "ghost account" on Instagram. She had created the account freshman year, and over time and with careful gossip curation, the majority of East River High and students from neighboring schools followed the account. Within seconds, she had found a photo, prepared a post, tagged Sarah, and uploaded it for the world to see.

With a long exhale of pride and relief, she handed me the phone to review her handiwork.

My stomach churned as I read the post. The picture was a random stock profile of a girl with long brown hair standing front of a building.

"You're starting a rumor that she was in California last summer because she got sent to *rehab*?"

She lifted a shoulder indifferently. "It could be true. She was in California for over a month."

"She was visiting her Grandma."

"Whatever," she replied, retrieving her phone. "She has the nerve to try to move in on Seth only a couple weeks after we break up? The gloves are off."

We watched in silence as the like count came alive, slowly ticking higher and higher. As much as Brae hated gossip about her, she was a master at spreading it about others.

"Okay," she sighed, settling back onto the bed. "Now I can refocus on me and my journey." Returning to her main account, she went back to Seth's profile. With a sigh of resignation, Brae clicked the mute button, pulling my mind back to the present, and I watched as the little red icon showed he was muted from her profile.

I gave her a supportive squeeze, even if guilt did knot in my chest at what she had just done to Sarah. While I wasn't the one to start the rumor, I was a witness and did nothing to stop it. Shame heated my face, even though I knew there was no way I could have stopped Brae without a fight. A fight I knew I wouldn't win. It was times like this that I was reminded just how ruthless Brae could be when it came to her popularity.

I shook the feeling away, trying to regain my own focus.

"I'm proud of you," I said, rocking her gently. "For completing the step, not for starting a rumor about Sarah, just so we're clear."

"Thanks," she snorted, resting her head on top of mine. "I just wish I hadn't thrown out my junk stash in one of my step one freak-outs. I could really use some Twizzlers right now."

I grinned. "I left some on the kitchen counter downstairs."

Brae laughed before pulling away to kiss me on top of the head. "You're the best," she said. She jumped up from the bed and bounded out the door with newfound vigor.

Lying back on her bed, it was time to release the tension of the day with some mindless social media time by scrolling through Instagram and catching up on everyone else's less complicated and non-best-friend-betraying lives. I steered clear of Brae's ghost profile, not interested in seeing just how tightly the new rumor about Sarah had taken hold. I had barely finished liking the latest news about a book series I loved when a text came through, causing me to gasp and almost drop the phone on my face.

Seth: *Hey. What are you up to?*

Confliction overtook me as I stared at the text with wide, nervous eyes before immediately feeling guilty for the reaction. I stared at the door, waiting for Brae to come in and catch me red-handed.

I shook my head at myself, cringing for my overreaction. He probably just wanted to meet up and work on our English assignment. Or maybe calculus again since my test was Tuesday. It was stupid of me to have such a visceral reaction to a freaking text.

Before I had the chance to figure out what to do, Brae came bounding back into the room. The bag of Twizzlers dangled from her hand, one hanging from her mouth as she balanced a carton of ice cream and two spoons in the other.

"Good news," she mumbled despite the licorice between her teeth. "My mom had a carton of ice cream in the freezer, so we can still binge my emotional sorrows thoroughly."

Forcing a fake smile, I accepted the spoon she passed me. We sat on her bed, switching between ice cream and Twizzlers, exchanging very little in the way of conversation. While usually this would annoy both of us, at this moment, I had a feeling she was thinking about her latest step in getting over Seth and dealing with the feelings associated with it.

I, however, was thinking about how to deal with the fact that step two, ridding yourself of reminders of him, was pretty damn hard when he kept texting you out of the blue.

CHAPTER TWELVE

"I'll catch you after class?" I asked Brae as I closed my locker, tucking my books under my arm.

"Yup. Did you want to grab lunch off campus today? I forgot to bring something, and all I have in my bag is some random granola bar that I'm pretty sure has been there since beginning of the semester."

I grinned at her misfortune. "Sounds good."

She had been practically buoyant the entire week as the rumor she had cultivated about Sarah made the rounds. Not only did Sarah look awful: pale, tired, and stressed at trying to convince people she had not been sent to rehab, but this new gossip took the attention off Brae and her breakup. In her mind, it was a win-win.

We waved goodbye as she disappeared around the corner toward her geography class, and I merged into the flow of students toward the science wing.

I had barely made it more than halfway down the hall before a tall figure slid up beside me.

"Hey," he said, catching me off guard. He seemed to have developed a habit of appearing out of thin air since breaking it off with my best friend.

"Hey," I replied as I adjusted my books. I felt on display, like a spotlight was shining down on me from above, eager to showcase my fraternizing with the enemy. I couldn't help but clench in my stomach, wondering if somehow Erin would see us together a second time, and immediately question whether our ongoing encounters were as innocent as English assignments and academic responsibility.

"So?" he prodded, lifting an expectant brow. "How did you do on your calc test the other day?"

"Oh," I sighed. "Pretty good, actually. I pulled off a B."

Before I knew it, he was pulling me into a tight embrace. "That's great! I knew you could do it."

My head swam, consumed with his scent, the feel of his body against mine, and the overwhelming realization at how natural and comfortable it felt. When he released me, I almost whined at the loss of him.

"Come on, I'll walk you to your next class," he said. "You can regale me with tales of your harrowing conquer of mathematics."

I snorted but followed his pace toward my biology class. We walked in silence for several moments, no tales of battling equations and derivatives to be told. I glanced at him from the corner of my eye before facing forward again. It had been about three days since his last text that left me boggled, and I quietly hoped that he hadn't noticed I never responded.

"Did you get my text?" he asked, falling in step beside me.

Damn.

"Yeah. Sorry I didn't respond. I was in the middle of something and kind of forgot."

I was a terrible liar.

"Too busy on a hot date?" he teased.

I didn't clarify that my "hot date" was with Brae, ridding him from her surroundings.

Glancing to him, I found him gnawing on his bottom lip. His hands were shoved in his pockets, his shoulders tense and rigid. He seemed lost in thought, and whatever those thoughts were must have been causing him worry, because he was lacking the casual, comfortable confidence he usually carried himself with.

Finally, I couldn't take the silence any longer.

"So what did you need?"

"What?" he asked, my question pulling him out of his thoughts.

"When you texted?" I explained, pausing outside my biology class. "What did you need?"

Seth seemed thrown by my question, an uncertain expression falling over his features, pinched brow and tight jaw, before he slowly regained his composure. Seeing him so out of sorts only further heightened my own nervousness.

Pulling his hands from his pockets, he cracked his knuckles in a gesture I had noticed him do before he took the mound in baseball. A little quirk he told me that usually went along with his inner pep talk.

"Remember when you asked me at The Diner why I broke up with Brae?"

I balked, my brow furrowing.

"Yeah . . .?"

"I told you that I just felt like we were too different and that if I stayed with her I might miss out on something that was . . . a better fit?"

He took a step toward me, his posture relaxed, but I suddenly felt cornered against the lockers at my back. He towered over me, the scent of his cologne making my head swim in combination with his proximity. I swallowed against the lump in my throat, hypnotized by the intensity of his stare.

"Yeah . . .?"

He took a deep breath. "Well, that wasn't the *entire* reason."

"What do you mean?"

Again, he hesitated, and I could see him trying to gain the confidence to purge the truth to me. "I know this will make me sound like a horrible person, and I completely understand if you think I am. I honestly never wanted to hurt Braelyn, but . . . I kind of have feelings for someone else."

My mouth fell slack, all the air in my lungs rushing out in a gust.

He liked someone else? He was with the most popular girl in our class, and he liked someone *else*?

Immediately, I considered the possibilities of who it could be. There was no shortage of pretty, popular girls in our school, any of which would give their left arm to date Seth Linwood. As I stared at him blankly, the seconds ticking by, my overactive imagination went to the one place it knew it shouldn't go.

What if he liked . . . me?

Immediately, the rational part of my brain told the irrational lovesick side that it was mental, kicked it in the shin, and locked it away. To even entertain something so ridiculous was both traitorous to my friendship and dangerous to my heart. It was a foolish, stupid, careless thing to—

"Who?" I asked, the irrational side of my brain somehow controlling my power of speech for one last second. Immediately, I cringed, stammering in apology. "I'm sorry, you don't have to answer that. It's really none of my business, and—"

"No, that's fine," he said, seeming much more relaxed now that part of his secret was out in the open. He gave me a nervous little smile, chewing on the inside of his lower lip. "That's kind of what I wanted to talk to you about—"

"Linwood!" a voice bellowed, causing both of us to turn.

Alex Shaffer strode over to Seth, slinging his arm around his shoulders roughly.

"Come on, dude, we're going to be late for class."

Seth's eyes flickered to me for a split second, a beautiful flush coloring his face. Alex looked to me, oblivious to the tension between us.

"Hey, Hannah," he greeted with a friendly smile. "What's up?"

Despite the fact it was Alex addressing me, I couldn't seem to tear my eyes away from Seth.

"Not much," I lied. Because there was *so much* up in this particular moment, all I wanted was for Alex to go away so I could find out exactly *what* was up.

But, like most boys, Alex was completely ignorant to timing.

"Well, c'mon, Linwood."

It was clear Seth wanted to say something more, either to explain or to apologize, but he never got the chance as Alex began to pull him down the hall by his collar. I was left watching in bewilderment as the two boys headed down the hall and around the corner out of sight, leaving me outside my classroom in complete perplexity.

For the rest of the day, I couldn't seem to retain anything in my classes. No lessons, no questions stuck in my mind. Only one thing dominated every corner of my conscious.

Seth liked someone new. A terrifying, exhilarating thought that sparked my imagination and let it wander down the dangerous path of: *What if it's me?*

CHAPTER THIRTEEN

Adjusting my position in my bed, I was enthralled in the book in my hands as I drank in the words. Reading had become my latest form of escape from my messed-up life. Not romance, of course. No one needed that kind of influence right now. Currently, I was lost in the latest thriller that was conquering the charts, letting my overanalytical brain focus on who the killer was rather than love and all that mushy stuff.

I was just about to turn the page when my phone buzzed gently at my side. Bringing it to my face, my brows rose in surprise to see a new text from Seth. I hadn't seen or heard from him since our strange encounter in the hall two days before. For him to be touching base again already only further increased wariness. Which, of course, I immediately felt guilty for.

The message caused me to snort. It was from one of my favorite Instagram profiles that posted funny, cute, and down-right adorable animal videos, photos, and gifs. We used to exchange them fairly frequently when we first met to tease and irritate each other, but sometimes there were some that were just too perfect not to share.

The current image was of a tiny kitten sitting on the floor, staring off into the distance with the caption "when you're at a party and your friend disappears."

Lord knew I had been that kitten on more than one occasion. With one or two people, I was okay. But put me in a party situation where I knew virtually no one? Yup . . . despondent kitten.

Hannah: *So cute!*

I replied, adding a heart eye emoji. Three little dots appeared at the bottom of screen. I had to wonder if he had been staring at his phone waiting to see if I would respond.

Seth: *I've been scrolling through that profile for the last little bit and thought you would like that one.*

Hannah: *You've been looking through a profile about baby animals?*

Seth: *You've been a bad influence on me. I've been addicted to it for months.*

Hannah: *lmao*

Seth: *Don't tell anyone. I don't want the whole school to know I'm obsessed with random animal humor.*

I shook my head at my phone.

Hannah: *Your secret is safe with me.*

Watching my phone, I waited for another reply, but nothing more came through.

Hannah: *Is that all you wanted? To share a kitten?*

There was a momentary pause, and I wondered if he had let the connection drop, when again the dots appeared. Then disappeared. Then reappeared. This happened several times, making it seem like he was typing, then erasing whatever he wanted to reply. After much longer than normal, a message came through.

Seth: *Sort of. What are you up to?*

Hannah: *Reading.*

Seth: *Anything good?*

I rolled my eyes with a grin.

Hannah: *A creepy thriller. Pretty sure half the characters are going to be murdered.*

Seth: *Morbid, Hannah. Hope you're not getting any ideas from that book.*

Again, I laughed at his banter.

Hannah: *I guess you'll just have to wait and see.*

And just like that, the tension eased, leaving us with the familiar comfort we used to have between us. For the next hour, we chatted back and forth with a relaxation I hadn't felt with him since before Brae first entered his life.

Another short pause broke through our conversation as I watched those telltale dots come and go. Again, he wrote, hesitated, and erased his message several times; the longer he took to message, the more nervous I became.

When his message finally came through, I was left speechless.

Seth: *What are you doing Sunday?*

I hesitated, wondering if I should answer with the truth or a lie. The truth was nothing. A lie would be something with Brae or working, because that would be the most logical and most likely to keep Seth at arm's length.

But, it would seem the irrational, heart-guided part of my brain had escaped her cell of solitude, taking over control of my fingers.

Hannah: *Nothing.*

This time, he answered quickly.

Seth: *Can we get together for a bit?*

My brow furrowed.

Hannah: *For English? Yeah, we could meet up at the library if you want.*

Seth: *No, not for English.*

My stomach flipped. He wanted to get together? With me? That couldn't be good.

Hannah: *Is everything okay?*

I asked, hoping to gain a little more insight into this out of the blue request. Possibly he had questions about school? Perhaps he wanted to talk about Brae? Maybe . . .

Seth: *There's something I wanted to talk to you about.*

Obviously, I thought with a touch of sarcasm. I started to type back, asking him what he wanted to talk about, when another message popped up.

Seth: *It's kind of important.*

Again, my stomach tensed uncomfortably, a thrill of nerves climbing up into my chest. I considered yet again going with a lie, saying I was busy. That would be the most logical, the most appropriate response considering our circumstances. But for some reason, I couldn't lie. I couldn't tell him no, because deep down, I wanted to know what was so important to him that he wanted to get together this way.

Before I could stop myself, my fingers followed my heart rather than my brain.

Hannah: *Sure.*

Seth: *Great. How about the park by the library?*

I nodded as if he could see me, my lip trapped between the vice of my teeth.

Hannah: *Sure. See you there around one.*

Seth: *Thank you.*

With those two words, I felt our thread of a connection break, leaving me with racing questions and an equally racing heart.

CHAPTER FOURTEEN

I paced back and forth with my hands shoved in the pockets of my light jacket, counting down the minutes with tense anticipation. The light breeze blew through my hair, pushing a few strands across my face, but I didn't bother brushing them back. I was far too distracted to care.

It was just before one in the afternoon on Sunday, and I was currently wearing a line in the grass behind the East Park library while waiting for Seth. A rather unremarkable park in comparison to the others in the area, but this one held special meaning for me in more ways than one. It was where I kissed Johnny Mahon in seventh grade, in the quintessential awkward first kiss where you don't know where your noses are supposed to go and wonder if it is really supposed to be so sloppy. I immediately raced home to tell Brae. It was where I met up with Brae late one night when we both snuck out of the house to go to an upperclassman's party just last year, ending in her getting drunk, me trying to sneak her back into my house, and both of us getting grounded.

So many memories of this simple place, so many of them with Brae. And as much as I tried, I couldn't seem to push those thoughts from my head as I paced back and forth, waiting for the boy we were both supposed to be getting over.

A car pulling into the parking lot broke me from my despondent thoughts, my eyes lifting up to see Seth sliding his blue Civic into an empty spot. I froze in my step, my body chilling with adrenaline at the sight of him. God, what was I thinking, meeting him here like this? Surely this was against the rules somehow, even if it was just meeting up with a friend. But when that friend is now your best friend's ex, there was nothing simple about it anymore. Especially when that friend is also the boy you're head over heels for.

He slid out of the car with an enviable grace, striding over to me with a nervous smile. Seth rarely appeared nervous, but even I could see that there was something in the set of his shoulders, in the tension in his eyes, that screamed "abort mission."

"Hey," he said, licking his lips. God, it shouldn't have made me groan inwardly with such a simple gesture, but wow. How could he even make *that* look sexy?

Jesus, Hannah, get a grip, I scolded myself. *You don't like him anymore, remember? He's old news. Completely off-limits, which doesn't matter ' cause you don't want him anymore, anyway.*

God, I was a crap liar, even to myself.

"Hey," I replied, ignoring my inner ramblings.

"Thanks for meeting me," he said, gesturing toward a nearby bench.

"No problem."

Following him to the bench, I sat down as far from him as socially acceptable without making it obvious. It was clear we were both feeling the tension of the situation, our gazes flickering toward each other, but neither of us seeming to know what to say.

"So what's up?" I finally asked, angling myself toward him.

He smirked before biting down on his lip. Another shockingly sexy habit of his.

"Right to it, huh?"

I shrugged. "Well, you said it was kind of important. I figured you would want to just get it out."

He nodded, his attention falling to the grass behind me. "Yeah. Yeah, I do."

As he turned back to me, I steadied myself for whatever it was he was about to say. There were many possibilities, all of which equally as daunting for me. That he wanted Brae back and needed my help to know how to do it. That he liked one of our other friends and didn't know how to go about asking her out. I let my mind run wild all weekend on what could possibly be so important to schedule a secret rendezvous and tried to steel myself for finally learning what it could be.

"I really don't know how to say this," he started, giving a little shrug. "I've been trying to think of ways that won't make me sound like a jerk, but I honestly couldn't think of any, so I'm just going to blurt it out."

I waited with bated breath as he took a deep inhale, letting the words escape him with the air in his lungs.

"I like you, Hannah."

His words struck me, my body leaning back and eyes widening to an abnormal size in my shock. It was clear that my reaction only heightened Seth's anxiety, because he started to babble, frantic to explain.

"I know this is probably the stupidest thing I could ever say to you right now, considering I only broke up with Brae a few weeks ago. And you probably think I'm the biggest jerk in the world for putting you in this situation, but I meant it when I said I ended things with Brae because I felt like I was missing out on something that fit so much better. Because I already know that you and I are a better fit, Hannah. We have been since before Brae and I even met." Since I still held an expression of disbelief, he seemed to feel the need to continue. "Look, Hannah, I've liked you since I knocked you on the ground in that stupid English class. And the more we work on that *Romeo and Juliet* project, fighting over the merit of tragic teen romances, I like you even more. I've *always* liked you."

My mouth opened to say something in response, but nothing came out. I stared at him in confusion, trying to piece together everything he was saying and decide if it was the truth or some horrible trick of my desperate heart.

"How?" I blurted, immediately shaking my head at myself. Hearing everything you ever wished your crush to say to you, surely your first response to it shouldn't be some mortifying brain fart turned verbal diarrhea. "I mean . . . why?"

"Why do I like you?" he asked, genuinely confused.

"Well, yes, that too. But . . . why now? Why are you telling me this?"

Again, he bit down on his lower lip as he assessed how to answer my question.

"I knew I made a mistake not saying something to you when we first met. I wanted to so many times but always talked myself out of it. I figured you just thought of me as a friend and that you weren't interested in me beyond that."

"Why did you think that?"

He shrugged. "Self-doubt, I guess. Any time I tried to get a feel for if you might be interested in me, you brushed it off and swore fealty to your spinsterhood. I assumed you just saw me as a friend and figured I had to accept that. Plus, when Brae asked me out and I asked you about it, you said it was okay. I mean, girls tell each other when they like a guy, right? If you had told Brae you liked me, she wouldn't have asked me out in the first place, and you probably wouldn't have told me it was all right. I figured that was my answer."

A cringe ran over me like a bucket of cold water was dumped over my head, the memory of that afternoon still so clear that I could still feel the pang of pain in my heart as I watched Brae swoop in and steal his attention away.

"Brae is great," he continued, still rambling. "I liked her. A lot. She was fun and spontaneous and just a blast to be around. But the longer we were together, the more obvious it was that it wasn't really what I wanted. That while I liked her, I didn't feel more than that. I didn't feel that connection with her. Not like I do with you."

My head swam, struggling to keep it above water and failing.

"But, why now? I mean . . . are you saying you broke up with Brae . . . for me?"

His eyes crinkled with a smile as my mind struggled to understand.

"I guess, yeah," he admitted. "I mean, things really weren't working out between Brae and I, and I knew I needed to break it off either way. But a big factor of actually doing it was this stupid little hope that maybe if I told you how I felt, if I got the courage to actually say it, that maybe you felt the same. I tried to push down my feelings and told myself it didn't matter, that you didn't like me that way, but it just kept haunting me until I decided I had to do something about it." He paused, considering a thought before letting out a single laugh. "Remember how I said *Romeo and Juliet* was only tragic because of a lack of communication? That if they had just been more open, that maybe all that bad stuff wouldn't have happened?"

"Yeah."

"Well, I don't want to end up like that."

"You mean, dead?" I laughed, shaking my head.

"That too." He laughed, probably realizing the absurdity of his reference. "But I guess I mean I don't want to leave something unsaid, open to interpretation, or to be missed because I wasn't clear in what I wanted. I don't want to lose out on something that could be amazing, because of a lack of communication. So here I am . . . communicating."

I was mesmerized by his vulnerable, nervous expression, his green eyes flickering between my own, searching for any hint of my feelings to his confession.

Seth Linwood had always been larger than life to me; this mystical, unattainable person that I knew I could never have. And yet, here he was, looking at me with those eyes, saying those words, and throwing me for the biggest loop of my life.

It was clear that he was waiting anxiously for me to say something back. Now, it was up to me to decide what I wanted.

That answer was easy. I wanted *him*. I had wanted him then, and I still wanted him now. He fit with me unlike anyone I had ever met, a perfectly matched puzzle piece that made me feel secure but also challenged me. Even from afar, I knew he was everything I wanted, and now I had the chance to have him.

But the reality wasn't as easy as that. Because the barriers between us were not as simple as a lack of communication. It wasn't even as dramatic as feuding families. It fell somewhere in between.

Braelyn. Not only has liking Seth been a betrayal to her, now I was faced with actually being with him after he broke her heart. I was the cause of everything that hurt her in these last few weeks, and that realization hit me like a slap in the face.

Because liking him was bad enough. But being with him was against one of the core rules of friendship.

Never, *EVER*, date your best friend's ex. Rule five was absolute, no matter your heart's desire.

Seth waited patiently for me to process everything he had said to me. I wondered if my emotions were as evident on my face as his were on his, but at the same time, I prayed they weren't. I knew I had to answer him, and I needed to explain.

"I like you too," I said, starting off with the most important part of this exchange. His reaction was nothing short of comical; a long gust of released breath he had been holding, followed by a single laugh and a shake of his head.

"God, that was torture waiting for you to say something." He laughed, looking back to me, with his green eyes shining in a heart-wrenching way.

I froze as he slowly slid a little closer to me. He kept a noticeable gap between us, but no longer was there that socially appropriate space that we had started with. I felt the warmth of his body, smelled the hint of his cologne—like cedar and rain—and it was almost too much for my frazzled emotions.

"I like you, Seth," I said, trying to pull together my confidence. "I have since before Brae even met you. I only said it was okay for you guys to go out because I was too scared to say anything else. I never could have considered that you would actually like me more than a friend."

"I do though," he reminded me, showing off that adorable smirk.

"But things aren't as simple as you liking me and me liking you," I continued, trying to rush through the difficult part of this conversation. "Because it isn't just about you and me anymore."

Realization slowly crept across his face.

"Brae."

"Yeah." I nodded. "Brae. You guys *just* broke up. She's still trying to get over it, and for me to go and tell her that you dumped her because you like *me*? I mean, I'm sure I don't have to tell you that she would have a bit of a meltdown."

"But you can't tell me she would be more concerned with her own ego than with you being happy."

"It's not just that," I interrupted, my heart hammering in my chest.

"What else is it then?"

Words came to the tip of my tongue and died off. I wasn't sure exactly how to explain it. It was as basic as loyalty, and because of that, I couldn't do this to her, no matter what my heart wanted.

"I know it doesn't feel fair and that it doesn't make sense. It's something as simple as girl code."

"Girl code?"

"Yeah. You boys have bro code, right? Certain rules of engagement when it comes to being friends with each other?"

"I guess."

"Well, Brae and I have the same. She's my best friend. She's stood by me when I felt like things were falling apart, when kids used to make fun of me for having two moms. And I've been there for her through all the drama with her parents, holding her up when she was going to fall. I like you . . . so much, but I can't do that to her. I'm sorry."

I could see his mind racing as he tried to come up with a way to change my mind, a pucker in his cheek indicating he was biting on the inside flesh. But the longer we stared at each other, the more he seemed to realize that nothing he said would matter. Even if it meant we were both unhappy, I couldn't be the girl who betrayed her best friend.

"What does that mean for us, then?" he asked, his thumb stroking along the back of my hand comfortingly.

I tried to give him a reassuring smile. "We stay friends," I said simply. "We can still talk, work on our assignment. Things can stay as they are now."

We sat on that bench, the air turning cooler along with our mood, watching each other silently. During that time, I memorized every facet of his face, the feeling of my hands in his, and the way the wind rustled through his hair. Even as my heart twanged with pain, he still made it skip a beat.

"I want to be more, Hannah. I really do, but I get it. If being just friends is what you want, then okay. Friends," he finally said, seemingly resolved.

I squeezed his hand, praying that he understood just how much I hated that that was all we could be. "Friends."

STEP THREE:
FOCUS ON YOURSELF

Block his number, love yourself,
and focus on your eyebrows.

CHAPTER FIFTEEN

"He's obviously going to regret it." Erin shook their head. Their eyes were downcast, focused intently as they moved the file across their nails. Their short hair was pushed back by a headband, their face slathered in a deep green cleansing mask Brae had assured them would do miracles. "I mean, you're the most popular girl in our class. What was he even thinking?"

Brae shrugged. "I honestly don't even know. It's just so stupid. But you know what? I'm over it."

Michelle cackled loudly, earning herself a glare from Brae. Her eyelids were bare of the splash of color that was her trademark, and her dark brown skin practically glowed from the serums and masks we had been applying all evening. Returning an innocent smile, she flicked her hand dismissively. "You're not over it, Brae. Even *you* don't get over a guy that quickly."

Brae tsked with annoyance, reaching out to steal the chips from in front of Michelle. "Okay, so I'm not *over* over it. But I'm not going to let myself dwell on it anymore." She turned to me then, an encouraging smile now on her face. "We're on to step three: focus on yourself. Right, Hannah?"

Clearing my throat, I nodded. "Right."

Brae continued. "I did the whole 'let myself grieve' thing. I did the relationship cleanse thing. Now, it's time to get back to paying attention to myself and to quit worrying about stupid boys and their stupid decisions that they will no doubt regret."

Again, Michelle laughed as she attempted to take a chip from the bag Brae had confiscated. "Yup. You're totally over it."

"Oh, eff off," Brae snapped, pulling the bag further away.

It was Friday night, and Brae had announced that she was officially ready to move on to step three, therefore a friend night was in order, full of junk food and boy bashing.

How talking about boys (and Seth in particular) was going to help Brae get over him was beyond me, but I had to admit she did seem much more self-assured than she had in weeks. She was slowly starting to return to the girl I had known for so long.

I, however, felt like a traitorous fraud. It had been five days since my emotional meet-up with Seth in the park, and in those few short moments, any minimal progress I had made in separating myself from the hold he had on me was erased with three little words.

I like you.

His voice echoed in my head like a broken record set to torture me, the mere memory of it causing my heart to race in my chest. I still couldn't seem to grasp the fact that he liked me . . . that he truly *liked* me. Enough to break up with someone like Brae Walker to be with me.

That was the kind of stuff you read about in cheesy romance novels. Not real life. Not to girls like me.

It had been five days. Five days of repeating his declarations in my mind like an echo while simultaneously telling myself it didn't matter. Five days of pushing him from my thoughts any time he crept in. Five days of standing at Brae's side, knowing that I could have everything I wanted, yet choosing her over my heart. Five days of pretending that his presence, his casual glances in the hall at school, and his confession meant nothing.

Five whole days of pretending later, and I was actually getting pretty good at it.

Stretching out farther onto my beanbag chair, I listened as the others complained about various people in our class.

"Well, at least Seth broke up with you rather than mess around with someone behind your back," Michelle commented casually, almost causing me to choke. "Rumor has it that Adam Mathers is cheating on Sarah Staples with Lindsay McLean."

Of course this new morsel of gossip caught Brae's attention. "You're kidding!"

"I heard they got caught making out behind the bleachers after the last baseball game," Erin added as they casually twirled a Twizzler between their fingers. "And when Sarah found out, she freaked, calling Lindsay a backstabber in front of a bunch of people at some party last weekend."

They giggled in the thrill of teenage drama before Michelle added, "Adam is pretty hot. I'd make out with him."

"Please, you'd make out with anyone on the football team," Brae coughed in a teasing manner.

This caused an eruption of giggles from my friends, followed by a crescendo of gossip about various boys on the football team. It was so normal, so typical every day, I felt the tiny thread holding my heart together tighten just a little more. Maybe more evenings like this were what I needed? More time focusing on myself, remembering who I was beyond Brae's best friend or Seth's . . . whatever I was. Step three finally felt like something I could achieve, reaffirming completion in myself without the necessity of another person. Maybe this was finally going to start getting easier?

I like you, his voice echoed again, shoving my head back underwater.

I closed my eyes, holding in the groan that threatened to betray me. Okay, so maybe not *easy,* but the most important things in life never were. I had to do this. I had to forget what he told me and move on one way or another.

"Hel-lo!" Michelle's hand waved in front of my eyes. "Are you okay? You totally zoned out."

A flush heated my face for being caught thinking about Seth in front of everyone. While there was no way for them to know what, or who, I was thinking of, the warmth on my cheeks felt like it was branded into my skin.

"Just judging you guys silently," I teased, earning myself a round of groans for my sarcasm. If only they knew it was merely self-preservation.

Rolling onto my stomach, I tuned back into the conversation with renewed intensity. This was about being with my friends, talking about all the things we did with or without boyfriends. Now, more than ever, I needed to stand my ground against my treacherous heart and come out on the other side of these steps no longer bound to the boy that stood between me and my best friend.

CHAPTER SIXTEEN

Turning the page of my book, I gasped at the latest twist in the story, nestling deeper into my bed. I drank in the words like I was dying of thirst, my heart hammering.

So far, step three was my favorite in this little venture of trying to get over Seth Linwood.

Focusing on myself so far this week had consisted of curling up in my bed reading, watching Netflix, random internet time, doing homework, or scooping iced cream. All the things I used to do but never put much conscious thought into. Now, they were done purposefully, with determination, to put Seth, his confessions, drama, and dimples far from my mind and escape into the world of make-believe.

I was strategic about my choices, however. No stupid, sappy love stories. No boy likes girl, they fight, they make up and live happily ever after. That wasn't real, and even if it was, I didn't need that crap in my life right now. I had finished the thriller I was reading a few days prior. Since Seth's confession, however, it wasn't quite strong enough to hold up against such a revelation.

I like you, whispered in my mind, rising over the words on the page until they were like a tornado siren, warning of impending doom. His face would appear, handsome and earnest and hopeful, until the book would lay forgotten at my side as I was swallowed whole by frustration.

What I needed was violent horror, thrilling drama, or just plain distraction.

Hence my current literary thrill of Stephen King's *IT*. I had read it before, and it had scared me to the point that I had to put the book in the bathroom cupboard because I didn't want it in my room. I was convinced for weeks afterward that Pennywise was hiding in my closet, ready to jump out and consume my soul at any moment. I swore to myself that I would never read it or anything like it again. But that was before I needed something so drastically captivating and horrifically disturbing to occupy my mind.

I was completely wrapped up in Pennywise stalking the characters to the brink of terror when my phone vibrated on my nightstand. I shrieked loudly, dropping the book onto my chest, my entire body quivering.

Picking up my phone, I scowled as I slid my finger across the screen. "You scared the hell out of me."

"Why?" Brae asked curiously. "What were you doing?"

"I'm reading Stephen King."

"Again? I thought after the clown fiasco of three years ago you wouldn't dare read something like that again."

"Yeah, well I felt like giving it another try. I need something different."

"Same here," she replied with newfound enthusiasm. "And that's why I'm calling."

"Okay . . .?"

"Part of step three is to focus on myself and find something new that will help me get out some of the feelings and stuff, right? A new hobby and a new start and all of that."

"Yeah."

"Well, I want you to take me hiking!"

My brow furrowed as I considered her announcement. Brae wasn't exactly the most coordinated or athletic person I knew. In fact, I couldn't remember a single time since ninth grade when she had voluntarily taken part in any kind of sporting activity that wasn't mandatory gym class.

"Seriously?" I asked, pushing up into a seated position. "Brae, you've tried hiking with me and my moms a few times, and—"

"I know, but what better reason than to try something completely out of the normal for me? Hannah, come on! I need a new hobby, and I could use something athletic to burn off my fury. And it will make me buff and hot, and then Seth will regret ever breaking it off!"

"First of all, the point of this is to do it for yourself, not to get back at Seth."

"Whatever, stop arguing with me. I'm coming over in ten minutes. Get ready."

"Wait, what?"

"Get ready! It's great weather out, and I have energy to burn!"

"Why the hell am I being dragged along to this messed up therapy session?" I asked, shaking my head.

"Because I need someone to go with. You love hiking and know all the trails. And besides, you have to."

"How do you figure?" I laughed.

"Rule one: always have your best friend's back, remember? I need you to have my back in this, both emotionally and physically, since I am pretty sure I will die."

"Ugh. I hate when you bring out these rules to your benefit."

I could almost hear her smile through the phone.

"That's the best time to bring them out."

"I'm going to die," Brae huffed, barely able to catch her breath. "I'm sure this is how I die."

My cheeks ached from laughter against the constant spectacle Brae created just as much as my arms and legs did from the hike. "This was your idea, remember?"

"Yeah, well, it's effective in distracting me. Because all I can think about is my heart pounding out of my chest and how much my shins hurt from these stupid rocks."

"It's not the rocks' fault that you find every single one to trip over," I reminded her, earning myself a middle finger.

I rolled my eyes but couldn't wipe the smile from my face. As much as I was reluctant to come along on this particular venture, I had to admit that it was actually a lot of fun. It had to have been weeks since I had been hiking, too wrapped up in school and work and study sessions to find any real semblance of "me time." And as much as I wouldn't admit it to her, the exertion really did help clear my head.

The warm spring breeze toyed with strands of my hair that had escaped my ponytail, the light sheen of sweat on my skin cool against the air. The soft song of the trees bending to the wind above soothed my mind, the heavy, earthy scent invading my nostrils and grounding my soul.

The occasional grunt, usually from Brae, would break into the mix against the squeak of shoes against rock. She was living up to her *I don't do sports* reputation. She tripped over every rock along the trail, fell down once when her foot caught on a wayward branch, and I swore I could hear her breathing from where I stood. She was sweating profusely, taking breaks to stand with her hands on her knees, and panting whenever possible.

"Having fun?" I asked as she straightened from her latest tripod position.

She stuck her tongue out at me before readjusting her form. "I know I suck at this, but I am actually having fun. Even if I won't be able to walk tomorrow."

"You'll be fine, drama queen," I laughed, adjusting my backpack on my shoulder. "Maybe you should do more exercise, and this wouldn't be so hard."

"That's the point," she reminded me. "I'm going to get good at this no matter what. Turn over a new leaf or whatever."

"Even if it kills you?" I asked, casting her a side-eyed glance.

She smirked. "Yup. Which I'm pretty sure it will."

We made it back to the parking lot just as the sun began to brush the treetops, descending slowly. I felt invigorated, alive, my blood pumping, and my lungs burning. And I loved it.

Reaching the car, we both leaned against its shiny white exterior. While I was basking in the sunshine, Brae took another opportunity to tripod herself and gasp for breath.

"Well . . . I did it," she sighed, sweat dripping from her brow into the dirt at our feet. "I'm dead, but I did it."

I couldn't hold back my snort as I pulled my water bottle from my bag. "You did pretty well, for a dead girl."

Clicking her tongue at me, she reached out and stole my bottle, drinking greedily. She swatted me away as I tried to reclaim it, water dribbling down her chin. For a girl who prided herself in looking put together and pristine twenty-four-seven, I had to admire how unfazed she was at her current state. Red faced, hair wind-blown, and sweat soaked, she couldn't have looked less "Braelyn" if she tried.

This little endeavor was proving to be much more difficult for both of us than I think we expected when it started, but today was the first day I actually felt like we could do it. That she could get over him, mend her ego, and move on. That she wouldn't blame him anymore or second guess herself because of his choice.

And despite my many setbacks, a renewed sense of determination flooded my system. I had been too wrapped up in the steps, in the task of it all, I wasn't letting it happen. Like, how can you get over something when it's all you think about? Finally getting out of the house and back into my life was the cleansing restart I didn't realize I needed.

I was finally feeling more like myself than I had in months. Today was a reminder that I could still be me, with or without Seth. Since the *without* was the only option, I was going to have to keep moving forward. Today had been a pretty good day and a few big steps in the right direction.

Maybe these steps were actually working after all.

CHAPTER SEVENTEEN

An eruption of giggles rippled across the three of us, all eyes turning to Michelle.

"Just hold still," Erin snickered, reaching out to push down on Michelle's knee.

"I can't help it! It tickles!"

"I swear to God, I can't believe you've never had a pedicure before," Brae commented, shaking her head in disbelief.

"I'm not a high maintenance pain in the butt like you three," Michelle snipped, gripping the armrests of her chair tightly with both hands. Her eyes were glued to her feet and the poor woman positioned near them as she struggled to file Michelle's toenails.

"Um, this is my first time, too," I said, raising a hand.

"Oh, shut up," Michelle whined, earning another wave of laughter at her expense.

The Saturday morning sun poured through the floor-to-ceiling windows of the salon, as we took part in yet another day dedicated to complete and total indulgence in step three.

For Brae, this step seemed to be the easiest to follow through on and the most natural to her.

I knew this was a positive sign and silently hoped that this meant the rest of the steps would go just as smoothly.

So when Brae suggested a spa day of relaxation and friend time, I decided it was much needed and deserved. I needed some time with my friends, a little pampering, and a solid step forward after my weeks of falling behind.

And making fun of Michelle's inability to sit still during a pedicure was an excellent pastime.

Leaning her head back against her chair, Brae sighed.

"This is exactly what I needed," she said softly, a gentle smile on her face. "I don't even remember the last time I had a real girls' day."

"Me neither," I added, watching the technician buff my toenails until they gleamed.

"I think this is my best step yet. Getting back to myself, focusing on what I want and things that make me happy. Not worrying about if the things I do or don't do will affect anyone else. It's kind of nice just to be me again, you know? Even if that hike last weekend almost killed me."

I nodded at her reference to her "near death experience." However, I had no frame of reference for trying to find myself again after ending a relationship, so I could only go on observation. My observations of Brae weren't exactly the clearest picture, either, since she never really held herself back from doing what she wanted whether she was in a relationship or not. I didn't necessarily agree with her assessment that she was getting back to focusing on herself, since she never really stopped, but I was glad she was feeling better all the same.

"Did you guys hear the rumor about Seth?" Erin asked, casually picking at a loose thread on their sweater. Both Brae and I sat up abruptly, our previous calm evaporating.

"What?" we said in unison.

Erin kept their face impassive, the least gossip addicted of our group. Normally, they would listen while the rest of us dissected the latest event, offering their comments on occasion. But rarely did they open those gates. We had been hanging out together for over an hour, and they only decided to mention news about Seth now? Normally I didn't care. But currently, I was as eager as Brae.

While I knew Erin was not the malicious type, I couldn't help but wonder if their latest gossip morsel was somehow about me. They had yet to bring up my hallway interlude with Seth again, but I couldn't shake the fear of having been caught.

Erin continued with a lift of their shoulder. "I heard from a girl in my history class that he told Adam that he likes some girl. He didn't say who, but it's someone in our class."

"What!" Brae and I shrieked again. I paled when I realized how indignant I sounded and prayed they assumed it was on Brae's behalf.

"Who is it?" she asked, leaning across me toward Erin. Her bony elbows dug into the flesh of my legs, her body practically crawling across my own in her desperation to get closer to Erin and their news.

"He didn't say. Or if he did, she didn't hear him. All she said was that she overheard Seth say to Adam that he's crazy about this girl, but that things are complicated and she just wants to be friends."

Michelle rolled her eyes. "What girl in their right mind would only want to be *friends* with Seth Linwood?" She turned to find Brae glaring at her. "I mean, no offense, but you know better than anyone how hot he is. That jawline could cut me like a steak, and I'd thank him for it. Plus, he is one of the few guys in our school who is actually nice, not a jerk looking to hook up."

"I can't believe he likes someone," Brae said, throwing herself back against her chair. "It's only been six weeks! How the hell can he be over me already and trying to score with some new girl?"

"Don't stress," Erin said quickly, coming to her defense. "The girl is probably just a rebound. He's just trying to get over you."

I frowned at the insinuation that this "girl" was just a rebound, the knee-jerk part of me wanting to tell her that the girl probably wasn't a distraction to get over Brae and was perhaps a very nice person. That she was possibly trying to do the right thing and not get involved in a messy and public breakup between high school royalty. That she was probably a great freaking friend and was choosing said friendship over the boy she was ass over teakettle for!

But, again, I kept my mouth shut.

"This is just great," Brae ranted, crossing her arms over her chest. "Seth is moving on before me. That just isn't right. He can't get over me before I get over him! I can't be the sad, single ex-girlfriend while he shows off whatever new little arm candy he picked up. That would be effing tragic!"

"Brae, calm down," I said, pushing her shoulder. "It's just a rumor. It probably isn't even—"

"Yeah, it's probably just a crush," Michelle interjected, cutting me off. "Besides, it sounds like the girl isn't interested, so you have nothing to worry about. Having him crushing on someone he can't have is awesome payback for what he did to you, anyway. This is a good thing."

Brae managed a nod. "Maybe."

"It's not like you don't have crushes on guys already," Erin smirked, sending a teasing glance toward Brae. "Hell, you even had them when you were with Seth."

"So what?" she shrugged, a smirk overtaking her frown. "A crush is innocent. We all have crushes and don't do anything about them."

Again, I felt a twinge in my stomach, as though I was being subtly called out. The subject of crushes and unrequited feelings was off-limits, the avoidance necessary to keep my mind in the game. The nerves I felt on the topic were ridiculous, of course, but any reference that resembled my current situation in any way seemed to be a trigger to my guilty conscience.

Michelle angled her body toward us and almost pulled her foot right out of the technician's grasp.

"This is a more fun subject. Who are you crushing on?"

"No one," Brae answered instinctively. "I just got out of a relationship for goodness' sake."

We all gave her dubious looks, causing her smile to broaden. "Okay, it's not a crush per se. But Liam Hutcherson is pretty cute. I'd rebound with him in a heartbeat."

"I knew it!" Michelle squealed. "I freaking knew you liked him."

Brae just cocked her head innocently. "I never said I *liked* him. I just said he was cute," she clarified, turning to Michelle. "How about you?"

"Me?"

"Yeah, you. Who's on the top of your list?"

Michelle pursed her lips in thought, resting her chin in her hands. "I'd probably say Oliver Trenner. He's got that lanky, artsy vibe that's kind of hot."

"Definitely cute," I agreed. "But you know he's gay, right?"

Michelle's eyes widened, her mouth falling slack. "He is?"

"Yes. He's been dating Matt Hennessy since before the end of last semester."

Erin sputtered a laugh while Michelle wallowed in her fake love lost. "Well crap."

"I'm totally down for a random hook up with Charity Newton," Erin said, leaning back in their chair. "She's got that edgy vibe."

Michelle and Brae both sang out enthusiastic "oohs," before bursting into laughter.

"She's definitely cute," Brae said, her previously sour mood now faded.

The three launched into an intense conversation about their respective crushes, analyzing aspects that they were certain made them perfect partner material. Even Michelle, despite her ill-fated crush on Oliver, was certain that there might still be hope.

"So, Hannah," Brae said in a singsong tone. "I noticed you haven't yet answered this particular question yet."

"Oh, I . . . um . . ."

"Come on, Hannah!" Michelle said, pulling on my arm playfully. "We all know there's someone. You might as well tell us now or we will be forced to go through the entire roster of East River until you give it away."

"Guys, come on," I whined, panicking internally. "Isn't today supposed to be about—"

"It's supposed to be about getting back to the things that we like to do and focusing on what makes us happy," Brae said firmly. "And what we like to do is talk about hot people, and what makes us happy is talking about the hot people who we have crushes on. Now come on!"

"Is it Ben Travers?"

"What? No!"

Erin rubbed their hands together. "Have you finally realized boys aren't worth the trouble and are ready to come to the rainbow side with me?"

I couldn't hold back my laugh. "Guys are definitely more trouble than they're worth, but no—"

"We'll keep guessing until you admit it!" Brae cheered, reaching out to sling her arm across my shoulders. "We all know there's someone. No one makes it through high school without crushing on someone."

"Dean O'Connell!"

"Garrett Davidson!"

My mind raced in a frantic panic, struggling to come up with a way to get out of this trap they had somehow cornered me in. I knew I couldn't admit the truth, because it would mean the end of my friendship with Brae. Breaking her heart all over again was not an option, but apparently, neither was pleading the fifth with these three treacherous brats.

In a flustered loss of control, my mouth blurted out the first name I could think of.

"Justin Ford!" I heard myself say, immediately cringing as a rush of anxiety gripped my chest for the lie. I tried to keep my face even as I watched my friends' faces change from pestering to elated before they all started to squeal.

"Oh, he's so cute!"

"Definitely crush worthy!"

"He has the most beautiful eyes, Hannah!" Brae added, pulling my arm until my attention was on her. "See, was that so hard?" She paused, slapping my arm. "I can't believe you didn't tell me!"

"Because you would tease me relentlessly or try to play matchmaker," I muttered, casting her a side-eyed glance.

She pursed her lips. "Yeah. That does sound like me."

I forced a smile as I sat back against my chair, my heart pounding and adrenaline zinging through my system thanks to the inclination to run for my life. My breathing was ragged, and I was pretty sure I was sweating through my T-shirt.

Pulling myself together, I was thankful to find that my friends had yet again changed topics. Now they were discussing options for lunch after our spa visit and the benefits of healthy options versus indulging in burritos and frozen yogurt.

I had never thanked God more for the short attention spans of my friends before in my life.

CHAPTER EIGHTEEN

"Ugh," I grunted, the edge of the freezer digging into my abdomen as I hung over the side. I struggled against the discomfort, convinced my organs were being popped like balloons. I didn't have time to focus on that, though, since my arms were mere moments away from frostbite.

I hated defrosting the freezers with every part of my being. While poking my head into the depths of the massive containers would sound like a nice reprieve from the heat wave that had taken over East River in the last couple of days, straining to scrape away the years' worth of accumulated ice and frost was worse than any workout I had ever endured. It was like brutal punishment, using the little scraper that was much too small to complete the job thoroughly when compared with the size of the freezer itself.

This particular task was supposed to have been done by the last shift. It was written on the schedule currently hanging on the clipboard by the door in big red letters. "Defrost freezer" right beside George's name. And yet, when I arrived for my shift twenty minutes ago, George rushing out the door with little more than a "Hey," I found this disaster waiting for me.

Brae would say for me to leave it. It wasn't my job this time around, and I shouldn't have to make up for what others lacked. But, as usual, I couldn't stand the idea of something not being completed, the owners of the shop being disappointed in me by extension. So, here I was, hanging precariously over the edge of the massive container, blasting cold air across my upper half as I struggled to reach the frost at the far edge.

The clearing of a throat caught my attention, pulling me away from my internal cursing at my lazy ass coworker and my own penchant for always having to be the reliable one. Straightening, I found Brae across from me, leaning on the wooden ledge of the window, watching me curiously.

"You look like you've done battle with a Demogorgon," she commented with a tilt of her head.

Reaching up quickly, I smoothed down my sweaty, messy hair self-consciously.

"I'm defrosting the freezer."

"Why?" she asked, genuinely curious.

"Because it needs to be done."

She watched me speculatively, and I could almost see her reading my mind.

"Let me guess. Someone else was supposed to do it, and they didn't? So you're stepping up to the plate."

I shot her an impressive scowl that only caused her to laugh.

"I'm not even going to bother telling you that you should just leave it for them when they come in next and that it isn't your job to do everything for everyone else."

"It sounds like you just *did* tell me," I snipped, closing the freezer door and placing the scraper on the top.

Brae shrugged, resting her chin on her folded hands, abandoning her favorite pastime other than gossip: telling me I was too nice. It was then that I noticed the despondent look in her eyes and the redness that surrounded them. Her hair was twisted into a messy knot on top of her head, a thin-strapped top hanging over her frame.

"What's wrong?" I asked immediately.

"What makes you think something's wrong?" She didn't even bother to look up at me.

"The same way you knew that defrosting the freezers was supposed to be someone else's job. I can read you as well as you can read me."

My logic caused a small smile to form on her face, but she still didn't lift her head from her hands. Instead, she stared straight ahead into her reflection in the glass of the freezer.

Finally, with a resigned sigh, she told me what I already suspected.

"My mom," she said. "She started in on me again about Seth, asking me if I've tried to fix things with him. When I told her no and that I've accepted our relationship being over, she then asked if I've found anyone new. Like I should just jump from one boy to the other because the idea of being single is so damn tragic, she can't bear the thought of her daughter not having a guy in her life."

My blood boiled, simmering like a pot under the surface of my skin. As much as Mrs. Walker was lovely in many ways, her obsession with relationships and the dysfunctional approach she had to them was nothing short of toxic. Especially when Brae was finally making progress toward mending her dented heart.

"You know that's not true, right?" I said softly, hoping that Brae hadn't let her mother's Sanctuary mantras get into her head.

"I know," she nodded. "It's like, if I can't get him back, she basically wants me to replace him as quickly as possible. Because if she could have found someone as a quick and easy replacement to my dad, preferably rich with a nice car, she would do that, too. As long as we have a man at our side, nothing else matters."

I couldn't deny her that assessment since I had witnessed Mrs. Walker's meltdown after her husband's departure and the subsequently twisted rebuilding that came after. Since her divorce, she had taken on a belief system of over-attentive desperation when it came to relationships. Before, she had been much like Brae. Confident, self-assured in the knowledge that she was attractive and desired. Her husband had pursued her rigorously, and for the majority of their marriage, she had held the power. But when he left, that power had shifted, leaving her questioning her entire understanding of what made relationships work.

"When I told her to stop trying to force me to follow some kind of twisted crap that she learned at that crazy place, she completely ignored me and kept asking who else I could be dating. And not like we were joking at the spa the other day. She's actually serious, almost desperate in wanting me to get back into another relationship. Like I'm not a whole person unless I'm with someone. She was driving me freaking crazy, so I had to get out of there."

Exhaling a deep sigh, I turned and exited the shop to come and stand beside Brae in the alley. The blazing spring day fell over me the moment I was no longer protected by the shade of the shop, the humidity sliding over me like a veil as I came to her side. Wrapping my arms around her, I rested my head on her shoulder as she continued to stare at her reflection.

"Before you ask, yes I know that isn't true. That I don't need a guy to validate me and all that crap. And I know Seth and I are done, even if sometimes it's hard to really accept. It's just exhausting having to listen to my mom tell me over and over that a relationship is all that matters. That people will talk about me, say it's my fault that things fell apart, and judge me for not moving on fast enough. It's all the things she worries about for herself, and she's pushing it on me. Eventually, you just kind of want to give in to her just to make her shut up."

"People talking about your breakup isn't the end of the world," I reminded her. "Any more than not being in a relationship means you're not enough. I get that your mom is still struggling to come to terms with all the stuff with your dad, but you can't let her mess with your head."

"I feel almost vindictive about being single now, because of her crap. Like, if I force myself to be single, it's like it's just to prove a point to myself or my mom rather than what I really want." Pausing, she rolled her eyes toward the sky. "Ugh. I think I've been thinking about this crap too much, I'm losing my mind."

"No, you're not." I laughed lightly. "You've been doing so good with the steps, Brae. Really, you're like a rock star. If you want to be in a relationship, then give yourself some time and see if you meet someone new. If not, you can be a spinster like me. We can live in a two-bedroom apartment and buy a lot of cats. Knit them little sweaters on weekends. Either way, you're still the most popular girl in our class, and everyone adores you. Having a boy at your side doesn't change that."

I meant every word, and yet, the image of Seth and I side by side invaded my mind. Like no matter how hard I tried, I would always be trapped in his orbit.

I lifted my chin in determination and pushed the mental image away harshly. I needed to start taking my own advice and just get over him, no matter what. Maybe, eventually, my mind and my heart would give in and accept it.

Watching her reflection in the glass, I saw the corner of her lip turn upward. After a moment, she pushed off the counter and turned to me.

"This is why I came here," she admitted, pulling me in for a hug. "I needed your special brand of logic and gentle sarcasm to reset my brain."

I chuckled against her hold as I smoothed her hair. "I thought you just came for the ice cream."

To this, she laughed genuinely. "That too."

STEP FOUR: GET BACK INTO YOUR LIFE

*Good friends don't let you do
stupid things . . . alone.*

CHAPTER NINETEEN

The crack of the bat broke through the tense silence of the crowd, and as the ball soared over the field, everyone rose to their feet, cheering with excitement. All eyes were trained on Alex Sheffield as he took off toward first base, sliding in safely before the opposing team's outfielder could even chase after the ball.

Sitting back down against the hard, cold bleachers, I shoved my hands back into the pockets of my jacket. It was Friday night, and our school's baseball team was currently in battle against our biggest rivals, Stratford. The buildup to tonight's game was steady during the week, most people talking about little else in the halls between classes. I was not a big sports fan myself, but even I was getting caught up in the excitement of watching our team crush our enemies.

Initially when it was suggested we go and cheer on our school, Brae opted to sit this one out. That was when I stepped up and reminded her that step four was now underway, and it required her to go out and be with her friends, get back into her social life, and rebuild her networks. What better way to do that than the season's biggest match up? Plus, it would let her show everyone, including Seth, that she was over him.

That got her attention, and eventually, her participation.

During the lead-up to the start of the game and all through the first inning, she was nervous and quiet. Her eyes constantly darted to the bench, locking on Seth before her bottom lip pulled between her teeth. But slowly, she relaxed, to the point where she was now cheering, dancing, and carrying on like she always had, like Seth was no longer an issue or concern. It made the twist of guilt in my chest ease just a little. Except when we saw Sarah several bleachers away, sitting alone and looking exhausted. Then, a whole different kind of guilt simmered under the surface.

My distraction, or punishment, was watching Seth from the bench with my lip between my teeth. Mainly because ever since the fourth inning, when he looked our way and found me staring at him, he had taken to smiling, unable to help himself. This kept me on my toes, jittery with the thrill of catching his eye while also thoroughly enjoying the view he gave me each time he stepped up to bat, which he was about to do at this very moment.

"Let's go Eagles, let's go!" the crowd called, clapping in sync with the cheer as Seth stood from the bench, stretching his arms behind him with the help of the bat in his hands. His previously flirty looks in my direction were gone, his focus now on the game. It was hypnotizing to watch him go from playful to determined in the blink of an eye, and I constantly had to remind myself that such a train of thought was not helpful or productive.

As he stepped up to the plate, I couldn't help bringing my fingers to my teeth, nipping at my nails. The bases were loaded, and all the pressure was on Seth to get at least one runner home. He was easily one of the best players on the team, but I still couldn't help but feel the anxiety of the situation.

As he took his stance, my eyes draped over his long, lean form. Wow, he was gorgeous. My ogling was interrupted by the crack of the bat and Seth taking off toward first base before I even had the chance to realize which direction the ball had gone. Again, the crowd was on its feet, the bleachers shaking as people stomped, jumped, and danced for the two runners coming home as Seth slid into second base. My cheeks started to hurt from smiling, but I didn't care. It was nice to be able to watch him participate in something he loved.

Seth pushed back to his feet, dusting the dirt from his pants. Immediately, he turned toward me as if unable to resist, causing my breath to stall. Even from this distance, I could feel the passion in his gaze, and it shook me to the core.

Sitting down quickly, I tried to break the connection he trapped me in, shoving my hands back into my pockets. I glanced to Braelyn, praying that she didn't notice the direction of Seth's stare, and was glad to find that she was too wrapped up in an animated discussion with the girls behind us. This gave me a few minutes to pull myself together.

As the next batter took to the plate, Michelle turned to me.

"Guess what?" she said, looping her arm through mine.

"What?"

"Jeff Watkins, that senior whose parents are totally loaded, is having a party tomorrow night."

"Okay?"

Michelle stared as if that simple sentence was all the information I needed. "We need to go!"

"Go where?" Brae asked, turning her attention to us.

"Jeff Watkins is throwing a party tomorrow night."

Brae's face was impassive, and again, Michelle sighed with frustration at our lack of enthusiasm.

"We should go!" she repeated. "It'll be a blast! And filled with hot senior guys."

Brae was already shaking her head. "I really don't feel up to it."

"Up to what?" Erin asked, now leaning forward to inject themself into the conversation.

"Jeff Watkins is—" Michelle started before Erin interrupted.

"I heard he's having a party! We're going, right?"

"Definitely," Michelle said firmly, angling toward us. "This will be the first big party since your breakup, Brae. You need to make an appearance and show everyone that you're over Seth."

Brae pouted in thought, shaking her head. "I don't really feel like it."

"But isn't step four all about going out with friends and to parties and getting back into the social aspects of life?" Michelle added, rocking Brae back and forth with a nudge of her shoulder. "What better way to do that than by showing up looking like a knock out and making Seth remember what he's missing?"

"You don't even know if—" I started to say before Erin interrupted me.

"Seth is going," they confirmed with a nod. "Stacey Richards heard Alex and him talking, and Seth said he would be there."

"See! He's going to show everyone he's over you! You need to show him that you are just as much over him!" Michelle shouted.

"I'm not sure that's how it works," I said before turning to Brae. "You know you don't have to go if you aren't ready. Step four is about going out and getting back into your life, but not with things that you don't feel ready for."

It was clear in the set of her features that she was weighing her own bruised ego against her desperate need to show the rest of the school that he didn't break her down. It was always about appearances with Brae, and Michelle and Erin had played to her weakness.

"We should go," Brae finally said. "They're right. I need to get out and do things I used to do, and before, I wouldn't have thought twice about going to this party. Especially if Seth is going to be there, I need to show up looking amazing and show him that I'm fine without him."

"Only if you feel ready," I emphasize, watching her closely.

She nodded. "I have to be ready. It's been weeks, and I've barely left the house. If I stay in much more, I'll be a social hermit, like you."

The gentle insult stung, even if it was kind of true.

"This will be a total confidence booster," Erin said with a wide grin. "You know half the guys at school think you're hot. You can flirt, dance, and chat them up, helping your self-confidence while also flipping a subtle finger at Seth. It's the perfect post breakup plan!"

My attention flickered to Seth, who had somehow made it to third base while we were deep in this social power struggle of a conversation. He bent over with his hands on his knees, rocking back and forth as he waited for the batter to give him the chance to head for home. My friends continued discussing the plans for the next night, ignorant to the fact that my attention was now completely on Seth, as another crack of the bat echoed through the night. Seth was off the base before the sound fully registered, and I sucked in a nervous breath. I didn't watch where the ball went, if it was caught, or anyone else on the field. My attention was glued to him as he dove forward, sliding on his front to the home plate long before the ball hit the catcher's glove.

"Safe!" the umpire called, and again the crowd was on its feet.

Seth stood, meeting teammates as he jogged back toward the bench with high fives, claps on the back, and fist bumps. The moment he sat, his focus was toward me, tying me to him. He was pleased to find me watching him, his mouth turning upward into a smirk.

Tearing my gaze away from him, I brought my nails back to the abuse of my teeth.

"So, you're in?" Brae said, oblivious to the sexual tension that was sparking across the field between her ex and myself.

"What?"

"Tomorrow night. The party? You're in, right?"

I groaned lightly. "I don't know—"

"You have to go," she said firmly. "I can't go without you. I know you plan on us being crazy cat ladies when we get older, but that's just my backup plan. I need to get back out there, and reclaim my throne, and I need my best friend there in case I do something stupid."

I couldn't stop myself from snickering. "You're the one who already has her cats named," I challenged.

She frowned. "There's nothing wrong with having a well-thought-out back up plan."

I shook my head. I had never been a fan of parties, mainly because they were loud, hot and crowded, full of drunk people bumping in to each other. Brae always tried to get me to come along, but when she had a boyfriend, I was usually able to avoid forced social interaction. Her reference to me being a social hermit wasn't far off. Maybe it was time for me to make a change, even if it was only for show.

"Okay, fine. I'll go."

"Good! You can help me figure out what outfit will make Seth the most jealous."

I nodded, my attention turning back to the subject of the conversation to find him still watching me intently, his playful smirk still in place as Brae looped her arm through mine.

I had never felt so torn.

CHAPTER TWENTY

"Wow. There must be half the school here already," Erin commented as they leaned closer to the steering wheel.

"That's cause we're late," I said, throwing a teasingly annoyed glance at Brae. Of course she flipped me the finger.

"My hair just didn't look right!"

"It looked the same an hour ago as it does now!" I argued, laughing at her affronted expression and crossed arms.

"It's not like you didn't take just as long trying to pick out just the right socks for tonight," Brae countered with a playful glare toward Erin.

Erin touched at their bright yellow socks adorned with little hedgehogs absentmindedly. "These socks are more likely to get attention than the single strand of hair that you were so upset about," they huffed. "Now would you two shut up, I'm trying to find a spot."

"Does their noise impede your ability to see?" Michelle teased, earning her a murmured profanity from Erin.

"Yes. You know I have to turn the music down when I'm trying to see something while driving. So those two bickering is basically the same thing, so everyone shut up unless you want to walk three miles in those shoes."

We all laughed at their expense, looking out the windows of the car in search of parking. Erin had been correct in their assessment that it felt like half the school was already lining the streets surrounding Jeff Watkins's house.

"Look! There's one!" Michelle shouted, pointing her arm forward.

"Thank God! You're a rock star." Erin sighed, gunning the engine to get to the spot a few milliseconds faster. They maneuvered awkwardly into the space, all of us clutching the seats waiting for the sound of the ominous crunch of metal that never came.

Stepping out of the car and onto the sidewalk, I ran my hands along the legs of my dark skinny jeans. I had taken longer getting ready than I usually did for nights like this, mainly for the same reason that Brae had worked herself up into a tizzy.

Seth.

This would be the first social outing since I discovered the truth of his feelings, and while I still stood firm on the belief that I would hold true to my friendship pact, that didn't mean I had to be a shut-in. Parties weren't necessarily my thing, but if Brae could take on the challenge of hiking, I could try to be more sociable and put myself out there. My shy, reserved nature and lack of confidence got me in this mess, maybe it was time to change that.

Following my friends along the sidewalk, the sound of music rose as we came closer to our destination. We turned the corner, and Jeff's house came into view, illuminated like a beacon in the night. It was a large two-story, red brick affair that always looked like it should belong in some Victorian-era film rather than on a usually quiet side street of suburban East River. The white columns that dominated the front gave it opulence, while the mass of teenagers in varying stages of debauchery spilling out the front door gave it realism.

Immediately, the music overtook my senses, my heart regulating to beat in time with the thrumming of the base. There were so many people crushed into the space; the sound of laughter, chatter, and the clinking of glasses blending together against the music into the white noise of festivity.

"Do you want to get a drink?" Erin shouted into my ear. Even being right next to me, I struggled to hear them.

"Doesn't matter. You guys lead."

Maneuvering through the throng of bodies, we clasped each other's hands like a train to keep from losing each other. Finally, we made it to the living room, which opened to the kitchen, giving us a good view of the majority of the partygoers.

"Look, there's Oliver!" Michelle called, watching from a safe distance. "Are you sure he's gay?"

I couldn't help but roll my eyes. "Yes, Michelle. He's literally holding hands with Matt right now."

Her face fell into a petulant frown. Stepping up to Brae's side, I noticed that her attention was locked on the kitchen. It didn't take long to realize why.

Seth lingered in the kitchen, leaning casually on the counter. The black button down he wore showcased his torso and brought out the lightness in his eyes when matched with his dark hair. He was currently laughing at something Brady Chandler was saying, his dimple on full display. Needless to say, he looked freaking hot.

"He looks so . . . happy," Brae said softly, a hint of sadness in her voice. "Like he doesn't even miss me."

I bit my lip, trying to think of the right thing to say. "I don't know if it's a matter of missing you. He doesn't have to miss you to mean that you were important to him."

This only caused her pout to deepen. "But does he have to look so . . . good?" she queried. "Ugh, I wanted to be the one to look amazing and make him want me back. And there he is looking all sexy, and all I want to do is go over there and kiss him."

"Just ignore him and have fun," Erin offered. "Don't let him win!" They capped off their point by passing Brae a red plastic cup of liquid that I had little doubt was not Kool-Aid. Brae looked at it skeptically before taking a deep breath and drinking. Her face contorted against the taste, but she didn't stop until half the cup was empty.

Finally coming up for air, she gasped. "Okay. Let's go."

For the next two hours, my time was alternated between listening to Brae talk about Seth and how he was over her to watching her flirt shamelessly with any boy within reach while I exchanged teasing glances with Seth from across the room. No matter how risky it was, neither one of us could seem to ignore each other completely. Whenever our eyes would meet, he would grin just slightly before dipping his gaze away again. It was a flirtatious, playful back-and-forth we had started, and it seemed to be a game as to who would approach who first.

Friends could do that, right? Two people who knew each other could talk at a party and it wouldn't be blasphemy? I wouldn't burn in hell for simply looking at him, right?

Maybe if I kept telling myself I was absolved, eventually, I would believe it.

Unfortunately, Brae seemed to have decided that the best way to make Seth miss her was to get messily drunk and hang all over half the junior class and a quarter of the seniors in attendance. My playful back and forth with Seth was becoming less and less the more Brae drank, as my attention was now focused on keeping her from making a complete fool of herself.

Catching sight of Erin, I waved them over.

"Can you keep an eye on her," I asked, nodding toward Brae as she chatted up a senior whose name I didn't know. "I need to pee."

They laughed, shaking their head. "She really is a lush, isn't she? This is probably why she doesn't usually drink."

"Yeah. Thanks for passing her the first. Real great idea."

"Hey, how was I supposed to know she would drown her sorrows in a little plastic cup?"

Shaking my head, I left them to babysit Braelyn and pushed through the bodies in search of the bathroom. I did my business as quickly as possible, checked myself over in the mirror, and stepped back out into the hall in record time.

Unfortunately, in my haste, I also stepped right into a warm, firm surface.

"Crap, sorry," I mumbled, stepping back to look up at the person I had just collided with. A pair of familiar green eyes shone down on me.

"Oh, hey." He grinned, tipping his cup toward me. "No worries, I was just in the bathroom line." We stared at each other for several moments, my previous reminders that it was a party and running into him would be inevitable rattling around in my brain as he continued. "Fancy seeing you here."

I snorted, shaking my head at him. "You mean at Jeff's? Or this particular hallway?"

He considered my question for a moment with a tilt of his head. "Both. You're not usually much of a party girl."

"Neither are you," I noted before cringing at my reference of Seth being a girl.

"Alex made me come," he clarified, not bothering to call attention to my error. "He figured it would be good for me to get out and have some fun."

"And how's that going?" I asked, glancing toward the red cup in his hands.

Seth followed my direction before shrugging. "Unlike half the people here, this isn't booze. It's ginger ale. I'm not much of a drinker." Looking down to my empty hands, he tilted his head. "No drinks for you?"

"Nope. Not much of a drinker either."

He leaned against the wall at his side. "We should set up a day to get together and try to get through more of that English assignment. We haven't really worked on it since . . ."

He trailed off, but I knew what he was eluding to. Since he told me he liked me and everything changed irrevocably between us. He had been giving me space, albeit marginally. I had been trying to push him from my thoughts, without success. Our mutual avoidance of each other had caused a serious backlog in our homework schedule.

Forced proximity made this whole "getting over him" thing so much harder.

"I'm sure we can find a day to work on it. We only have a few more acts left, anyway."

"Yeah, but they're kind of important ones. You know, the whole 'oh here, where I set up my everlasting rest' and such," he mused with a smile and a dismissive flick of his hand.

I snorted. "For a guy who isn't a big fan of romantic classics, you sure do know *Romeo and Juliet* by heart."

His smile grew at my assessment. "Only certain parts. And mostly because Brae made me watch those Twilight movies a million freaking times, so the parts that are quoted in it are kind of seared into my brain."

I coughed a laugh, knowing full well of Brae's obsession with the Twilight series. It still didn't negate the fact that Seth knew passages from *Romeo and Juliet* so fluently, and hearing them spouted in his deep, melodic voice was nothing short of erotic.

"We'll find time to work on the assignment," I assured him. "Although by the sound of it you could probably rewrite it all on your own. Since you know it so well and all." I shot him a taunting glare as I pursed my lips in thought. "You know, you are kind of like Edward in a way."

As Seth's eyes widened, his mouth falling slack, I had to fight against the initial impulse to laugh. It was the reaction I was hoping for.

"How the hell did you come up with that one?" he pressed, feigning insult.

I shrugged innocently, playing along. "Well, you always try to do the right thing. You're kind of self-deprecating at times, even if you don't realize it. And you both *love* romance."

The last similarity was merely to get a rise out of him, since we had battled more than once over his preference for romance against my hesitance on the subject. As his eyes narrowed playfully, his head shaking in disbelief and fake irritation, I smiled up at him.

He considered my assessment for a moment, and I fully expected him to return with his own comparison between myself and a Twilight character. Admittedly, I was curious which one he would choose.

"I guess you might be kind of right," he said, shocking me. I watched as his expression turned from teasing to thoughtful, lips pursed and eyes distant. "Mostly because I'm a bit of a masochist. At least lately."

I was ready to ask him to clarify his statement and his belief in his own masochistic nature, but my breath stalled. His gaze was heavy, penetrating, and I knew exactly what he meant.

Me. He knew wanting me, pursuing me, was a fruitless labor, and yet he still did. My refusal of him had to hurt, because having to turn him away hurt every part of my soul. Any response I could have considered died off on my lips.

His eyes were locked on my own, green meeting gray, the intensity almost jarring. Slowly, all the noise around us seemed to fade into a dull hum in the distance. I could still see everyone milling around us, could feel the music vibrating my body, but everything was much lighter. All I saw clearly was Seth, and all I heard was my heart pounding in my ears as his eyes flickered to my lips. His own parted slightly, his eyes lingering before returning to meet mine as they slowly rose along my face. The entire action caused my body to tingle, a ripple of adrenaline filling my veins. He repeated the action a second time, and I knew what he was considering.

He was thinking of kissing me.

I knew I had only milliseconds before he would lean in to me, and I used them to assess the situation. Firstly, I wanted him to kiss me. Completely, unquestioningly, without hesitation, I wanted to feel his lips against mine. I had fantasized about what they would feel like, what he would taste like, since meeting him all those months ago. It was a silly, schoolgirl crush that intensified over time to an all-consuming lust, and no matter the situation, that one little desire never completely faded.

Secondly, I knew he liked me. That if he was to kiss me, it wasn't just an emotionally charged reaction to a drunken ex-girlfriend, pressuring friends, and the surroundings of teenage hormones. He had already confessed his desire to be with me, and the only thing keeping us apart was me.

But thirdly, and most importantly, I thought about Brae. About the fact that she was currently downstairs in a drunken stupor fueled by her own dented ego, oblivious to the sexual tension passing back and forth between me and her ex-boyfriend at this very moment. I knew where my loyalty still resided, and the kind of person I wanted to be, no matter what my heart and lips might want in this moment.

So, when Seth moved that first little inch toward me, his eyes locked on my lips, I closed my eyes to break the hypnosis he had me entranced in and stepped back. The moment I moved, he paused, his eyes darting to mine. They were wide and nervous and even a little embarrassed once he realized what he had done.

"I'm sorry," I said softly as the intensity of our moment faded, allowing the world around us to flood back into my senses. "We can't."

Seth held his breath for a beat, then exhaled. I watched as he swallowed back his hurt, dropping his eyes before nodding. "I know," he replied, turning to lean back against the wall again. Running a hand over his face, he groaned. "Damn, I'm sorry. I shouldn't have—"

"Don't." I stopped him, reaching up and pulling his hand from his face. The muscles in his forearm flexed against my hand. "It's not that I don't want to. But we can't."

Again, he took a deep breath as if trying to cleanse himself of the charge that passed between us before nodding. We watched each other for a moment longer before I decided it was best that I walk away. As much as I knew the type of person I wanted to be, I wasn't sure my will power was strong enough to reject Seth Linwood twice.

"I better go," I said, stepping back from him and toward the stairs. "I'll see you later?"

He pushed off the wall, watching me retreat away from him with a look of longing that almost made me go back to him. "Yeah."

CHAPTER TWENTY-ONE

Rushing down the stairs quickly, I almost stumbled at the bottom, crashing into Tommy Heslip. He righted me as I stammered apologies, my body and brain finally catching up to what had just happened in the last few moments. It was like a tidal wave crashing over me; Seth's intensity, his lips, the way he looked at me, and the way the whole rest of the world faded away in that moment.

He almost kissed me. I almost let him.

Ugh, I was the worst best friend in history.

"I'm so sorry," I muttered once more, stepping away from Tommy's grasp. He smiled a crooked grin at me, his eyes heavily lidded.

"No worries, Hannah," he said, his eyes raking over me slowly from head to toe, grin widening. "You're looking hot tonight."

"Uh . . . thanks?"

He reached out to take my arm again. "Care for a drink?" I stepped away, keeping myself just out of reach.

"No, I'm good, thanks."

With liquid courage running through his veins, he didn't seem deterred by the gentle rejection. "Come on, you look much too sober to—"

"I'm good," I said quickly, rushing away from him before he could slur any more passes at me. Pushing roughly through the crowd, I desperately searched for my friends. The temperature in the house was suddenly much too hot, my hair clinging to the back of my neck. Jitters and anxiety twisted in my stomach, and I wanted nothing more than to go home.

Weaving through the kitchen, the familiar faces of my friends were nowhere in sight. The front foyer was the same, as was the kitchen. *Where the hell is everyone?* I thought as I squeezed my way down the hall toward a room at the far end of the house. Pushing a door open, I exhaled with relief when I found Michelle and Brae in what appeared to be an office. A large desk dominated the space, the wall behind it flanked with thick volumes. The girls were currently curled up on a small, plush couch, Brae's head in Michelle's lap.

"Thank God," Michelle sighed emphatically. "Where have you been?"

"I went pee," I said innocently, avoiding the real reason why it took me so long to actually do the deed.

"Well, Erin is off making out with Charity Newton and left me here with this hot mess," she huffed, gesturing to Brae who was muttering something incoherent from her place on Michelle's lap. "She tried to make out with Josh Brayden, drank directly from the kitchen tap, and then tried to climb up the banister cause she wanted to slide back down like when we were kids. I finally had to lock her in here with me to calm her down."

"Ugh. I'm so ready to go home. Do you want me to go find Erin?"

"Home?" she balked. "I don't want to go home yet. I was chatting up this cute senior before I got conned into drunk duty here. Can't you just sit here with her for a while?"

Shaking my head, I looked at her imploringly. "Michelle, come on. It's after eleven, I'm tired and hot and just really want to go."

"Well, maybe someone else can drive you guys? I don't want to—"

The door behind me pushed open, cutting her off in mid-whine. When her complaints choked off in her throat, I didn't have to turn around to know who it would be.

Brae's attention turned toward the door, a lopsided grin overtaking her. "Seth! My little dimple butt!"

Looking over my shoulder, I found him shaking his head at her. "Jeez, Braelyn. How much did you drink?"

She tried to push herself up into a seated position, limbs awkwardly flailing. "Not that much. Just one . . . two?" She paused counting on her fingers, her brow furrowing. "Four comes after two, right?"

Stepping forward, I ignored Seth to kneel by Brae. "C'mon, you mess. Michelle and I are gonna take you home."

"But—" Michelle started.

Brae began to protest. "I don't wanna leave."

"Brae, come on. I'm tired, and we need to get you home."

She frowned, swatting her hand weakly in my direction. "You are such a fun sucker," she huffed. Glancing at Seth, her head lolled to the side. "I swear, she can be such a loser sometimes. If it wasn't for me, she would be freaking tragic."

Blood drained from my face in embarrassment as Seth jumped in.

"If Michelle doesn't want to go, I can take you guys home," Seth said, causing all eyes to turn to him. "I'm leaving now, anyway."

My attention moved to Michelle, giving her a stern and obvious "Don't you dare!" expression. Unfortunately, she refused to look my way. Traitor.

"Really? That would be great! Seth, you're awesome, no matter what Brae says. And don't listen to anything she says. She's just drunk."

She was up and out of the room before I had a chance to stop her.

I stood up and turned to Seth. "You really don't have to. I'll figure out—"

He was already shaking his head. "I would feel better if I knew you both got home okay. I'm not leaving you to deal with her this drunk by yourself."

My heart stuttered at his concern while simultaneously choking at the awkward situation I was about to be placed in. Only minutes after an almost kiss, now we were about to drag a drunken Brae back to my house and pray my parents were already in bed. This was going to be just great.

"Fine," I finally sighed, raising my hands in surrender.

Seth chuckled at my reluctance as he took my place kneeling by Brae's head. She looked at him longingly before reaching out and running her hands through his hair. "You're so pretty," she muttered with a pout. "Why do you have to be so pretty? It would be so much easier to get over you if you weren't pretty."

He exhaled a long breath before sliding his arms around her. "Come on, sweet talker. Let's stand you up."

It was a disorganized, stumbling, and slightly frustrating mission to get Brae on her feet, through the crowd, and out the door toward Seth's car. I trailed behind as he carried her, having to listen to her swoon over him, kiss his cheek or any part of him she could reach, and whine about how much she missed the way he would run his fingers along her back when they would fool around. By the time we reached his car, safely and securely sliding Brae into the back seat, I was in a terrible mood.

Climbing into the passenger seat, I didn't even wait for him to make sure she was settled. This night was supposed to be about going out with our friends and having fun together. I knew there would be some interaction and some back and forth regarding Seth, but I never expected the party to turn into a veritable battleground. I was raw and dented and more than a little irritated at the opposing team who was currently slipping into the driver's seat.

Starting the car, he cast me a glance.

"Back to yours?" he asked.

"Yeah. She's staying over. Her mom would freak if she saw her like this, and my moms are supposed to be out at some awards thing. Even if they're home, they'll be asleep."

He nodded before pulling out onto the street and away from the party.

The short drive to my house felt more tension filled than our standoff outside the bathroom, but for completely different reasons. It didn't take long for Seth to catch on to my shift in mood, and while I rationally knew it wasn't his fault that Brae was hanging all over him and reminding me of everything they had shared, I couldn't help but be irritated. I didn't want to want him anymore, and yet, all I seemed to do since they broke up was fall even harder. I was supposed to be on step four of this stupid program, and all I had managed to do was almost kiss the guy I was supposed to be ridding of my system.

Step four freaking sucked. This whole thing *sucked*.

Pulling up against the curb outside my house, I breathed a sigh of relief to find no car in the driveway. My moms were still out, and Brae and I could sneak in without incident. Despite my annoyance, I helped Seth pull a now snoring Brae from the backseat and didn't even glare at them as he easily swept her up into his arms. I kept a few paces ahead of them so I wouldn't have to watch how perfect a scene they made; the beautiful tragedy and her handsome hero.

He followed me through the house and up the stairs, bringing her into my bedroom. Tucking myself into the corner like a creepy voyeur, I watched as he gently laid her on my bed, slipping his arms out from under her. The moment he moved to pull away, she reached up and clutched at his shirt.

"Don't leave," she whined, her eyes barely open. "Don't leave me again."

Kneeling down, he brought himself level with her, whispering softly. "It's late. I gotta go."

"Just stay with me," she pleaded, reaching up to run her fingers along his face. "We were so good together. Just stay with me."

Seth said nothing in response, instead brushing her hair from her face gently. Before she could hold on to him tighter, he gently slipped from her weak grasp, stepping away and coming to stand by me.

I reined in my wayward emotions just in time. "Thanks," I said, clearing my throat. "For bringing us home."

"No problem. Like I said, I couldn't leave you guys there if your friends were going to ditch you. Especially when she's like that."

I nodded, not knowing what else to say. We stared at each other awkwardly for several long moments, and I had to wonder if he wanted to say something more. But whatever it was died off in the silence between us, and he moved around me toward the door.

Pausing with his hand on the doorframe, he looked back to me. "See you Monday?" he said, voicing it as a question. It was a silly thing to ask since there was no question whether we would see each other. But considering the current tension filled-climate between us, I could tell why he felt the sudden uncertainty.

"Yeah," I finally said, trying to ease his nerves. "See you Monday."

He hesitated for another moment before shaking his head at himself and disappearing down the hall. I listened as his footsteps padded down the stairs, as the front door closed behind him, and as moments later, his car started. My feet carried me to the window on their own accord, watching as he pulled away and disappeared down the street, and only then letting myself exhale.

Methodically and slowly, the task of changing into my pajamas took longer than usual while I reined in my emotions. Washing the makeup from my face and twisting my hair into a knot on top of my head, only then did I turn my attention to my best friend currently sprawled across all four corners of my bed. I considered changing her into the tattered old pajamas she always kept under my bed but wasn't in the mood to struggle with her. So, instead, I climbed in beside her, throwing the comforter over both of us in the darkness.

Once I was settled, Brae rolled over toward me.

"Hannah."

"Yeah?"

"Thank you."

"For what?" I asked, turning to find her watching me.

"For always taking care of me. You're a great best friend. I don't deserve you."

I let out a small chuckle before pushing her messy hair away from her face. She said nothing more as she quickly and easily fell asleep, soft snores leaving her. I turned my attention back to my ceiling, folding my hands over my stomach.

My mind wandered over the events of the night; from the amazing to the frustrating to the downright exasperating. Tonight was supposed to be a venture of independence and solidarity in step four, and all it became was a drunken, emotional, confusing, tension-charged mess. I was torn between the elation of almost kissing Seth to the guilt of the same; from the frustration of a drunken Brae at my side to the acceptance of it all.

I sighed, forcing my eyes to close as I considered that maybe I wasn't meant to succeed at these steps. Maybe I wasn't meant to get over Seth Linwood. Because I was flunking miserably, and I was starting to not even mind my failure.

CHAPTER TWENTY-TWO

I kicked the door closed with my foot and it slammed loud and effectively, causing the person currently sprawled out in my bed to startle. Brae sat up quickly, her hooded eyes looking around for the source of the sound while her hair was a wild halo of blond sticking out in every possible direction.

"What . . . what was that?" she muttered in her confused state as I ventured further into the room.

"Morning, sunshine," I called, louder than I needed to. Setting the tray in my hands on the corner of my desk, I bounced onto the bed beside her energetically. Of course, Brae groaned as she flopped back onto the mattress, covering her eyes with her arm.

"Ugh . . . why do you have so much energy?"

"Oh, I don't," I said, crawling over her clumsily to lie on the other side of the bed. "I'm merely paying you back for my night of no sleep."

Brae's lips turned downward as she moved to face me, her arm staying secure over her eyes.

"What did I do? Or do I even want to know?"

"Well, that depends. Do you want the 'during the party' events, or the exorcism that you seemed to be enduring in your sleep?"

She groaned. "Ugh. Start with the exorcism. I have a feeling it will be less painful."

I crossed my legs beneath me on the bed. "Well, you fell asleep pretty quickly, which was good. I guess it was stupid of me to expect you to sleep through the night considering how much you drank, though, because just as I started to drift off is when you started to jerk and flail." Brae made an embarrassed groan, which I ignored and continued. "Twice, you flung your arm out and smacked me in the face. Once, you sat up completely confused and tried to strip. You got as far as taking your jeans off, then got stuck on your shirt and gave up."

She looked down at her body, which was half covered by the sheets. "Is that why I have one arm out of my shirt and it's hanging around my neck?"

"Yup. Pretty much."

"Kill me now."

The sadistic part of me enjoyed her misery, even if it was selfish. I was still bitter about the turn of events from the night before, and while I couldn't say or do anything about them, that didn't mean I couldn't torment her over the scene she created . . . just a little bit.

"I haven't gotten to the best part yet," I teased. "You saw Seth last night."

"I figured." She sighed, her mood immediately sullen.

"You decided to give up on the 'I'm totally over you' plan and went for the 'getting so drunk that you call him dimple butt and make him have to drive us home' option."

To this, her arm fell away from her eyes, which were now wide with humiliation. "I didn't really call him that, did I?"

"Oh, you most certainly did. Then you complained that he was too cute to get over and asked why he didn't love you anymore. This was all after you tried making out with random guys at the party, drank from the sink, and then climbed the bannister."

She reached out, weakly trying to cover my mouth with her hand. "Okay, okay. I get it. I was a hot mess. Please just stop with the play-by-play."

I grinned, obliging to her request as she covered her face with both hands, soaking in her humiliation. I knew I was probably being a little harder on her than I needed to be, considering that I had little doubt she had a rough night. But I also had a less-than-thrilling experience in part to her recklessness, and this was my way of getting her back.

Pulling her hands away from her face, Brae huffed toward the ceiling. Her makeup was smeared across her cheeks, her eyes red and swollen. She was paler than usual, her lips dry against the alcohol-induced dehydration our parents always warned us about. For the first time in our friendship, I could honestly say she looked like crap. Pathetically, I took a small bit of enjoyment from that fact.

Leaning across her, I pulled the tray from the desk onto the bed with us.

"Here," I offered, my tone much more comforting than it had been moments before. "I made you a hangover cure."

She turned, judging my concoction. I had Googled during the night in my sleep-deprived state the best way to cure a hangover. Apparently, lots of water, Advil, dry, bland toast, and Gatorade were the best options to avoid feeling like death for the rest of the day. I had seriously contemplated after the second time Brae smacked me in her sleep of depriving her of these treats, but of course I felt guilty for the consideration and caved to the better person in me.

She pushed up slowly, groaning loudly.

"For real, I think I'm going to die. I've never felt so nauseous in my life, and my head feels like it's going to split open. I'm never going to drink again."

I passed her a large glass of water. "I would say serves you right, but—"

"You literally just said it," she hissed, taking the water from me and drinking it quickly.

We sat in silence, sharing the little plate between us. Slowly, the color returned to her face, her movements less sluggish as she began to get her bearings.

"So I really outdid myself last night, huh?"

My irritation at the memory simmered under my skin, but I tried to soften the affirmation with a light shrug. "It certainly wasn't one of your classier moments."

Brae shook her head at herself. "God, I can't believe I humiliated myself in front of Seth. Ugh, in front of half the school. I'm never going to live this down."

I waved a hand at her dismissively. "Don't worry about it. I checked social media this morning and people aren't talking about you that much."

"That much, huh?"

"No. Apparently after we left, Taylor Smith fell into the pool, then started to strip. That's making the rounds more than you and your jungle gym showcase."

Brae exhaled, picking at the crust of her toast absentmindedly.

"I thought I was honestly getting over him," she said with a hint of sadness. "I mean, I wanted to make him miss me, because it still hurts that he broke up with me, but I was actually starting to feel better. Almost like myself again. I was actually even getting pretty good at ignoring my mom and her obsession with my failed love life. Now with this, maybe I was just lying to myself all along? Maybe I'm not over him at all?"

Her confusion caused a twinge of confliction in my chest. I wanted to tell her I knew exactly how she felt. That I had been struggling with getting over him for months but always tripped and fell right back down again the moment he looked at me. That I knew just how hard getting over Seth Linwood really was.

But I couldn't tell her any of that, because to do so would mean betraying my secret and my best friend. So, instead, I had to come up with an alternative.

"I think you are doing a lot better," I said, trying to encourage her. "You had one bad night. One really bad, embarrassing night."

"Screw off," she whined.

"But overall, you are getting over him, Brae. You only acted like you did because of the booze. Sure, you miss him, but you might always miss him. That's normal. But the booze made you over-the-top, and yeah, that was kind of unfortunate. But you've come so far, one setback doesn't mean you have screwed up the whole thing."

"Maybe." She nodded. After a beat, she looked up to me. "Have you ever felt like this?"

"Felt like what?"

"I don't know. It's hard to explain," she said, setting the now mangled toast back on the plate. "I mean, I understand why Seth broke up with me. I get it, and I know we don't have a lot in common, and it probably makes sense for him to find someone better suited for him. And if I'm being honest with myself, I feel the same way, but that doesn't mean I didn't really like him. It's just so frustrating and confusing, and it hurts to be the one left behind, you know?"

I nodded, unable to form words.

"Have you ever liked someone so much, but then something happens and they break your heart?" she asked, catching me off guard with the directness of her question.

My mouth opened to respond, but no words came out. Again, I struggled between telling the truth to the person I was always honest with and keeping my friendship with her intact through my fallacy.

Because yes, I had liked someone so much that it hurt. That watching them care for someone else broke my heart on a daily basis as I stood just at the edges of their life, wondering what it would be like to be that girl. I had to watch as the person I fell for was falling for someone else and keep those feelings inside. A deep-seated longing burrowed in my gut, latching on with claws and teeth. And now, I had to live with the knowledge that I could have everything I ever wanted, but it could cost me everything I always had. The feelings were surprisingly similar.

So, again, I was forced to find a balance between the truth and a lie.

"I don't know," I said, my eyes dropping to the broken toast. "I mean, I can see how that would feel. But I don't think I've ever felt that way before."

"Well, I hope you never do," she said with conviction before taking a long drink of her water. "Because it frigging sucks."

I nodded, the tension around my heart seizing.

"Yeah. It sure does."

CHAPTER TWENTY-THREE

After the harrowing adventures of Friday night, by Sunday I was curled up on the swing on the front porch, my favorite place in my home, having some quiet alone time with a good book. After my epic failures in step four, I had reverted back to step three, which suited me much better than the social efforts and exploits of the more party-centric after step. At least step three allowed me to hide away in my own solitude and didn't judge me, didn't include mopping up after my messy best friend or require me to endure run-ins with sexy boys I was trying to forget.

No, step three was much more my style. It was a nice step, in my opinion, as from my experience, steps that required social outings just ended in disaster. Hence the porch, my book, and the quiet of the late Sunday evening.

Turning the page of my slightly less frightening but still intense novel of choice, the sound of approaching footsteps gained my attention. Looking up from my book, I almost choked in surprise at who I found standing at the foot of the stairs.

"Hey," Seth said, offering me a reserved smile. The gentle wind rustled through his hair, the lighting casting an almost ethereal filter over him. It was frustratingly unfair that he could always look so damn good when I was desperately trying to ignore my feelings.

"Hi," I squeaked in response. "What are you doing here?"

"I'm on my way to Alex's. I was walking by and noticed you sitting out here."

I nodded, unsure what to say.

"What are you reading?" he asked, nodding his head toward my book. Lifting it up, I glanced at the cover. *Girl on the Train.*

His brow furrowed. "Isn't that the one where the crazy girl kills her ex's mistress or something?"

"She didn't do it," I said firmly. "He did."

"Have you read it already?" he asked, smirking.

"No. I just figured it out."

He chuckled, rocking back on his heels.

"Mind if I sit?" he asked, nodding now to the empty space beside me.

Instinctively, my brain screamed "No!" because it knew as well as my heart that I would only fall deeper the longer I allowed myself to be with him. But it was my heart that ruled in this moment, and I nodded.

Jogging up the stairs, Seth eased himself onto the swing, using his long legs to gently rock us back and forth. We said nothing for a long while, simply content with the silence and each other's company, listening to the soft sounds of the coming night.

"I haven't seen you since the party. How was the rest of your weekend?" he asked, turning to glance at me.

"Okay. Pretty boring in comparison."

Seth snickered. "Yeah, well, drunken best friends and rumored skinny dipping is hard to top."

I giggled. "I still can't believe Taylor did that."

"Yeah, well, she was about as drunk as Brae, so I'm not too surprised."

I angled myself toward Seth. "Thanks for that, by the way."

"For what?"

"For bringing us home. For taking care of her like that."

He shrugged, looking down to his hands in his lap. "You took care of her. I just drove."

"Hardly. I wouldn't have been able to carry her upstairs like that," I laughed.

"You could've dragged her. She probably wouldn't have felt it."

"Probably not," I agreed with a giggle. "But still, thank you. That was really nice of you."

"No problem," he said softly, his eyes still on his hands. He was twisting his thumbs around each other, his body language making it seem like his mind was far away. I left him to his thoughts, again a comfortable silence falling between us.

"Can I ask you something?" he finally said, turning to me with new-found resolve.

"Sure."

"Do you ever wish things were different?"

My brow furrowed as I considered his question. "How do you mean?"

"With us," he said directly. "That we hadn't let our doubts stop us from admitting how we felt months ago? That we hadn't spent all this time going in the wrong direction? That your rules weren't there."

I balked at the boldness of his question, my mouth dropping open. I meant to respond, but no words came out. After a beat of silence, Seth continued.

"Because I think about it all the time. I think about how mad I am at myself for not having the balls to tell you when we first met that I liked you or for convincing myself that you didn't think of me that way rather than just finding out for sure. I think that maybe if I had just had the courage, then maybe I wouldn't have wasted all this time being with the wrong person. Don't get me wrong, Brae is awesome. She's a great girl and a lot of fun. Maybe eventually we can be friends like we should have been all along, and maybe we won't. But what I can't stop thinking about is the fact that if I hadn't convinced myself to go out with her because the girl I really wanted wasn't interested, then there would be nothing standing in our way now. That all of this mess is my fault because I didn't just ask you months ago to go out with me." He paused in his rant, his eyes boring into mine, before he shook his head and revealed a small, sad smile. "I kind of hate myself for it."

Again, I moved to respond, but I couldn't think of a single thing to say to such an honest and heart-wrenching admission. It was hard to hear because it so closely resonated with everything I had been feeling about my own part to play in our little drama.

I knew I needed to say something, anything, to show him it wasn't his fault.

"I do," I admitted with a sigh. "I wonder all the time if I had just told you I liked you or told Brae that I didn't want her to date you, that we could have avoided all of this. But I honestly never considered someone like you liking someone like me."

"Someone like me? What does that mean?"

I couldn't help but laugh. "Come on, Seth. You're handsome, smart, funny, and athletic. There is basically nobody at school who has a bad thing to say about you. You're pretty much perfect, and I'm . . . well, I'm me."

"And who are you?" he asked, tiling his head in query.

To this, I had an immediate answer. "I am Brae Walker's best friend."

Shock overtook Seth's features. It started out as surprise, then quickly turned to irritation.

"You obviously don't see yourself clearly at all," he said with a lace of anger. "Hannah, you're the one who's smart, funny, and enchanting. You are fiercely loyal, determined to face your challenges no matter how difficult. You turn heads more than you realize, and you captivated me from the moment I first knocked you over in that hallway. It was humiliating at the time, but I am thankful for being such a klutz because if I hadn't done it, I don't know if I would have ever gotten the nerve to talk to you on my own. You are the most beautiful girl I have ever met, inside and out. I wish you would stop comparing yourself to Brae, because to me, there's no comparison."

Rendered mute by his declaration, my mind slowed down to a crawl as it absorbed each and every one of his words. I had never had a boy say anything like this to me before, and to hear them from Seth left me struggling to stay in my seat and not jump across the swing and into his arms. My fingers twitched to reach out and touch him, to feel the stubble on his cheeks beneath my fingertips, but I dug my nails into my palms to keep myself from falling further under his spell.

Tears brimmed in my eyes, a burning that flowed down into the lump at my throat. I felt elated and excited but trapped and frustrated all at once.

"It's like without meaning to, we became our two greatest literary heroes," he said softly, a teasing grin curling his lips.

"Who?"

"Romeo and Juliet," he clarified. "Star-crossed lovers, and all that, kept apart by circumstances beyond their control."

My chest clenched, invisible hands twisting at my heart. I didn't know what to say in return, but I didn't have to say anything. Seth reached across the small space between us and gently pried my fingers from their torture on my palm. Lacing his fingers with my own, he held my hand tightly, his warmth radiating along my skin.

His eyes scorched along the angles of my face, as if committing them to memory. It was almost sensual, the look he was giving me. I held my breath, afraid that if I exhaled, he would disappear.

Without another word, he leaned toward me, slowly. So slowly, it was almost painful. His eyes flickered to my lips, his own parting, and I knew this was it. And I knew, no matter how badly I wanted to be a good friend, to stand my ground and be the person I hoped I was, I didn't have the strength to turn away from him again.

But just as he neared, leaving only an inch between our lips, his path veered upward and to the side. When his lips landed on my temple in the softest, most tender kiss, my eyes closed, and I exhaled.

Pulling away, he faced forward again, his long legs returning to the gentle motion of rocking the swing soothingly. I watched him for what felt like hours, but was probably no longer than a few minutes, before I regained control of myself and followed his gaze out toward the street.

We fell back into our silence, the only sound being the creaking of the swing under our influence, as our hands linked together between us. And while I wanted so much more, for now, this would be enough.

STEP FIVE: TRY DATING AGAIN

*Me: I met someone. *two days later*
Me: Never mind.*

CHAPTER TWENTY-FOUR

———

We walked shoulder to shoulder, taking up more space in the crowded hallway than we really needed to. Normally, I would be the one to try to corral my friends into a more acceptable cluster rather than parting the seas of student bodies like a social status Moses, but our current line of conversation was more intense than was my penchant for appropriate hallway etiquette.

"Hannah, what's step five again?" Erin asked, eyeing me from their place on Brae's other side.

"Try dating again."

Erin grinned wickedly as they turned to Brae. "You said so yourself that you feel like you messed up on step four because of the party. Which, by the way, wasn't even that bad. It was a momentary lapse. Which means it's even more important for you to keep a forward motion and get past it by grabbing step five by the balls."

Brae gave Erin a dubious look. "I don't think that is how it works."

"That's exactly how it works," Erin said firmly. "It's been over two months now, and it's time to get back out there and date! Get back to the old Brae and remind these boys why you're the girl they all want."

A corner of Brae's mouth turned up at the compliment, her eyes still focused on the floor as we stopped at our lockers. I concentrated on my uncooperative lock while I listened to Erin and Michelle continue to persuade Brae to get back in the game.

"I heard a rumor that might make you change your mind." Michelle smiled with an evil glint to her eyes.

Immediately, a flush of anxiety flooded my system. Images of Seth and I standing in the hall at the party, dangerously close with our little bubble of sexual tension vibrating all around us. Had someone noticed? Had I been branded a traitor without even knowing it?

Or maybe someone had seen us on my porch the other day? Someone else casually walking down the street, unexpectedly catching Seth and I holding hands like an old married couple.

My stomach churned as I cast my gaze to the floor.

Of course, this got Brae's attention immediately. "What is it?"

"So apparently Liam Hutcherson was at Jeff Watkins's party the other weekend."

Relief surged through me at the realization that I was not caught red-handed. Brae paled quickly. "Oh God, please don't tell me he—"

"No, no!" she laughed, waving off Brae's concern. "He didn't see your sloppy display."

"Thank God. So what about him?"

"Mitch Martin told Andrea Sanderson who told me that Liam Hutcherson told Mitch that he thinks you're hot."

My brow pinched. It took me much longer than it should have to finally understand that the that the boy Brae thought was cute apparently thought the same about her.

Brae seemed to decipher the code at the same time, her face lighting up.

"You're kidding?"

"Nope. He's thought you were hot for a while but obviously never said anything to anyone 'cause you were with Seth. Now that you're single, I guess he mentioned something to Mitch but isn't sure if he should ask you out 'cause he is kind of friends with Seth and doesn't want to cross a line."

Blood drained from my face at her statement . . . Liam didn't want to ask Brae out and risk crossing a line with Seth. And yet, here I was having romantic interludes outside of bathrooms and sharing porch swings like a traitor.

I was the absolute worst.

"So he wants to ask her out on a date?" I asked.

"Basically." She nodded.

I looked to Brae, finding her staring into the depths of her locker with a contemplative expression. I let her consider this new information for a few moments before stepping up closer to her.

"What are you thinking?" I asked, leaning against my locker.

"I'm not even sure," she laughed. "I mean, obviously I'm excited. I've thought he was hot for ages, but I've always been dating someone else or he has. I don't really know what to think about this right now. My mind is still so all over the place."

"You know you don't have to do anything with this information. You can just wait and see what happens."

"I know."

Her expressive features spoke volumes, and I could see her swaying toward doing more than just waiting. I knew her too well, knew the way her mind worked. Waiting for someone else to make the move was never Brae's style.

"Do you *want* to do something about it?" I finally asked, putting her on the spot.

"I don't know. I mean, it's been over two months. You said yourself that it should take me half the time of the relationship to get over it, which means I have just shy of three weeks to feel like I have closure."

I rolled my eyes. "Brae, it isn't an exact science. You don't have a deadline for this, you—"

"But I do," she said sharply, turning to look at me. "I can't keep letting myself fall back into this pattern of wallowing or doing stupid things just because he hurt my ego. I need to move on, and to do that, I have to keep moving forward, not back. Here I find out a guy I think is cute actually likes me too, and if I don't do something about it, then I feel like I'm not moving at all. Does that make sense?"

Maybe I had been listening to Michelle too much, or maybe I just understood Brae's rambling better than Michelle's, but I did actually understand what she meant.

"Yeah. It makes sense."

"So what do you want to do?" Michelle asked eagerly, practically bouncing on her toes.

Brae pursed her lips in thought. "I'm not going to say anything to him. I don't feel like I'm ready to be that direct yet. But if someone," she paused, giving a poignant look toward Michelle, "were to say something to him, like that if he asked me out I wouldn't say no, that wouldn't necessarily be a bad thing."

Erin laughed with a shake of their head. "Always so strategic. I swear, you're going to rule the world one day."

"That would be a scary freaking world," I joked, pulling my items out of my locker just before the warning bell sounded.

It didn't take long for the game of messenger to make its rounds to Liam. By fourth period, he had already come up to Brae outside her English class and asked her out for that Friday. She met me at our locker with an excited, beaming smile that was the first I had seen on her face since her breakup with Seth. She was light and happy and finally back to her old self.

We were already discussing date options animatedly as we found a table in the cafeteria at lunch when Michelle and Erin exchanged knowing, scheming glances.

I had barely sat down with my tray when they rounded on me.

"Okay, so don't be mad at me," Michelle said, immediately making anxiety rise in my chest.

"If you didn't do anything stupid, I won't have a reason to be mad at you."

"It wasn't stupid!" she said indignantly. "I just figured since things worked out so great for Brae, that I would keep the good luck train moving."

The knot in my stomach tightened, and I already knew I wasn't going to like where this particular line of discussion was going.

"What. Did. You. Do?"

The tone in my voice alerted Michelle to the fact that quite possibly what she thought was a great idea was, in fact, not.

"I . . . um . . . I kind of told Justin Ford that you thought he was cute."

"You *what*!"

"You said you liked him!" she rambled in a panic. "You haven't dated anyone in ages and—"

"Why would you do that!"

"Because I was trying to help?" she said uncertainly. "You've seemed kind of down lately, and I thought maybe you just needed a little nudge. Justin said he thinks you're cute and asked if I thought he should ask you out."

"What did you say?"

"I said yes, obviously."

"Ugh! Michelle—"

"This is great!" Brae squealed, grabbing on to my arm. "Hannah, this is perfect!"

Nervousness in my stomach crawled its way upward and threatened to spew from my mouth. Although, as panic started to take over, it might have actually been vomit.

"How do you figure this is perfect?" I asked incredulously. "This is mortifying!"

"No, it isn't! You like him, he likes you! It's just like me and Liam!"

I rolled my eyes so hard, they almost toppled right out of my head. "This isn't like that at all."

"Of course it is. You never would have done anything about it on your own. Hell, you almost never even tell us when you like a guy."

"And now I remember why," I muttered sullenly.

Of course since Brae was already on a high from her own successful match, trying to talk sense into her was pointless. She was like a hamster on a sugar high, her eyes wide and elated.

"Oh my GOD! We can go on a double date!"

"What!"

"This is so awesome! Hannah, come on! I'm already nervous enough about all this. This is my first date since breaking up with Seth. I could use your support."

"You have my support. You don't need me there in some uncomfortable matchmaking deal."

"Yes I do," she stated plainly. "And you will feel better if I am there on yours. We have each other's back. Rule one in full effect!"

"Brae—"

She turned away from me, scanning the crowded cafeteria for her prey. I followed her line of sight and froze when she found the object of her desire.

Justin Ford sat with his friends a few tables over from ours. His light brown hair was falling into his dark eyes; a warm, broad smile on his face. He really was cute, and I did have a bit of a crush on him before Seth ambled his way into my life. But things were different now; my heart belonged to someone else completely, and I couldn't imagine dating anyone else just yet.

Unfortunately, Brae wasn't on the same level of understanding, rising quickly out of her seat. I grappled for her arm, but she shook me off easily.

"Brae, don't!" I whispered loudly, too afraid to yell in case I drew attention to myself. "Don't you dare!"

She sauntered over to Justin with the quiet confidence she always held, and immediately, all eyes turned to her. Pausing at their table, she looked at Justin's companions with an expectant lift of her brow and a flick of her hand for them to make room. Once they moved over, she sat down, leaning toward Justin with a commanding air. I seriously contemplated running for my life, or maybe crawling under the table to hide from the humiliation, before Justin's eyes turned to me. He looked at me with confusion for a moment, my own face pale and surely panicked. Slowly, a smile came across his features as he said something back to Braelyn. She clapped her hands together excitedly, saying a few things more, before standing up and practically skipping back to our table.

The moment she sat down, I wanted to throttle her.

"It's all set," she said happily. "You, me, Liam, and Justin are going to a movie and dinner on Friday."

"Brae, I really don't want to," I practically begged. "I can't believe you did this. I am so embarrassed."

"Don't be! He thinks you're cute! You like him. This is a good thing, Hannah." Taking a moment to observe my confliction, she furrowed her brow. "Give me one good reason why you don't want to do this."

I panicked as a myriad of reasons circled around my head.

First off, it is humiliating to be called out by your friends to a boy that you only mentioned to keep the attention off of the boy you actually longed after.

Secondly, it is mortifying for your best friend to go up to him and ask him out for you in front of the entire school.

Third, I don't actually want to go out with him, since I am head over heels for another boy, who just happens to be said best friend's ex and is off-limits.

Fourth, to tell her that I didn't want to go would require me to tell her why I didn't want to go, which would mean to have to admit that I lied all along to keep the truth of my obsession with Seth from her attention.

And finally, I couldn't help but feel nauseated at what Seth might think if he was to hear that I was going out with Justin only a day after we had a moment together on my porch.

But, as usual, I couldn't voice any of these reasons aloud to Brae or my other friends. Because just like everything in my life lately, I was trapped in my own secrecy if I was to keep my friendships intact.

So rather than telling the truth and outing my broken heart, I sighed. "Fine. I'll go."

CHAPTER TWENTY-FIVE

"What does one wear to the date equivalent of a firing squad?" I pondered to the silent room.

Staring into the depths of my closet, my eyes passed over each item with only minimal interest. More than half an hour had already passed, and I was still in the exact same place I had been when this venture started. I didn't really know what I expected to happen; that the right outfit would somehow jump out at me, declaring that it was the perfect option for a night of forced and awkward socialization, or if eventually, I would just give up and grab the first thing I saw.

The latter was obviously more likely, but I hadn't quite reached that point of giving up yet.

The looming date with Justin, Brae, and Liam was the following night, and I was currently at just as much of a loss on what to wear as I was on how I felt about the entire situation.

Rationally, this was probably a good thing. A date with Justin Ford was a pretty big deal. He was cute, sweet, and popular. Apparently, he thought I was attractive and had agreed to go out with me even after being cornered by Brae in the cafeteria. Under normal circumstances, I would be spending the eve of this date anxiously anticipating every little word, exchange, and glance, like most girls did before a big date. But instead, I was standing here feeling like I was cheating on the boy who wasn't even mine to betray.

Really, this was a perfect opportunity to get back on track with my mission of getting over Seth. Each step thus far had been one step forward, two steps back for me while Brae was messily but consistently moving in an onward direction. I knew I needed to refocus my attention on the mission at hand, and going on this date was the epitome of step five.

This was the perfect opportunity for me to get my feet back under me. They had been quickly and thoroughly swept outward by Seth in recent days, and I had to nail them back to the ground. I had spent most of the day giving myself frequent pep talks on how this was a good thing, and it would help me redirect my attention.

Unfortunately, anytime I tried to think about what I wanted, the traits I desired in a partner, Seth's face popped into my head.

My phone singing to life broke my already distracted attention from my boring closet. Plucking the device from my bed, my eyes widened at the name on the screen.

"Hey," I called, my voice betraying my surprise.

"Hi," Seth answered, his deep, smooth voice sending a shiver down my spine. "Sorry to bug you, but I have an English question."

I tilted my head. "Okay."

"I'm trying to plot out a bit of our project, and—"

I covered my eyes with my hand. "Oh God, I'm so sorry. We were supposed to make plans to work on it this week, weren't we? Seth, you don't have—"

His deep chuckle echoed through the phone. "Don't stress, Hannah. I'm just preparing my offensive for when you inevitably lay down a power play for the benefits of having Juliet ditch Romeo completely and go off on her own adventure."

I snorted, unable to deny that he was right that I would much rather have Juliet forge her own path, sans Romeo.

"So if I was to suggest that Juliet and Romeo do still end up together in the end, but with the stipulation of a long distance relationship as they go off to college and experience life apart, would you be agreeable to that?"

My smile widened, a burn coming to my cheeks. "I would consider it. So long as there were ground rules."

"I would expect nothing less." He was quiet for a moment, and I could hear papers shuffling around through the line.

"So, what are you doing?"

Sitting back on my bed, I tucked my legs under me. "Just staring into my closet."

Seth was silent for a moment as he considered my odd answer. "Is that something you do often? Expecting to find the gateway to Narnia in there?"

"No, smartass," I snorted. "Just looking through my clothes."

"Do girls do that? Just stare at their clothes? You all are weird."

I stalled for a moment, unsure what to say in return. There was little doubt that word would get back to him eventually that I was going out with Justin. Did I want this information to come from a random person, or did I want to admit it to him myself?

If the tables were turned, finding out from someone else, or at all, that he was going out with another girl would suck no matter what. But maybe a little less if I had a bit of warning.

Clearing my throat awkwardly, I tried to think of how to explain.

"Well, I kind of have a date tomorrow," I started, cringing immediately at my less-than-gentle introduction into the topic.

Seth was silent for a long moment, and I could almost picture the look of surprise on his face.

"Oh?"

"Yeah. Brae has a date tomorrow with Liam Hutcherson."

"I heard about that," he said with an eerie calm. "I'm glad she's moving on."

"Yeah, well, then Michelle told Justin Ford that I liked him, and then he told her that he thought I was cute. Brae decided it was the perfect excuse for us to go on a double date and kind of ask him out for me."

"Why would Michelle tell Justin that you liked him?" he asked, a steady calm in his tone.

I closed my eyes, feeling cornered. "I kind of told them that I did."

Again, he fell silent, trying to understand my reasoning. "Why?"

"We were out for a girls' day a couple weeks ago, and they got talking about guys they liked. They kind of cornered me and kept bugging me to tell them who I liked, and I panicked. I couldn't very well say you because Brae would freak. And somehow, Justin's name just came out. Then after Liam and Brae matched up, Michelle got it in her head to keep the ball rolling since I haven't been out with anyone in a long time. I kind of got trapped."

A long and weighted silence rippled through the phone, and I listened intently for any sound on the other side. My heart was pounding in my ears, my mind racing with how Seth might respond to this news.

"He's a good guy," he finally said, his voice distant and monotonous. "You will have a nice time."

My heart broke a tiny bit at the sound of his voice. "I'm so sorry."

"It's okay. Hannah, really. I get it. You couldn't really tell them the truth because Brae would lose her shit. I don't expect you never to date anyone when we can't even be together. That would be a real dick move on my part to be mad at you for that. So really, don't worry about it. Have fun."

"Seth."

"I better go," he said quickly, clearing his throat. "I still have a history paper to work on, and it's due on Monday."

My throat ran dry with emotion, everything in me longing to tell him to forget it, that I would call off the date and tell Brae the truth. But I couldn't bring myself to do it, because I knew the consequences of that decision. To keep Seth, I would lose Brae. To keep Brae, I would lose Seth. No matter what I chose, I lost.

"Okay," I answered solemnly. "I'll see you later?"

"Yeah. Later."

The click of the line cut me off from him. My arm fell to my side, my phone still in my hands as my eyes rose back to my uncooperative closet.

But now, I had finally reached one side of the push and pull game it had me in before. Standing up, I strode over to it with angry determination and yanked the first pair of jeans and blouse my hands touched. Throwing them over the chair in the corner, I tossed myself back onto my bed, my eyes on my ceiling.

CHAPTER TWENTY-SIX

"What's up with you?" Brae finally asked me as we stood outside the theater. "You look like someone stole your last Twizzler or something."

I forced a smile, my eyes still on the ground. I had tried to remind myself to keep any sense of despondence from my face so she wouldn't notice my hesitancy. Unfortunately, that was easier said than done, because the date hadn't even officially started, and it appeared that I was already failing.

I had spent the majority of the day putting on an excited and happy face at school, talking about the date with Brae, and even chatting with Justin when he came up to me before third period. He really was a sweet guy, which only made me feel even worse for putting him in the middle of the cluster eff that was my love life. All the while I was getting ready, I tried to pep myself up for the evening. That tonight may be great and Justin and I would really hit it off. Perhaps there would be a second date, maybe a third, and eventually this barrier between Seth and I wouldn't matter anymore because my heart wouldn't be so tied up in him. That maybe, just maybe, I could be happy with someone else.

But pep talks and false smiles only get you so far before your traitorous mind takes over. All I could think about was the fact that I was standing in front of the Regal Cinema waiting for a boy who I already knew wasn't going to sweep me off my feet.

Shaking myself out of my mood yet again, I tried to sound convincing. "I guess I'm just nervous."

"There's nothing to be nervous about. You both admitted you like each other. Just enjoy it. This is going to be a blast."

I nodded just as Justin and Liam rounded the corner. The moment Brae saw them, she let out a little squeal, grabbing on to my arm.

"Oh, there they are. Shit, Liam looks so good. Justin does too. I'm so excited."

Despite my own reservations about tonight, I had to admit that seeing Brae this excited about her date did help a little. She had become more of herself this last week than in all those previous, and I could only hope that meant she was in the home stretch.

As the boys approached us, I took a deep breath to ready myself for the next few hours. Justin was as adorable as ever; his hair that perfect blend of style and intentional mess, his eyes bright and eager. He was slender and tall, his tanned skin golden under the lights of the theater front. If I hadn't been noticing all the differences between him and Seth in these few moments, I probably would have swooned.

"Hi." Justin smiled, looking me over. "Wow, you look great."

I had gone for the simple and casual look of dark jeans and a black button down that crossed at my waist. It was classy, but still comfortable since I knew I was already going to be uncomfortable enough with the setting.

"Thanks. So do you."

"Liam and I already got the tickets online," he said, holding up his phone. "You girls ready?"

I glanced at Brae to find her already fawning over Liam. Her hand was on his forearm, and she had her "flirty laugh" already in full swing. Turning to us, Liam nodded.

"All set."

The next two hours weren't nearly as tense as I was afraid they would be. I guess that is the benefit of choosing a movie for a date; it was socially acceptable, and preferred, not to talk. I sat with Justin on my right and Braelyn on my left, although she was leaned right up against Liam for the majority of the movie. Justin offered me some of his candy, and we exchanged a little small talk before the trailers started, but overall, it was fairly casual. I was nervous that Justin might try to hold my hand or do the cheesy move of "yawn and stretch" to put his arm around me, but other than the occasional candy offer, he kept his hands to himself. Plus, watching a movie about a dinosaur park run rampant by its residents isn't the best atmosphere for romance. Although, my occasional glance toward Brae would seem that her and Liam did not hold to that same belief as her arm was looped through his, their fingers entwined. They looked completely comfortable in each other's company, and again, I found myself happy for her progress.

Filing out of the theater two hours later, my nerves returned as the boys guided us to the small café we had agreed upon for a little post-movie snack. The Soda Parlor, a hybrid soda shop and arcade, was a great place to take the edge off a first date with a little competitive face off. Leading us to a table near the back, Justin placed his hand at my lower back. Again, I was torn between the desire to move on—to give Justin a chance—and my thoughts of Seth that never seemed to truly leave my mind.

Sliding into the booth, we took a few moments to scan over the items. It was a sweet tooth's paradise, and my mouth watered as I scanned the options.

"I've always wanted to come here," Brae mentioned casually. "But Seth never brought me."

I glanced at her quickly at the mention of Seth. She was still scanning the menu, and I had to wonder if she even realized she had said his name. Looking to Liam, I found him watching her much like I was. He said nothing in return.

"Do you want to share something?" Justin offered. "I've been here before, and the Cookie Monster is amazing, but it's huge. Even my brother couldn't finish it, and he's never full."

I laughed, nodding in agreement. "Sure. That sounds good."

We placed our order, filling the wait with casual chatter. I was now expected to truly focus and take part in this date, to really give it a chance, but my attention was not on Justin. It wasn't even on Seth. It was on Brae and her inability to stop talking about her ex.

"I bought Seth a shirt like that," she commented as she reached out and ran her fingers along the arm of Liam's shirt. "I don't even know if he ever wore it. His style was so casual, he never dressed up unless he was going to a funeral. It drove me crazy."

Again, Liam's lips pulled tight, his eyes flickering to me. I tried to give him an encouraging and slightly apologetic smile, hoping that he wouldn't take offense to Brae's lack of filter. She asked Liam about his classes, his family, and his plans for college, but every once in a while she would throw in another comment about Seth. I could see Liam growing more annoyed as the night went on, the tension in his jaw rising to an almost grinding pressure.

Shaking my head, I decided to leave Brae to her own sabotaging ways. Instead, I tried to focus on Justin, to ask him things about himself. I could tell he was a great guy once I let myself stop worrying so much about the situation and just talked to him.

His parents divorced when he was five, but there was none of the drama that Brae was used to. He wanted to go to college for graphic design, hopefully to eventually work for Disney or Pixar. It was fascinating listening to him describe building characters on his computer, creating individuals that would later form the avatars for adventures in worlds that had yet to be.

Finishing the last of our dessert, he pushed the plate away with a grin. "Do you want to try your hand at a few games?"

Glancing toward the arcade, I felt my inner child grow excited. It had been years since I had played any kind of video game, but the lights and sounds of the arcade had me sliding out of my seat.

I had never been very good at games, and it would seem that the years hadn't changed that. I lost four different games to Justin, each time him assuring me that it was just a matter of practice.

Returning to our table, I found Liam completely exasperated, and Braelyn wide-eyed. Justin and I paused at the edge of the table, stepping into their heated argument.

"I have not," Brae said, looking affronted.

"You definitely have. I don't even know if you realize you're doing it, but you've brought him up at least ten times in the hour we've been here."

Brae was quiet for a moment, and you could almost see her mind trying to recall if she had in fact brought Seth up.

"I . . . okay, maybe I mentioned him a couple times. But we just broke up, I—"

"Didn't you guys break up like two months ago?" Liam challenged. "Look, Brae, I get it. We've all been there. But if you're still hung up on him, then I don't want to get involved. I don't want to be your rebound."

Brae stared at Liam with wide eyes, her mouth slightly slack. I looked back and forth between them, Justin at my flank, both of us seemingly too unsure to move or breathe in case we drew attention to our presence. Like flies on the wall, captivated by the drama, but uncomfortable by the tension.

"I like you," Liam said firmly. "I've always had a thing for you. But I mean it when I say I'm not going to be your second choice. If you have shit to work out about Linwood, that's fine. But if you want to date me, you're going to have to date *me*. Not spend the whole time you're with me talking about another dude."

I could tell Brae's mind was racing; her fingers twisted together rhythmically, shoulders tense and leg tapping against the floor. I knew her well and had no doubt that this was probably the first time a guy had spoken to her like this before. It appeared that Liam was not the kind of guy to stay silent and was certainly not going to let Brae get away with her usual behavior. I couldn't tell yet if that was going to be a good thing or a complete disaster.

Brae swallowed audibly. "Okay," she finally said. "I'm sorry."

Liam offered her a nod for her apology. "Now, if you're ready to continue *our* date, how about I let you beat me at Skee-Ball?"

Brae's smile slowly returned, and I watched in awe as the two of them headed off toward the arcade. Once they were out of earshot, Justin and I turned to each other with wide eyes.

"Well, that was awkward," he laughed, sliding back into the booth.

"Yeah. I can't believe he told her off like that. Not that she didn't deserve it, but wow. No one has ever talked to her like that."

"Maybe she needed it," he commented gently. "She is kind of known for being pushy. Maybe she needs a guy who will push back once in a while."

I nodded, my hands folding on the tabletop. "Yeah. You're probably right. Even I always let her get away with things. She's kind of hard to say no to," I replied with a small smile.

"I can see that," he laughed, leaning on the table. We sat in silence for a few awkward moments before Justin broke it. "She really is the center of her own universe, isn't she?" When I gave him a look, he was quick to explain. "I don't mean that as an insult, Hannah. But she knows she rules the junior class and isn't afraid to use that to get her way. Most people look at her as a high-maintenance bully sometimes."

My mouth dropped open quickly to defend Brae, as I had countless times before. "I know that's how she comes across at school, but that honestly isn't how she really is. It's hard to explain. But when she is just with me or her family, she is almost like a different person. She's so much more relaxed and doesn't care what everyone else thinks. Sometimes we spend whole weekends in our pajamas."

Justin laughed. "I find that hard to believe, but okay." He shrugged. "Maybe it would be nice for people to see more of that side of her. She doesn't always have to be two different people like that."

"I know." I nodded. "I guess it's just hard once you reach a place like Brae has in the high school hierarchy. You're afraid to lose it, like it is something that actually has real meaning."

Justin nodded, his eyes falling to the table thoughtfully before they returned to me. "Can I ask you something?"

"Sure."

"I don't want to seem like a jerk, but I kind of got the feeling that your mind has been elsewhere most of the night."

Immediately, I tensed, a ripple of fear and guilt sliding over me as he continued.

"Michelle said that you liked me. Then Brae came and asked me out for you. Don't get me wrong, I think you're great. I just get the feeling that maybe this wasn't really your idea."

Again, I was rendered speechless, unsure how to respond. I never expected Justin to call me out, albeit gently, on my distraction. I had tried so hard to not let it be obvious, to keep Seth from my thoughts and be truly present in the night, but it seemed that even in this I had failed.

"Justin, I—"

"Did you really say you liked me?" he asked, no hint of anger or accusation in his tone. He seemed genuinely curious.

Sighing, I started twisting my thumbs together nervously. "I did. But it was kind of because they all cornered me into admitting to who I liked, and at the time, I didn't know what to say. Your name came out, and then I didn't have the courage to correct them. I never expected them to actually drag you into this. I am so sorry."

"So . . . you don't like me?"

My stomach dropped. "I do! I do like you, Justin. You're amazing, and I've had a lot of fun tonight."

"But?"

A small smile overtook me. "But I kind of like someone else. I like you, just not as much as I like him." I reached out before I could stop myself, taking his hand. "I'm so sorry. I never should have agreed to go on this date. It wasn't fair to you, and I'm really sorry."

Surprisingly, Justin smiled at me. "It's okay. You don't have to feel bad. You can't help how you feel, Hannah, or who you like. I had fun tonight, and if at the end of it we're just meant to be friends, that's okay with me."

"Ugh. Justin, you're being too nice about this," I groaned, my guilt surging. "Just call me a bad name or a liar so I'll feel better."

To this, he burst out laughing. "Sorry, Hannah. Can't do that. First, because I would never call a girl a bad name, and second because I get it. We both kind of got sucked into Brae's little plan here, and you said so yourself. It's hard to say no to Brae Walker."

The sound of bickering garnered our attention, and we turned to see Liam and Brae shouting at each other in front of the skee-ball game. Neither looked genuinely angry, but there was obvious disagreement in however their game had turned.

"Doesn't look like Liam has any trouble telling her no," Justin laughed, sitting back against the booth.

"It's about time she met her match."

The remaining time of our date passed in a much less tense atmosphere. Now that the truth was out between Justin and I, I felt as though a weight had been lifted. I was able to enjoy his company, to truly interact with him without worrying how the actions would be taken.

Stepping out onto the sidewalk an hour later, the previous tension of the night had faded into happy laughter.

"I had fun," Brae said, her arm still slipped through Liam's. "Even though you shouted at me."

"Well, you needed it," he said with a shrug. "And once you stopped talking about Seth, I had a good time, too. Maybe we can do it again?"

"Definitely," she smiled.

As Liam led her a few paces away, I gave them a few private moments to end their date. This in turn left Justin and I alone, smiling at each other awkwardly.

"I had hoped on kissing you goodnight, but I figure that's kind of off the table now," he joked, moving in to hug me tightly. I let myself mold into his embrace before turning my head and kissing his cheek.

"I did have a good time," I assured him as he parted. "And I am sorry."

"Stop saying you're sorry!" he warned with a stern glare. "It's fine." He paused, glancing over my shoulder before he grinned. "Looks like they had an even better time."

Turning around, Liam was kissing Brae like it was their last day on earth. She was on her toes to close the distance between them, her arms slung around his neck.

As they parted, Brae was beaming before placing one last kiss on his lips and bounding over to me.

"You guys all set?" she asked, eyeing us mischievously.

"All set."

Justin and I said our goodbyes, and I offered a wave to Liam as Brae and I headed down the street to her car.

Turning to her, I found her smiling. "You and Liam certainly had an interesting night."

Her expression changed from confusion to pure elation. "Yeah. He's so hot."

"I thought you were going to slap him when he told you to stop talking about Seth so much."

"Ugh, was I really doing that?" she asked as we reached her car. "God, I am so embarrassed."

"Yes, you were. But at least Liam called you out and didn't just let it piss him off all night."

"To be honest, I kind of liked it." She grinned as we climbed into the car. "No guy has ever done that before. It was kind of hot. The rest of the night, he didn't let me rule, which was so weird. He handles me but does it in a way that I don't feel like punching him in the face."

I couldn't help but laugh loudly, rolling my eyes at her. "So you actually like that?"

"Yup." She nodded as she pulled out into traffic. "Who would have thought? Oh my God, I wonder if he is that dominating in other ways?"

"Ugh, Brae, let's not get on that topic," I groaned, causing her to cackle.

CHAPTER TWENTY-SEVEN

It was only just after eleven at night as I entered my room, kicking off my shoes, but my mind and body felt weary as though it was the early hours of the morning. Even though the date had turned out well, everyone involved finding the ending they needed, I still felt an edge after spending so many hours in weighted tension.

I stripped off my jeans and blouse, threw them into the hamper, then I pulled on my most comfortable pajamas. At this point, the warmth and familiarity of my bed was so desperately needed, I sighed the moment I slid between the sheets. I didn't even bother scanning through social media, which was my usual pre-bedtime ritual, in favor of succumbing to the exhaustion that I felt to my core.

Only moments after I turned my bedside light out, however, a strange sound brought me out of my quickly approaching slumber. My ears perked for any hint of the sound. It came again only seconds later: an odd, clicking sound coming from the window beside my desk. Quickly, I pushed back the covers and scrambled to the window, hiding under the cover of darkness to keep my presence away from whatever may be on the other side.

Peering out into the night, I never would have expected the sight that I found. I gasped before my brow furrowed in confusion.

Seth stood in the middle of the lawn, staring up at my window intently. His bottom lip was pulled between his teeth in concentration, and I watched as he pulled his arm back, jerking it forward with a snap.

Less than a second later, the clicking sound rang out as a pebble hit my window with shocking accuracy.

My heart fluttered at the realization of what was happening. That Seth was in my yard, in the middle of the night, throwing stones at my window.

And all this time, he had thought the tales of Shakespeare had no merit, when he himself was acting as a modern-day Romeo.

Moving toward the window, I pushed it open quietly to stick my head out before Seth had the chance to lob another stone toward me.

"Seth!" I hissed. "What are you doing?"

The smile that broke out the moment he saw me was enough to make my insides melt before he faltered into a look of embarrassment.

"I . . . I wanted to see you," he said, dropping the few little stones remaining in his hands.

"It's eleven thirty," I whispered, hovering at the window ledge. "Why didn't you just wait until tomorrow?"

"I couldn't," he said plainly as his eyes scanned the side of my house. He assessed the façade before he began to stride toward it. "I'm coming up."

"What?"

He didn't answer me. Instead, I watched in shock as he linked his fingers around the trellis that edged the front face of the house and pulled himself up.

"Seth! For goodness sake, be careful!"

But he didn't need my warning as he hoisted himself upward with expert skill until he reached the roof of the porch just below my window. Once sure-footed, he straightened, bringing himself almost eye level with me. He placed his hands beside my own on the windowsill before he smiled at me.

"Can I come in?"

I gaped at him in romantic gesture overload, saying nothing as I stepped back to allow him to climb through the window. He swung his long legs over the windowsill, slipping into my room silently, until he was standing just in front of me.

"You threw stones at my window," I said, staring at him in shock.

"Yeah. I meant to go for a walk to clear my head and just found myself in your driveway. I wasn't sure if you were home or asleep or—"

"You could have texted me," I reminded him with a tilt of my head.

"Yeah, well, where is the romance in that? Remember, we had Romeo tossing stones at Juliet's window in our story. It felt kind of fitting."

A rush of excitement slid over me like a crashing wave. He was barely lit in the dimness of my room, the angles and lines of his face so much sharper from the contrast.

"What are you doing here?" I repeated, my voice weak from the lack of air left in my lungs.

Staring at me, Seth seemed suddenly at a loss. "I needed to see you."

"And it really couldn't have waited until tomorrow?"

"No," he said firmly. Reaching out, he took my hands in his and led me to my bed. Sitting down beside me, he kept both my hands firmly grasped in his as he stared at me imploringly. "Look, Hannah, I know you probably think I've lost my mind. Like I said, I honestly hadn't planned on showing up like this, and I really hadn't planned on climbing through your window." He took a moment to glance toward the window, a small laugh escaping him. "I guess I didn't really think most of this through, but all I knew was that I needed to tell you something."

He looked at me with an intensity that set my blood on fire, turning to face me almost completely.

"I've spent this entire night going out of my mind thinking about you on a date with Justin. Seriously, it's been driving me crazy because all I could think about was what if you really did like him? What if you decided to really give him a shot, knowing that you and I couldn't happen? Then I got to thinking about what it would be like to have to watch you with him every day and how much that would kill me."

"Seth—"

"Hannah, I know you don't want to hurt Brae. I don't either. I know you guys have your rules or whatever, and you want to be a good friend. But isn't there a rule about doing what is right to make your best friend happy? Those rules shouldn't only apply to Brae, Hannah. I know you are used to always taking the back seat to her and her always getting her way. But I'm fucking crazy about you, and it's really hard to sit back and see you every day and know the only thing standing between you and me is her and some stupid rule."

"Seth—"

"I know I'm probably being a hypocrite, because you had to watch me be with her all this time, so you've already had to go through the whole thing of her being what stands between us. And maybe I'm being egotistical to think you like me as much as I like you, but I know what I can lose now by not saying what I feel and not acting on it, and I don't want to do that again. I don't want to fuck this up a second time by being quiet or polite."

"Seth! Just shut up for a second!"

His speech died off in his throat with a little choke, and it almost made me laugh.

"First of all, you need to keep your voice down. My moms are asleep, and if they catch you here, they will kill me."

His mouth snapped shut, and again, I almost giggled.

"Second of all, I do like you. A lot. Definitely more than I should considering everything. I've liked you since I first met you, and even though watching you with Brae sucked, those feelings never went away. To be honest, I've been trying to get over you."

To this, he startled. "You've been trying to get over me?"

"Yes."

"But . . . why?"

"Because it's too hard to want to be with you and not be able to, you know? When you guys broke up, I decided I needed to get over my crush on you once and for all because it was never going to happen. I started helping Brae through these steps to get over you and was secretly trying to follow them too. I was doing okay for the first little bit. Then you told me that you liked me and kept showing up whenever I was trying to get my feet under me, and now you crawl through my damn window like right off the pages of those stupid novels we fight about, and it's only making me fall harder for you. And I'm trying to be a good friend to Brae because she's always been there for me, and I don't want to hurt her, but I am falling so hard for you and—"

My words died off against his mouth as he closed the space between us in the blink of an eye, crashing his lips to mine. I gasped a small sound, my body stilling, as he brought a hand to my face, cupping my cheek. His kiss was urgent, passionate, and all consuming, and within seconds, my head was spinning.

I had always wondered what kissing Seth would be like. I was learning now that all my fantasies and all my dreams were nothing compared to the reality. His lips were soft and skilled, and he tasted like the faint hint of vanilla. As I tried to draw in a breath, he used the opportunity to part my lips with his, his tongue invading my mouth with gentle, intoxicating strokes. Slowly, my body relaxed, melting to his control, as I started to respond to him.

He kissed me unlike I had ever been kissed before. He didn't take my breath away. I gave it to him willingly.

Slowly, he eased me back against the mattress, his long, hard body following along until he was positioned over me. The feeling of his weight along me left my head swimming when coupled with the skill of his mouth as the hand on my cheek began to slide his fingertips along the curve of my neck. My skin reacted in the wake of his touch, goose bumps coming alive at the sensation.

Adjusting his body, Seth went to push himself up further in the bed, his foot connecting hard and loud with the chair at my desk. The force caused it to topple with a clatter, causing both of us to jump. We froze, a mess of limbs, panting breath, and electricity, before Seth turned his gaze to me.

"Oops." He smiled, bringing his hand back to my face.

I couldn't hold back my girlish giggle. "You are so lucky," I laughed. "You could have woken my—"

"Hannah?" Ma's voice sounded, followed by a gentle knock on my door.

"Shit!"

Sitting up quickly, the force caused Seth to all but fall onto the floor. We both scrambled to our feet, desperately trying to be quiet, but failing.

"Honey, are you okay?"

"Crap, crap," I cursed, frantically moving around my room. "You woke my parents. Crap." I glanced to the window before grabbing Seth by the arm and dragging him toward it. "You gotta go."

"Hannah, I—"

"Just go!" I fluttered as he tried to carefully climb back out onto the porch roof. His previously nimble dexterity seemed to have been absent in the fluster of the situation as he lingered on the sill looking downward.

"This is higher than I remember."

"Hannah," Ma said, my doorknob beginning to turn.

In a frantic and desperate effort, I pushed on Seth's shoulder, sending him falling onto the porch roof that angled outside my window. He landed with a light thud and a small grunt before staring up at me wide eyed.

Mouthing a panicked "sorry," I quickly turned my back to the window just as Ma entered my room. She looked around in the darkness before finding me standing with my hands behind my back.

"Hannah? What are you doing?"

"Nothing," I squeaked, shaking my head unconvincingly.

Ma's brow furrowed as she looked at me skeptically. "I heard a noise. Is everything okay?"

"Yup, all good," I replied, reaching down to pick up the fallen chair. "I just got up to go to the bathroom and tripped over the chair in the dark."

She looked at me with knowing "mom eyes" before she turned her attention to the window.

"Why is your window open? It's cold out tonight."

"Oh, I just wanted some fresh air," I explained as she moved toward the window. I fluttered in a frantic panic, trying to think of something to say or do to keep her from looking outside and seeing Seth sprawled on the roof. "I'll close it, no problem."

But it didn't stop her from coming over and peering out into the yard below before I had the chance to close the window. I followed her gaze nervously, exhaling a sigh of relief to find that Seth was nowhere to be seen. Ma scanned the lawn for several moments before straightening and closing the window herself.

"You'll catch a cold if you leave this open," she said firmly while rubbing my arm.

"Okay."

"Don't stay up too late. Remember, we're going hiking at Greenway tomorrow."

"No problem."

The moment the door closed in her wake, I was back at the window overlooking the lawn. There was no sign of Seth or his mangled body—if he had fallen from the roof—causing a sigh of relief. Seconds later, my phone vibrated gently on my bedside table.

Seth: *You pushed me!*

I giggled like a schoolgirl as I flopped back onto the bed, bringing my phone closer.

Hannah: *I'm sorry! Are you okay?*

Seth: *I'm fine. I've never climbed so fast in my life. I hid on your porch until I heard your mom leave.*

Hannah: *I am so, so sorry!*

Seth: *It's okay. You can make it up to me ;)*

I felt a warmth rise in my stomach, the feeling of his lips on mine lingering on my skin.

Hannah: *Presumptuous.*

Seth: *Hopeful ;)*

Again, a giggle escaped me as a feeling of elation overtook my body.

Seth: *Goodnight, Hannah.*

Hannah: *Goodnight.*

Setting my phone on the corner of my desk, I crawled back between the sheets. Where moments ago, I had felt tired and weary, now my body was like a live wire. Every nerve was alert as the scent of Seth's cologne still lingered in the air. Bringing my fingers to my lips, I ran them along the skin, feeling the exquisite swollen sensation he had left.

STEP SIX:
ACCEPT IT'S OVER,
PLAN YOUR FUTURE,
AND DON'T LOOK
BACK

That awkward moment when your laptop screen is brighter than your future.

CHAPTER TWENTY-EIGHT

Sliding into Brae's car, I barely set my butt onto the seat before she started talking.

"Guess what?"

"What?" I replied as I tossed my bag into her backseat.

"Liam called me yesterday, and we met up again."

"Already?"

She squealed excitedly before putting the car in reverse and backing out of the driveway. Once we were safely on the street, she launched into her tale.

"He said he wanted to go out just the two of us. We met up for ice cream at the Pied Piper, then just walked around. It was so nice, Hannah. Like, we just talked for hours and wandered the streets with no real direction in mind. I didn't even realize how long we had been out until it started to get dark."

I grinned at her enthusiasm. "So you had a good time?"

"I had a great time! He is so amazing. I mean, I felt really bad and kind of embarrassed for talking about Seth so much on Friday, and I honestly thought that I had royally screwed it up and that he probably wouldn't call me again. But we had a really good time just hanging out. He's so different from Seth, too. Plus, it got my mom off my back about the whole dating thing. Not that it should matter, but it is definitely a bonus that she's no longer looking at me like I am some sad little reject destined to become a spinster."

At the mention of Seth, I tingled with nerves. I flashed back to Friday night, to his appearance in my yard and his assent into my room. But most importantly, to the feeling of his lips on mine, his weight over me, and the thrill of his touch on my skin.

Guilt rose up from my core, and I so badly wanted to tell Brae what happened. I wanted to tell her I was sorry for betraying her but that I was truly falling for him. That it wasn't just a crush or wanting something I couldn't have. That for the first time in my life, I was starting to understand what all those corny romance novels were talking about.

But I held my tongue, the words dying off in my throat. Because as much as I wanted to come clean, to be the good person I thought I was, I knew doing so would cost me the best friend I had ever had. Again, gaining one good thing in my life would mean the sacrifice of the other, and I just wasn't ready to take that leap.

"That's good."

"I know!" she exclaimed, thankfully ignorant to my sudden despondence. "With Liam, he makes decisions for me, and I actually *like* it. Like yesterday, he chose the ice cream place and a few other little things. It was like he wasn't letting me lead all the time."

"I never thought I would see the day where Brae Walker likes being told what to do," I joked, nudging her with my arm.

"Me neither. But it's kind of hot. Plus, we like the same things. He likes going out and partying, hanging out with people. He is more in the loop for school gossip than I am, which is a lot of fun," she giggled. "He kept brushing my hair behind my ear and holding my hand. Just little things that were so sweet." She paused for a moment, considering her next statement. "Can I tell you something?"

"Always."

"It was the first time in forever that I felt like I could just be me. That I didn't have to be the hot girl or the popular girl. The one who everyone watches and knows all the rumors about everyone else. I didn't have to put on the show that everyone expects of me all the time. It was kind of nice to just . . . breathe."

I turned to her as if seeing her for the first time. "Brae, no one expects any of that from you. Seth never—"

"He didn't expect it, I know. But I felt like I had to all the same. I can't explain it, Hannah. I guess it's kind of what you said about some people fitting better with others. That sometimes you find someone who just clicks with you and everything falls into place even though you didn't know it wasn't right before."

I silently took in everything she was telling me. Brae was the person I felt I knew better than anyone else. Maybe even better than myself in some ways. But I would never have expected to hear her say she felt like she was always on a stage, acting out the role of the perfect popular girl every day like it was her job. All this time, I thought she loved that life, that role and the perks that came with it. She loved the eyes on her, the looks and admiration. I never considered how exhausting that could be after a while, until now.

"I'm happy for you," I said, reaching across and pinching her side. "It looks like you've officially passed step six."

Brae emitted a happy giggle as she pulled her Jetta into an empty spot in the school parking lot. "I never even thought of that, but yeah. I guess so. Step six is acceptance and planning your future. I've pretty much accepted that Seth and I are done and that it's probably for the best. And right now, Liam is a pretty good thing to look forward to in my future." Cutting the engine, she turned to me with a sly grin. "Speaking of which . . . how did you and Justin work out? How was the rest of your weekend?"

I bit down on my lip instinctively, taking the opportunity to step out of the car as a chance to delay my response. At the question of Justin, the answer was easy. We just didn't click. But in terms of the rest of my weekend . . . that was a different story.

"Justin's a great guy," I said, as we headed toward the entrance to the school. "We had a lot of fun."

"Why do I feel like there is a 'but' coming?"

"But . . . we just didn't click. He's fun to hang out with, but I just didn't feel a spark."

"A spark?" she snickered. "Hannah, he's hot, funny, and nice. He's on paper perfect, and you're looking for a spark?"

"Yes, a spark. Isn't that what we all want?"

She rolled her eyes. "Sparks only happen in fairy tales and romance novels our moms read, Hannah."

My lips turned downward in a frown. "I don't think so. I think they can be real, with the right person. Don't you want that? Someone who makes us feel alive? I'm looking for the someone who makes my pulse race. Someone who gets me and who makes me think. I want to be challenged and excited and hopeful all at once. I want something more than just a decent match or on paper perfect."

I saw her considering my words, trying to meld all the aspects of a relationship, its endless facets, into a theory such as a "spark." It felt almost cliché; a term used as a scapegoat when things just didn't fit.

But I believed in it wholeheartedly despite Seth's teasing at my less than romantic nature. Maybe romance only meant something in real life when it was with someone who made you feel all those things and more?

Brae stopped in her tracks, appraising me as if meeting me for the first time. I met her gaze evenly, no hesitation or uncertainty in the statement I just gave. I wanted all of that and more, and I had found it in Seth. I wasn't going to settle for something that could be good when I knew there was the existence of something exceptional.

Finally, Brae smiled, shaking her head lightly. "Sometimes I forget what a romantic you can be," she laughed, slinging her arm over my shoulders as she led me toward the school. "Don't worry, Hannah. We will find you someone who is perfect for you and all your crazy expectations."

I chuckled just once, saying nothing more as we stepped through the threshold into the school.

CHAPTER TWENTY-NINE

After a week of school, work, and listening to Brae gush over her new romance, it was finally Saturday night, and I was enjoying some much-needed peace and quiet. My moms were out at a school function, celebrating the retirement of one of their colleagues. Brae had a date with Liam, which left me with nothing requiring my attention or time other than the beauty of fiction. Not long after my parents left, I pulled on my pajamas, twisted my hair into a knot on my head, and curled up on my bed to lose myself in another world.

The world beyond my window was dark, the sun long ago set below the horizon. It was a peaceful darkness, as if the world had been erased. Just as I was about to move on to the next chapter of my book, my phone buzzed at my side. I was tempted to ignore it, my captivation in the fantasy world hard to break, but I picked up the phone with a groan, my brow furrowing at the confusing message.

Seth: *Incoming*!

I barely had time to consider what it meant before a distinct clinking came from my window. I paused, turning my attention toward the direction of the sound, listening closely. Seconds later, I heard it again.

I grinned, setting my book aside and moving toward the window. Just as I knew I would, I found Seth in the yard, grinning up at me like my own private Romeo calling me to my balcony. Sliding the window up, I leaned on the sill.

"Making a habit of throwing stones at my window, huh?"

"I don't want your parents to catch me."

I couldn't help but laugh. "They aren't home."

The look on his face was the perfect mixture of surprise, confusion, and adorable embarrassment as he looked down to the remaining stones in his hand.

"Well, there goes that romantic gesture," he called, moving toward the trellis. I stepped back as he scaled the side of the house, clambering onto the porch roof and swinging his long legs over the edge of the window. Once safely in my room, he grinned down at me.

"You know you could have just come in the front door," I commented with a raised brow.

"But where would the romance in that be?"

I giggled before moving to sit on the edge of my bed. He followed, leaning over to place a gentle kiss on my lips before he was even completely seated. Unlike our previous encounter, this kiss was purely sensual. Soft and beckoning, relishing in the feeling of us together. When he moved to pull away, I couldn't stop myself from following in his wake, causing him to chuckle.

"I've been dying to do that since the last time I climbed up here," he said before finally taking in my attire. My tiny boy shorts and oversized T-shirt hanging loosely from my shoulder made me feel incredibly bare. His eyes widened in appreciation before he pulled his lip between his teeth.

Reaching up, I pulled the loose shoulder of my shirt up in a weak attempt to cover myself. "Sorry. I wasn't expecting any visitors to climb through my window."

"You're gorgeous," he stated firmly, without reservation. Within seconds, I could feel a flush crawl over my cheeks.

I cleared my throat nervously, tucking my legs beneath me. "So what brings you here this time?"

A determined expression overtook his features.

"I've been thinking."

"Is that so?"

"I think you should talk to Brae about us."

I leaned back as though he had struck me, my mouth falling slack. Immediately, Seth raised his hands in defense.

"Just hear me out, okay? I know you guys have your pact and all that, and you have this rule not to get involved with each other's ex. But I know Brae, and I really don't think she would care more about a stupid code than your happiness. Honestly, Hannah, if she is really your best friend, would she truly expect you to be unhappy just to stick to some law you made up back before it was ever an actual possibility? Plus, she's clearly moved on. Wouldn't she want you to have the same happiness as her?"

"It's not that simple," I argued.

"I think it is. You're using this rule of yours as if it is doctrine, without even really trying to see if Brae would ever expect you to stick to something that makes you unhappy. You haven't even tried to talk to her about how you feel about me or how I feel about you. You even admitted she didn't know that you had feelings for me before she and I got together, so maybe if you explained to her that you've liked me all along, she will understand and—"

"Seth, you're rambling again."

"Well, I ramble when I am passionate about something. And I am passionate about you." He paused, reaching out and taking my hands in his, his eyes imploring me. "I want to be with you, Hannah. I want to try and make this work. But I won't go against your wishes and say anything to Braelyn because I know it would hurt you. I just ask for you to consider talking to her. To give it a chance that she will understand and choose your happiness over some stupid rule. She's happy with Liam now. You never know, she might surprise you and give us her blessing."

Guilt burrowed in my chest for thinking Brae wouldn't understand. That she would hold our rules over my happiness, even despite the circumstances. But I couldn't rid myself of the fear that polluted my veins at the idea of having to purge all my dirty little secrets. That I liked him first. That I lied when I said it was okay for her to date him. That I harbored these feelings for months, never telling her.

Then not only urging her to make it through these steps to get over him like I pathetically attempted the same but that I was the reason for her heartbreak.

She was understanding, was my soul mate, and my best friend. She would do anything for me, just as I would for her. But I wasn't sure I hadn't sabotaged myself by continuing to doubt my feelings and her faith in our friendship. Now, hiding it for so long felt like more of a betrayal than if I had just been honest at the start.

I had to tell her. I knew I did, no matter what happened with Seth and I in the long run. But I couldn't deny that I was a coward, scared to face my role in everything that had happened.

"I don't know," I said, anxiety taking hold. "What if she blames me for you breaking up with her?"

"But what if she doesn't?" he replied. "I mean, yeah, she'll probably be a little hurt and maybe mad. But you can't tell me she wouldn't want you to be happy."

My mind raced with all the scenarios of how telling Brae the truth might go. Some with her crying and screaming, and some with her crying but hugging me saying she understood. There was equal chance for each of those possibilities, but it didn't lessen my fear that the first would be the most likely.

"Just think about it," he urged, closing the distance between us. "I'm not trying to pressure you, I'm just asking you to consider fighting for this. To put yourself first."

I looked to our linked hands. Everything he said made perfect sense, in turn making it so much harder for me to hide behind my fear of losing Brae. But at the same time, I knew her better than he did. I knew how she felt about loyalty, how she felt about her friends, and her biggest law of friendship is to never betray each other. For me to come to her and admit that all this time I liked her ex, that for the last few months I had known he felt the same about me, would cause her to question my loyalty. The fear that so many girls held, deep down, that their friends would choose a boy over them.

"Just think about it," he repeated, reaching up to place his large, warm palm against my cheek. I leaned into the feeling, the way his fingers curled around the back of my head, as he moved forward and placed his lips against mine.

With just his touch, my worry and fear evaporated, leaving in its place nothing but warmth spreading through my body. I responded to him instantly, my lips following his lead, tasting the hint of vanilla on his tongue as he brought his other hand to cradle my face. He kissed me slowly, consuming me, before his body angled me back against my bed, the soft mattress cradling me as his weight pressed against me. The feeling of him left my head swirling, all thoughts of Brae, of my friendship, and all the reasons this was wrong fading in favor of the tingle along my skin. He slowly pulled a hand from my cheek, his lips becoming more urgent, as his fingers began to tease along the bare skin of my leg that was bent at the side of his hip. My fingers wound in his hair, pulling lightly, and I felt as though I was another person in this moment. Someone brave, someone passionate, and someone who wasn't afraid to show what she wanted. Seth made me feel this way, made me want to be bolder, even as his wandering hand began to tease at the skin of my side under my shirt. It was like he was fighting the urge to touch me, to feel every inch of me the way I so desperately wanted to feel him, instead choosing to explore with soft, tentative strokes of his fingertips. It was a sweet gesture that only made me groan into his mouth as he rocked himself against me.

I was enveloped in him, my every sense completely overtaken, which was probably why I didn't hear the sound of the door until her voice called out.

CHAPTER THIRTY

"What the hell is happening here?"

Seth jumped back, his hands falling away from my body before sitting up quickly, and we both turned toward the source of the sound. Brae stood in the doorway of my room, her gaze flickering between us in disbelief. In her hand was a plastic bag; over her shoulder, her overnight bag.

The silence in the room was the loudest sound I had ever experienced as we each stared at each other, no one knowing what to say. I could almost see Braelyn's mind racing to comprehend what she had just walked in on—the confusion, hurt, and anger moving across her features—until she dropped the plastic bag of treats onto the floor along with her overnight bag.

"What the hell, Hannah!"

I was on my feet instantly.

"Brae, I can explain—"

"Explain what? You've been screwing around with my ex behind my back?" Her attention moved to Seth before quickly going back to me. "How long as this been going on?"

"It isn't going on!"

She scoffed, crossing her arms over her chest. "Really? So, you stick your tongue down all your guy friends' throats? Good to know. I'll make sure to keep that in mind next time I bring Liam around you."

"Brae—" I was cut off by Seth standing from the bed, moving to bring himself between us.

"Brae, this is my fault. Not Hannah's."

"Funny, I'm pretty sure you weren't kissing yourself, Seth!"

Unfazed by her venom, he continued. "I told Hannah a while ago that I had feelings for her."

Oh crap. Thanks a lot, Seth. That's a great start, I thought bitterly as Brae's eyes burned with anger toward me.

"I've had feelings for her since before you and I even got together, and that's part of the reason I knew I had to end things with you. I knew I couldn't be with you when I had feelings for someone else. When I told her how I felt, she told me that she felt the same about me."

"Seth, for God's sake," I groaned, grabbing his arm. "You're making this worse!"

Still, he continued. "But you know what she said to me?" he asked Brae, ignoring my pleas.

"What?" Brae asked, indignantly.

"She told me that even though we both had feelings for each other, that we wanted to be together, that she couldn't do that to you. That her friendship with you meant more to her than being with me."

I stood silently, waiting for any change in the blazing fury that overtook every feature on Brae's face. Her attention was on me now, the heat of her stare scalding me, but no measure of softening could be found in her eyes.

"So she shows me that my friendship means something to her by messing around with you behind my back?" she accused, turning her eyes to me. "I came over here because I wanted to surprise you with a pre-exam girls' night. I knew your moms were out, so I brought over all your favorite junk food. I noticed that you've been acting kind of weird lately and thought you were just going through something you weren't ready to tell me. I never expected to find what you were going through was my ex's boxers."

"Brae."

"You are my best friend, Hannah!" she shouted, losing her momentary composure. "You and I have rules! We always promised each other that we would never betray each other, because we never wanted anything stupid to risk our friendship. I took those things seriously since we were kids, and I thought you did too!"

"I do! Brae, I do, that's why I told Seth we couldn't be together. I didn't want to hurt you—"

Brae sneered. "Yeah, 'cause I feel just great finding out you two were messing around by walking in on you!" She shook her head at me in bewilderment. "If I hadn't just caught you, would you have ever even told me? Would you have just been with him behind my back for who knew how long, hoping I never found out?"

"NO!" I cried.

"Braelyn, we haven't been seeing each other behind your back," Seth said, trying to be the calm voice of reason. "I just came here—"

"I don't care, Seth!" she screamed, throwing her arms out in frustration. "I don't care why you came here, the point is that you're *here*! That you're in my best friend's bedroom, making out with her! That you've liked each other all this time, and neither of you ever thought to *tell me* about it!" Again, she paused, turning back to me. "Do you honestly think that if I knew you liked each other, that I would have ever dated him? I asked you, Hannah. I asked you if you had feelings for him, and you said you were just friends. Do you really think that little of me that you would believe I would ever purposefully hurt you like that, going out with him if I knew you really did like him?"

"No, Brae, I know—"

"Brae." Seth moved to interrupt, but both Brae and I couldn't control our anger any longer.

"Shut up, Seth!" we shouted in unison, causing him to jump.

We all glared at each other, the tension in the room suffocating, until Seth ran his hands through his hair.

"I'm, uh," he said softly, turning to me with sad eyes. "I'm just going to go."

I wanted to tell him not to go, that I was sorry that I yelled at him and that I didn't want him to leave, but I couldn't. I couldn't stop him under Brae's hurt and angry stare, knowing that if I did, she would take it as a sign of me choosing him over her.

Instead, I said nothing. He moved carefully past Braelyn who remained hovering in the doorway like a rabid animal, both of us staring at each other silently until his footsteps on the stairs died away and the click of the front door sounded.

The moment we were officially alone, tears brimmed in her eyes.

"I can't believe you would do this," she said with surprising calm. "I can't believe you would fool around with my ex-boyfriend. All this time, you've been trying to help me get over him. Is that just so you could have him? Did you figure that if I got over him, then I wouldn't be so hurt to find out that you were the reason he dumped me?"

"Brae, I didn't know he had feelings for me until weeks after you guys broke up," I tried to explain, taking a step toward her. The moment she realized my intention, she took a noticeable step back, keeping distance between us at all times. "When I found out, I told him that we couldn't be together because I didn't want to hurt you. And I meant it! I *do* mean it! Brae, I've been going mental trying to figure out how to not hurt anyone in this situation, but I like him. I like him so much that it drives me crazy. I want to be with him, but I don't want to hurt you. I know that I shouldn't, and I hate that you had to find out this way. This whole thing is such a mess, and I don't know what to do."

Tears were falling from my eyes now, but I didn't bother wiping them away. Brae's cheeks became wet with her own tears, both of us hurt and scared and angry but not knowing how to find a solution to everything placed between us. I wanted her to prove Seth right; to tell me that she understood and that if he made me happy that she supported me. I wanted her to not hurt, to not hate me, and to just go back to how it was before.

"We swore never to let a guy come between us," she said softly, reaching down to pick up her overnight bag and sling it over her shoulder. "It may not have been important to you, but it was to me. And you broke it."

She moved toward the door as I took a step forward. Just as she passed the threshold, she turned back, glancing down to the plastic bag now on my bedroom floor.

"It's peanut butter, strawberry jam, and that weird whole grain bread you love. I figured we could make your favorite sandwiches and watch Netflix. Just be us for a little while, without school or parents or boys. But I guess that doesn't matter anymore."

"That isn't fair!" I shouted. "Brae, I didn't do this to hurt you! Do you think I would honestly do any of this intentionally? That this was some big master plan?"

She snorted. "This isn't *Law and Order*, Hannah! Motive isn't the biggest factor here!"

Her sarcasm only turned my vision red with anger. "Then what is? Because I've tried to do everything right in this messed up scenario and still end up losing! I told him we could only be friends even though it made me miserable because I didn't want to lose you. I chose you, and it's still never good enough!"

Her face turned an angry red, tears streaming down her cheeks as she swallowed back her emotions. I could almost see the thoughts racing, confliction between condemnation and forgiveness and everything in between. After several moments, she pulled her masterful mask of indifference over her eyes.

"Have fun," she said, gesturing to the bag of treats on the floor before disappearing out the door. I scrambled after her, but she was too quick, racing down the stairs and out the front door before I could get to the top of the staircase. By the time I reached the door, I could only stand on the porch and watch as she backed out of the driveway and onto the street, leaving me with my tears.

THE FALLOUT

Follow your brain.
Sometimes your heart is a moron.

CHAPTER THIRTY-ONE

"Brae, it's me. Again. Listen, I know you're pissed, and I get it. But please just let me explain. Just talk to me." A hitch in my throat cut off my plea, forcing me to pause to swallow it back. "Please, just call me back."

Hanging up the phone, I tossed it angrily to the side, watching as it flopped uselessly onto the bed beside me. It had become a vicious circle of the same for the last twelve hours, and I had made no headway for the effort.

The moment I made it back to my room after watching Brae speed away down the street the night before, I grabbed my phone and dialed her number. Tears blurred my eyes, guilt and fear swirling in my stomach as my shaking fingers struggled to dial her number. Of course it went to voicemail, and I left my first of what would become many, many, *many* messages. Ten minutes later, when I knew she would have already made it home, I tried again. When no response came, I started texting.

Hannah: *Brae, I'm sorry. I am so, so sorry.*

Hannah: *Please pick up the phone. We need to talk about this.*

Hannah: *You're my best friend. Please don't do this.*

Time after time, call after call, text after text went unanswered. I fell asleep sometime in the early morning hours, long after my moms had returned from their party. I heard them come through the front door, but I crawled into bed and pretended to be asleep. They popped their heads into my room as they always did, but I kept my back toward the door, concentrating on keeping my breathing steady and even, fighting against the tension and inclination to shudder with every inhale. Tears still fell from my eyes, soaking my pillow, cold against my cheek. I didn't want them to see the mess I had become, because then they would ask questions. And questions required answers or lies, neither of which I was prepared to provide.

Seth had texted me about an hour after the emotional explosion, asking me if I was okay. I stared at the message for at least ten minutes, not knowing how to respond.

Obviously, the answer was no. I was most certainly not okay because I had just had my best friend in the whole world walk out on me. I had little doubt that said friend now hated me and couldn't even think of a single good reason why she shouldn't. I wanted to be able to type back a simple "I'm okay" for no other reason than to ease his own guilt, but I couldn't bring myself to do it. I couldn't make myself do anything but feel the pit in my stomach and the pain in my chest. So instead, I rolled onto my side, curling into a ball, and tried to ignore the pain in my chest.

I woke to a cloudy, dreary June day, the rain tapping lightly on my window like the stones Seth had thrown the night before. The weather fit my mood perfectly, giving me every excuse to hide away from the world beyond.

Ma came into my room not long before lunch, curious as to why I hadn't come downstairs. I made some excuse of having a migraine and that I just wanted to sleep. It wasn't a total lie, since crying for hours dehydrated me to the point where my head felt like it was in the grips of a vice. She returned moments later with water, Advil, and a cookie, leaving them on the corner of my desk before pulling the drapes over my window and leaving me to my solemn mood.

The rest of the morning, I lay on my back, hands folded over my stomach as I stared at the ceiling. Every now and then, I would text, call, or email Brae; the flutter of hope in my chest refusing to fade no matter how long the silence stretched on.

It was now just after three in the afternoon, and I had lost count of how many messages, texts, and calls I had sent. All of them unanswered. I hid in my room, jumping at every little ping of my phone, hoping it was Braelyn, feeling the plummeting of my heart when each time it was nothing more than a notification on Instagram or a spam email.

The thought crossed my mind of just falling back asleep, letting the gentle sound of the rain lull me into a dreamless slumber where I could pretend that everything wasn't falling apart. I closed my eyes, trying to ease my breathing enough to find some kind of refuge, when the sound of my phone ringing brought me back to reality.

I almost threw myself at my phone, scrambling with fumbling fingers to slide my finger across the screen before looking at who was calling.

"Brae?"

"It's me." Seth's voice caused the hope that had bubbled up to plummet back into my stomach. "Are you okay?"

Disappointment overtook me. I remained quiet for probably much too long, but I couldn't think of an appropriate answer to his question.

"She hates me," I finally answered, my chin quivering.

"She doesn't hate you, Hannah," he said gently. "She's just mad and confused."

I shook my head as though he could see me. "You didn't see the hurt on her face when you left. I've never seen her look at me that way before. She hates me, Seth. She truly hates me."

"She could never hate you. I know you feel like she does now, and maybe she even thinks she does. But she'll calm down and eventually understand that—"

"You don't get it!" I interrupted with a shout. "I betrayed her. It isn't just about some stupid, childish girl code, Seth. We promised each other years ago that no guy would ever come between us. We watched other friendships fall apart because of guys and swore that would never be us. It is more than just girl code. This is about doing something I promised her I wouldn't. This is about her feeling like she wasn't enough, only to walk in on me in a place where she felt she should be. This is about her walking in and getting slapped in the face with every bad thing she ever thought about herself."

"Hannah, you're overreacting—"

"Ugh, just . . . just leave me alone, Seth. I need time to work things out, and you're not making this easier."

"Hannah—"

"I'll talk to you later." I hung up with the sound of my name being called through the line. Again, I tossed my phone aside like the traitor it was before rolling onto my side. Tears brimmed in my eyes, forcing me to blink to hold them back as the emotions coursing through my veins ran my throat dry.

I slowly calmed, using the sound of the rain to distract me from my thoughts. In my dark, lonely room, I drifted off to sleep, escaping the disaster my life had become in the only way I could.

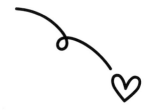

CHAPTER THIRTY-TWO

A tingle of adrenaline filled my veins as I entered the school, expecting all eyes to turn to me the moment the doors closed behind me. That the entire school would know what I had done, that I had betrayed my best friend, and I would be forever painted as a jezebel for falling for a boy who was off-limits. I wore my scarlet A as a brand on my skin, invisible but there, as I kept my head down and feet moving. But as I paused at the threshold, no one seemed to look at me any differently.

In fact, no one looked at me at all.

I supposed that could be counted as a good thing. It meant that Brae hadn't gone on a rant and told everyone at school what I had done to her and what a horrible friend I was.

Turning in the direction of my locker, I froze as I saw Brae standing at hers. Her back was to me, her attention focused on the books in her hands. Her hair was pulled up into a messy knot on her head, her clothing surprisingly casual for the usually dressed to the nines Braelyn. It was all signs that she was struggling just as much as I was, and it caused my heart to pang with guilt.

Moving cautiously toward the lockers, like approaching a wild animal, I paused at her side. Sweat coated my palms, my heart thrumming in my ears like a steady white noise of panic, as I tried to force the words to rise from my parched throat.

"Hi," I said softly, and she froze at the sound of my voice. When she didn't look at me, I wondered if she was actually going to speak to me. But after a beat, she finished shoving her items into her bag roughly before slamming her locker closed without even looking at me. My heart shuddered at the clang of her locker, like she wasn't just closing the container, but closing the door on our friendship with the action. She turned on her heels, storming away from me when I called out after her. My voice crawled up my throat, escaping in a hoarse and unrecognizable sounding plea.

"Brae, please!" I called, taking a step to follow her. She paused in her retreat, her back still to me. "Please just talk to me."

Brae stood in the hall, not moving to run or turn to acknowledge my voice, and I could see in the set of her shoulders that she was struggling to decide how to face me. As well as I knew her, I honestly couldn't imagine what she was thinking or feeling in this moment.

Suddenly, without warning, she rounded on me.

"What do you want to talk about?" she yelled, several pairs of eyes turning in our direction at her outburst. "What could you *possibly* have to say for yourself!"

I backed down at her public outburst, fearful of having this standoff in the middle of the hall in front of half the school. My stomach churned with unease, a chill sliding over my skin. Curious gazes darted in our direction, eager for some excitement, and I tried to take another step toward her. Of course she backed away as though I was something to fear.

"Brae, I didn't mean for any of this to happen," I said quietly, trying to keep my voice low enough for only her to hear. "When he told me how he felt, I told him we couldn't be together because I would never betray you like that."

She scoffed. "You would never betray me like that?" she repeated loudly. "Making out with my ex *in your bedroom* is how you don't betray me? You have a funny definition of what it means to *not* betray your friends, Hannah."

"Brae."

"You broke the rules!" she screamed, earning the attention of all eyes in the hallway. The usual flow of student traffic meandering in the halls came to a sudden halt as everyone now focused on us. I paled under the stares, the instinct to run and hide tingling along my skin, but I held my ground. "You knew that being with him after we broke up would hurt me! We agreed to never do that to each other, but the first chance you get, you run off and mess around with him behind my fucking back like a coward!"

I took a step back from her words as if they had struck me, several bystanders calling "oohs" at her harsh accusation.

A warmth rose from my core, but it wasn't the embarrassment I expected. This time, it was anger. It was a slow, steady rise, like the simmering of lava hidden under the ground. Always there, but never seen. Until something changed, a fissure appeared, and it surged forward.

"I had feelings for him long before he even met you," I said in a low voice. "Then you swooped in and put on your Braelyn show and took him like you do everything else."

"What's that supposed to mean?" she balked.

I snorted sarcastically. "You know exactly what I mean, Brae. Everything is always about you, and you love it. Guys think you're hot, girls want to be you. You're rich and popular and rule the school and expect everyone to fall in line behind you. If something doesn't go exactly your way, you either try to railroad it into submission or you kick up a fuss."

"Don't act like this is my fault!" she screamed back, taking a step toward me. "I asked you before I even went out with him if it was okay, and you said yes!"

"Because you knew I wouldn't say anything else! You played the entire thing to your advantage, and now you're trying to play the martyr for it because I didn't *tell* you that I liked him? You never gave me a fucking chance!"

She glared at me with fire in her eyes, her hands balled into fists at her side. Every line of her body was tense, quivering with the vibrations of her anger as her eyes narrowed into slits. Only a sliver of blue could be seen as she glared at me, teeth clenched.

"It's not my fault that you're a pushover, Hannah," she said with surprising calm despite her outward appearance. "You didn't tell me you liked him before I met him. You didn't tell me even when I asked you. Now you're pissed because I went out with him anyway? In case you forgot, he agreed. I didn't trick him into dating me for six damn months. Seth chose me, and you're pissed off about it."

"It isn't a choice when there is only one option, Braelyn!"

"Hannah! Brae!" a voice called, as a tall, broad figure stepped in between us. "Jeez, cut it out!"

I groaned, throwing my head back in exasperation as yet again, Seth chose the exact wrong time to make an appearance. When I brought my attention back to Brae, she was glaring at me as if I had planned for him to rush in as my savior yet again.

"Figures. You need him to come in and fight your battles for you, even with me. The person who is supposed to be your best friend!" she snorted, crossing her arms over her chest.

"Because my best friend is acting like an entitled brat and won't even listen to me when I'm trying to apologize for something I didn't even do!"

"You were kissing him in your room!"

"You—"

"Hannah, stop," Seth said, placing his hands on my arms and pushing me back. He was putting physical distance between Brae and me when all I wanted was to get in her face. We rarely fought, and in all our years of friendship, I couldn't recall an instance when we were at each other's throats this way. Usually, I would do just as she said and back down or wait until she was calm and try to talk it out. But in this moment, with this situation, ten years of pent-up frustration for taking second seat to her was rising in my core, and I wanted nothing more than to hash it out regardless of the public setting.

Moving himself into my eye line, Seth tried to calm me. "Just calm down. You're making a scene."

"I don't care!" I shouted, pushing him out of the way. Once my eyes set on Brae again, a lump formed in my throat. "I've always been there for you. No matter what stupid shit you did, I stood by you. I always gave you the benefit of the doubt even when I knew you were being a brat, and I always forgave you because I knew you never meant to hurt me with your dismissive comments. I stand up for you with your mom, and I stood by you with all her crazy crap. Yes, I broke one stupid rule, but it was one that only benefitted you from the start, and we both know it. But you are breaking all the others right now if you walk away and don't talk to me like a damn adult!"

Brae glared at me silently, and I waited for her to make her decision. Her body remained rigid, like a bow pulled taut, shoulders raised and jaw tight. Either she would choose the high road, go off somewhere private, and have our face-off one-on-one or she would walk away from me and our friendship.

Usually, I could tell what she would choose before she did. But this time, I honestly didn't know.

The hallway was eerily silent as we stared at each other, and it seemed as though they were waiting just as anxiously to see what she would decide as I was.

Biting down on her lip to stop it from quivering, to stop from showing any sign of weakness in front of the general population, Brae looked upward to the ceiling for a moment. In that action, I seriously thought she was going to choose me. That she was going to listen and let me explain. But without warning, she spun on her heels and stormed away, pushing through the crowd that had gathered and out of sight before I could even take a step forward to stop her.

Once she was gone, all eyes turned to me. I stared at the space where she disappeared, secretly hoping she would come back. But as the bodies that formed the wall around us began to move and disperse, I realized that she wasn't going to return.

"Hannah," Seth said softly, reaching up to place his palm on my cheek. "Are you—"

I slapped his hand away harshly, stepping away from his touch.

"Seth, just stop!" I shouted, tears brimming in my eyes. "Stop getting involved in this!"

The shock and hurt at my rejection flashed across his features before he pulled himself together. "Whether you like it or not, I *am* involved in this, Hannah."

"Well then stop making it worse!" I cried, covering my face with my hands. "You just keep showing up and taking my side, and it's just making things even worse than they were!"

"I'm sorry," he answered sadly. "I'm just trying to help."

"Then just let us work this out on our own," I replied. "Just give me time to figure this out."

I didn't wait for him to respond. I didn't even bother gathering my books. Instead, I turned away quickly and practically ran back down the hall toward the exit, bursting through the doors and back out into the Tennessee summer day.

CHAPTER THIRTY-THREE

The gentle knock at my door broke me away from my feigned attempts at studying. I sighed as if it was a huge inconvenience to be pulled away from the lessons of literature and history, when in reality I had been doing nothing more than staring at the pages in alternating attempts to retain anything. Finals were upon us, and I was struggling to clear my mind of the recent gaping hole of despair I had been residing in to make some form of an effort to pass my classes. I had already taken my calculus final, and despite turning down Seth's offer of help, I passed . . . barely.

Lifting my head from my history book, I let my hands fall lifelessly to my lap.

"Come in."

The door opened slowly, my moms appearing at the threshold with furrowed brows. I exhaled again, my attention moving back forward to stare toward my window.

I knew it was only a matter of time before they showed up. They had watched me from a distance as I withdrew more and more from daily life barely saying a word. There were the typical parental "Is everything okay?" or "Do you need to talk about anything?" questions asked, but other than that, they had left me to deal with my problems on my own.

But it had been over a week now, with Brae and I nothing more than cold, distant strangers in the hallways, and my mood becoming increasingly sullen. Seth had honored his promise to give me space, but now his gazes in the hallways were ones of longing and sadness rather than passion and intensity, and it only served to make me feel worse for the role I had played in everything that had happened. It would appear that a week was as long as my moms were willing to wait on the sidelines before confronting me on my fractured friendships.

My moms entered my room, hovering at my desk. Mom was her usual self; contained and strong, but I could still see the lines of worry in her face. Ma was the opposite; nervous, hands twisting, her desperate need to reach out and hug me being held back by a lecture from Mom, no doubt. Usually, the balance worked perfectly, but right now I just wanted them to say whatever they came to say so they could leave me alone.

"Hannah," Ma said gently, using the tone she used to use when I had done something against the rules. The soft warning before Mom stepped in and was the heavy hand. "Your mom and I have been trying to give you space, because we don't want to pry or push. But we know something is bothering you. We've also noticed that Brae hasn't been around lately." She pulled out the chair from the corner of the room to sit. "We really wish you would talk to us and let us help. Did you guys have a fight?"

I dropped my eyes to my hands, my bottom lip finding its way between my teeth. Biting down, I let myself focus on the sting of pain I inflicted rather than answer her question. I didn't have to answer for them to take my nonverbal cues as confirmation.

"What happened?" Mom asked, sliding my beanbag chair over to sit beside Ma. They looked almost comical, like a strange little support circle looking at me with worry.

I shook my head, the rush of memory coming back to me at their questions. The look on Brae's face when she walked in on Seth and I mid-kiss. Our standoff in the hallway; the angry hurtful words we had slung at each other. The cold, unfamiliar silence that had followed. All of it because I couldn't be the friend I should have been.

My chin quivered involuntarily, and Ma sighed.

"Oh, honey, it's okay."

"No, it isn't," I interrupted, my voice cracking. "I screwed up so bad."

They exchanged a glance, and I could only imagine the myriad of possibilities flying through their creative minds. As much as I didn't want to have to admit what I did, I had a feeling that telling them the truth would be far less traumatic than whatever they were conjuring in this moment.

"What happened, Hannah?" Mom asked, her voice even and calm.

I inhaled a shaky breath, trying to figure out where to start. It was all such a confusing, interwoven mess; almost a year of kept secrets, of lies and wounded hearts, all over a boy. It was so tragically teenage, it would have been funny if it hadn't been my life.

"You remember Seth Linwood?" I asked, glancing toward them.

"Of course," Ma said, encouraged by my participation. "He's that nice boy in your English class."

"Brae's ex-boyfriend," Mom corrected, and I could see that she was starting to figure out where this might be leading.

I nodded. "The thing is . . . I like him. I've liked him since September, way before Brae and him ever got together."

Ma raised an eyebrow. "If you liked him, why would Brae—"

"She didn't know," I clarified quickly. "I never told her. I didn't tell anyone."

Mom pursed her lips. "What happened?"

I exhaled, trying to calm my breathing. "When they broke up, Seth told me that he liked me. That he had liked me since we first met, just like I liked him. But he didn't think I felt the same, so when Brae asked him out, he accepted. She asked me if it was okay, but I just couldn't tell her the truth."

Mom made a little noise.

I shrugged in response. "Anyways, when he told me that he liked me, I admitted that I liked him too. But that we couldn't go out because he had just broken up with Brae, and it was against the rules."

"The rules?" Ma asked with a curious expression. Mom, however, seemed to know exactly what I was talking about.

"Hannah, you two still have those silly friendship laws from when you were nine?"

"They aren't silly," I defended quickly. "They mean something to us. And there's one about never dating a friend's ex, so even though we like each other, Seth and I can't be together because that would mean I had to betray Brae. We agreed to be friends, and everything was fine for a while."

I was trying to help Brae get over him and even tried using the same steps to get over him myself, but it was a disaster. She was doing great, but I just kept falling for him harder. We have so much in common, we like the same things, and he makes me feel like no one else ever has."

My moms exchanged a glance, the type parents show when their child is talking about the boy or girl they like. That embarrassing "young love" smirk that drives all kids crazy.

"So what happened between you and Brae?" Mom asked, keeping us on track.

I swallowed deeply, knowing I was about to get myself in trouble for my admission.

"Seth came over the other night. When you guys were at the retirement party for Professor Kalheed."

Ma gasped in shock while Mom just shook her head. "Hannah."

"I know, I know! I didn't invite him over, I swear. He just showed up, and we started talking. He wanted me to talk to Brae about us, to tell her how we felt about each other. He figured that if she was really my best friend, then my happiness would mean more to her than some stupid rule."

"He's a smart boy," Mom said with a nod.

"Yeah, well. After we talked, he kind of kissed me. We were kissing, and I didn't hear the door open." I closed my eyes as the memory returned to my mind. "Brae came in and kind of caught us."

Neither of my parents said a word, both watching me silently. I could feel the heat in their stares of disapproval, and I wanted nothing more than to shrink away into the floor. Finally, I couldn't hide any longer, turning to meet their disappointed expressions.

Of course I found what I expected. Frowns, contemplative eyes, and folded hands. It was the exact same stance they always took when I screwed up. Although, slightly less threatening when Mom was awkwardly perched on my beanbag chair.

It was Mom who spoke up first.

"Well, I can't say I approve of the fact that you had this boy in the house when we weren't home. You know the rules, Hannah."

"I know."

"And I'm sure you know you're going to be in trouble for that."

"Yeah, I know."

"But . . ."

My gaze jumped to Mom in surprise, my expression causing her to grin.

"You shouldn't be so hard on yourself," she continued. "You didn't go out to hurt Braelyn. You've always been a good friend to Brae and always stood by her. I have to agree with Seth that if she was the type of friend that you are to her, she would want you to be happy. Some silly rule shouldn't mean more to her than that. You need to apologize to her for your role in all this, because you aren't blameless, honey. But you didn't do it on purpose, either."

"Hannah, honey, you know we love Brae," Ma added. "You two have been joined at the hip since you were small, and we consider her one of our own. But you know better than anyone that she's a handful. She loves the attention, and everything always seems to circle around her. She knows exactly how to get what she wants, and while I have no doubt she would never intentionally hurt you or anyone else, I think sometimes she doesn't put enough thought into her actions before she follows through. I think you end up as collateral damage more than either of you realize." Brushing my hair from my face, she leveled me with a firm parental stare. "But I agree with your mom. You both had a hand in this fallout, and you both need to own up to it. Apologize; try to make it right. If it's meant to be repaired, it will be."

"What does Seth have to say about all this?" Mom asked, leaning to rest her elbows on her knees.

I began to twist my thumbs together absentmindedly.

"He figures she will come around, but he doesn't know her like I do. When she caught us, he kept trying to explain, but it only made her more mad. Then, at school Monday, we were fighting really bad in the hallway, and he came up and just made it so much worse. I know he's just trying to help, but it isn't. I've asked him to just give me some space until Brae and I can work this out between us."

Mom's face pinched, thoughtfully. She seemed to consider her words before speaking, and I knew from experience that usually meant I needed to listen carefully.

"I understand how you might feel that he is making it worse, but remember, he's just trying to help. He has a hand in all this, too. Maybe a bit of time for you to sort through things on your own will help all of you." She reached out, taking my hand in hers to force me to look at her. "You can't always control who you fall in love with, baby. I wish you could, but it doesn't work that way. I know you're struggling to figure this all out, but can I offer a piece of advice?"

I nodded, my voice failing me.

"You don't always get a second chance when it comes to love. You lost out on this boy once. I would hate to see you do it again because you were too busy pushing him away to protect Brae than accepting the fact that you deserve to be happy."

"I agree with your mom," Ma said. "It's not always easy to admit you like someone and impossible to do it when they are right in front of you, but you should have been honest with them both from the start. Brae especially. What's done is done, and you can't keep blaming yourself or punishing yourself by pushing Seth away. It's not going to make Brae accept it, and it's not going to make you feel any better. It's just going to make you lonely, and the whole situation will have meant nothing in the end."

"So . . . you don't think I am a horrible person?"

My parents laughed. "Of course not," Ma said, pushing up to hug me tightly. "Hannah, you are a caring, sweet, wonderful friend. You've spent all this time putting your happiness second to Brae's. She is hurt right now, but if she is the girl I think she is, she will come around."

"And you deserve to be happy just as much as she does," Mom added. "Stop always thinking you have to stay in second place just because your best friend is Braelyn Walker."

I nodded against Ma's shoulder, letting the warmth and constriction of her embrace hold me together. I inhaled the familiar scent of her shampoo and allowed myself a hint of forgiveness for the state I had put myself in.

My moms stood, Ma squeezing my shoulder and Mom kissing my forehead before heading for the door.

"We will let you get back to studying. Let us know if you need any help," Ma said.

"Okay."

Mom paused at the door, turning back around. "Oh yeah, and Hannah."

"Yeah?"

"You're grounded for a week for letting Seth in here when we weren't home."

CHAPTER THIRTY-FOUR

I made my way over to my porch swing, book clutched in my hands. I had long ago given up on avoiding all forms of romance and boys in literature on the foolish and misguided belief that they would help me keep my thoughts from Seth. That was a pathetic bust of a mission, and in all honesty, gave me nightmares.

Now I held a new romance to occupy this second week of summer break. I needed something light, something funny, and something that would restore my belief that not all love was destined to fail no matter the obstacles in its path.

Curling up on my spot, my legs tucked beneath me as I set the book at my side. I took a moment to take in the warm summer afternoon, the breeze through the trees emitting a soft white noise that calmed me as my mind trailed off.

School had ended almost two weeks ago, and that was the last time I saw Brae. We had passed in the hall after our Spanish final, neither of us speaking to each other; no acknowledgement beyond a cursory glance in the other's direction. The hole in my chest that formed with her absence swelled, searing at the edges painfully, but I couldn't bring myself to break our silence.

I couldn't seem to make my voice work or bring air into my lungs to force words out. By the time I reached the end of the hall, I turned in time to watch her sashay through the front doors of the school like she didn't have a care in the world.

I had been replaying that encounter in my head every day since, wondering if I should have just talked to her. Should I have just reached out and touched her arm, hoping she would stop? Should I have just apologized, screamed it out into the space between us before it became a void? Maybe we would have had a chance at mending our broken friendship.

Or maybe that was the first example of how all our encounters would go from now on.

Erin had texted me the week before in preparation for Brae's seventeenth birthday, asking if I was going to her party. I explained that I knew she didn't want me there and that I didn't want to show up and ruin her time. That as much as it hurt to spend the night at home knowing she and all my friends were having the time of their lives, I would never crash her party that way.

"I know things with you guys are messed up," they said, their tone soft. "But she wants you there, even if she doesn't say it out loud."

I shook my head as if they could see it through the phone. "You didn't hear her," I replied, my voice cracking. "She's never been so angry."

"That doesn't mean she hates you," they pressed. "Mad and hate are two different things."

"I'm surprised she hasn't started a rumor or a social destruction campaign against me."

Erin snorted. "That is her style, it's true. And if this was anyone else, she probably would have unleashed a hurricane of retaliation by now, but I think even she can't bring herself to do that stuff to *you*."

A long silence fell over the line, tears brimming in my eyes. Finally, Erin sighed.

"You could have told me, you know," they said, no accusation in their tone.

"What?"

"That you liked him," they explained. "I mean, I kind of figured, even before Brae and him got together. You were different those few weeks you kept him as a sexy little English project secret . . . happier. I wondered if there was someone you liked but didn't want to ask."

My stomach churned, remembering the early days of my crush on Seth.

"Then, when Brae and Seth started dating, the way you would look at him . . ." They paused, as if trying to find the right words. "I wondered if there was something there."

I laughed almost manically, exasperated. "I kind of wish you had called me out on it back at the start. Maybe it would have prevented all of this."

"I do, too," they admitted.

In the end, I declined Erin's offer to attend Brae's birthday. The day of the party, I walked the several blocks to her house, pausing on the sidewalk. Balloons were draped along the tall oak trees out front, a banner strung across the porch reading "Happy Birthday, Braelyn." I could hear voices calling from the backyard and the faint sounds of music. The house looked so familiar, but at the same time, so foreign to me that I scrambled to complete my mission. I placed the wrapped gift of a jumbo box of Twizzlers along with coupons for free ice cream from Alley Scoops on her doorstep with a note. I didn't go into a long, apologetic sonnet explaining my reasons and begging her forgiveness. Instead, written as neatly as I could on the blue card with a unicorn on the cover, I wrote *Happy Birthday, Love Hannah*. Once the gift was delivered, I quickly made my escape before anyone noticed my presence.

I finished the English assignment of *Romeo and Juliet* on my own, emailing Seth the final version for his approval. I hated that the closing of our partnership with this project was being done via the invisible lines of the internet, but it was a necessary evil. I wasn't ready to face him. To have to sit beside him again after all this and spill lines of love everlasting onto the page. I did so in private, crying as I ended our tale.

Seth replied an hour later, saying I had done a great job. This only served to make me cry harder.

Finals passed in a blur, merging into the final summer of my high school career, and all I planned to do was read, sleep, and work. Even though the trip to Paris was unofficially off the table, I kept my job for the routine and the money. It gave me a distraction and the funds to go on my own adventure once senior year came to a close. It wouldn't be the same, but it was better than nothing.

I had barely made it to the end of the second chapter of my book before footsteps stole my attention. I wasn't that surprised to find Seth standing there. I had learned he had a habit for showing up randomly, like a secret sense of knowing when I needed him. My chest swelled at the sight of him, a mixture of nerves and relief.

He looked as beautiful as ever, of course. His green eyes looked impossibly light in the sunlight, the brightness hinting to brownish hues in the blackness of his hair. Wearing a fitted white T-shirt over khaki shorts, his hands shoved deep into his pockets, he watched me with uncertainty as if trying to assess if I would ask him to leave.

Only this time, I didn't even consider it. The moment I saw him, I knew I was done blaming him. I was done acting like he was the reason for the demise of my friendship. It was like taking that first breath after a long dive, filling your lungs with what gives you life.

I had fallen for him, and I was finished pushing him away.

"Hi," I said casually, my eyes drinking him in.

"Hey," he replied, clearing his throat. "How are you?"

"Okay. You?"

"Okay."

Again, silence, as neither of us seemed to know how to navigate the awkward terrain between us. Finally, I pushed up onto my feet.

"Seth, I am so sorry. I know I pushed you away when all you were trying to do was help. You didn't deserve that, and I'm sorry."

He shook his head. "Hannah, no. I'm sorry. I've liked you for so long, I kept pushing you when you said we should just be friends. It was selfish, and I made this so much harder on you than it should have been. I am so sorry."

"I like you, too. I always have. I'm not sorry you pushed me because if you hadn't, I probably would have just accepted never having more. I never would have realized I deserve to be happy, too." I approached the top of the stairs, looking down at the boy in front of me. My heart swelled at the sight of him, and I knew in that moment, I wanted nothing but him. "I'm crazy about you, Seth. I want to be with you. If you still feel the same."

His eyes widened in surprise, making it clear that my statement was the last thing he expected me to say. I could almost see his brain processing this information before a wide, dimple-accented smile slowly overtook his face.

He said nothing in return before he scaled the steps between us, picking me up clear off my feet and into his arms. His lips crashed into mine, soothing an ache in me I felt was branded into my soul. I hung in his arms, my own wrapped around his neck, before giggling at the sight we made. Even then, Seth refused to stop kissing me, as if he was afraid it would be the last time we ever would.

Finally, I pulled back, dodging his lips. "You can put me down, you know?"

He shook his head. "Nope. You're mine now. Get used to it."

A fit of giggles overtook me as he moved to kiss me again, turning my head so it was planted on his cheek. After another moment, as though making a point, he set me on my feet and took my hands in his.

"So . . . we're really going to do this?" he asked as he stared down at me. "Rules be damned?"

Nodding, I laughed. "Yup."

Seth's smile returned, igniting my heart. "Should I ask you to be my girlfriend? You know, to make it official and stuff?"

"Are you getting cheesy on me?" I laughed, pushing at his shoulder.

"Hannah, I've already thrown rocks at your window, climbed into your room in the middle of the night, twice, and let you push me onto the roof, once. I'm pretty sure I've already crossed the line of cheesiness."

"That's true," I admitted, reaching up to place my lips to his. "Then, yes."

"I didn't even get to ask!" he laughed against my lips.

"You don't have to. The answer is yes."

CHAPTER THIRTY-FIVE

"Finally, a nice day," I said, turning my sunglass-covered gaze to the sky. "I'm so tired of the heat."

"Thank goodness, too. You've done nothing but complain about it all week," Seth teased, earning himself a pinch in the side.

"I don't like it when it's humid," I defended with a pout. "Besides, it makes my hair go frizzy."

Seth snickered at my side, swinging our linked hands between us.

It was nearing the end of July, and Tennessee was finally feeling a reprieve from a month's worth of sweltering heat. It was the type of weather that drained you of energy from the moment you woke, leaving a coating of sweat on your skin and your clothes sticking to your back. It was too hot to do anything other than park yourself in front of the air conditioner, dreaming of Iceland, Canada, or anywhere cold.

The only amnesty I had been able to enjoy, however, had been quite pleasant indeed.

Most of my days had been spent lounging poolside at Seth's, alternating between tanning on the patio and cooling off in the most perfectly-mild water I had ever experienced. I couldn't tell if it was the temperature control on the pool or the fact that anything that wasn't a hundred and four degrees felt like heaven on my skin, but every time I dove in, the most exquisite relief overtook my body, and I swore I would never get out again. Of course, that was until I got pruney and my hands felt gross, then I would crawl back to my lounger in the shade.

My view during these days was also quite pleasing. I had always admired Seth's body from afar, thinking that there was nothing sexier in the world than him in a tight black T-shirt and jeans. That was, of course, until I saw him in nothing but swim trunks, with beads of water sliding down his bare torso. His wet hair looked jet-black, every muscle in his body tightening as he walked. It was a show that caused my mouth to run dry and my pulse to race, and just as much of a reason for my frequent cooling-off requirements as the sun.

We spent the last two weeks basking in the bliss of a new relationship, deciding to no longer let others dictate how we felt and what we did. It was freeing to finally be able to hold his hand and walk through town without fear of who might see us. I no longer let myself feel guilty for how I felt about him and knew without a doubt that I was falling in love with him. It had been a crazy, frantic, dramatic descent, but I didn't regret the landing one bit.

Today was the first day that the weather could be considered warm as opposed to scorching. I had awoken that morning with a cool breeze flowing through my open window, rustling the sheers softly. I felt like a kid on Christmas morning, peering out into the day with a sense of excitement. Within fifteen minutes, I was showered, dressed, and on my way to Seth's with the promise of a walk around town and ice cream.

And as always, he followed through with his promises. We had wandered the streets of town, peeking in store windows, up until one long, pouting look from me at the pet store made him pull me away from the puppy I had been playing with through the glass.

Which brought us to now; sitting across from each other at a small table outside Alley Scoops. The sounds of dogs barking, the breeze rustling the trees, and the faint smell of freshly-mowed grass was heaven. It was as if the weather had followed suit with the dramatics of my life over the last few months, going from burning and torturous to cool and serene.

We took our time with our ice cream, bickering over whose flavor was better. He had decided the only way to settle the debate was through a series of kisses, where we could taste each other's choices in the most delicious way. We never did agree on a favorite, but we certainly enjoyed the experiment.

Once finished, we just sat there, hand in hand, talking. The topics flowed from thinking of senior year to planning our first hiking trip together for the following weekend. I don't know what pulled my attention toward the street, but as I turned my gaze, I noticed another couple coming toward us. Like us, they were hand in hand, smiling and laughing, enjoying the day. But it wasn't the commonality that froze me where I sat. It was the fact that it was the first time I had faced Braelyn since our final passing in the halls at school more than a month ago.

She was hand in hand with Liam, and for a moment, she was oblivious to my presence. She looked happy, light, and free, much like I was feeling, and it made the guilt that still hid in the pits of my stomach both lessen and surge. I missed her so much and had been trying to go through the six steps of getting over someone to work my way through the loss of our friendship. But, much like with my application of the steps on Seth, I wasn't doing too well.

As if feeling my stare, she turned and met my gaze. Even from behind her sunglasses, I could see her eyes widen, her mouth stalling in her sentence as she stopped in her tracks. Liam jerked to a halt, turning back to question her, before following her line of sight and finding Seth and I sitting a few paces away.

We watched each other from a distance for a long time. Each minute passed by, bringing with it the next, but neither of us moved to speak or to walk away. I was too afraid to do anything, for fear that my choice would not be the same as hers. That if I moved, I would frighten her away, another opportunity for healing lost.

After a moment, she turned to Liam, saying something that only he could hear. He nodded at her before kissing her cheek and stepping up to the ice cream counter. To my surprise, she walked toward me, holding my gaze.

"I think I'm going to go say hi to Liam, okay?" Seth asked, squeezing my hand.

I nodded, keeping my eyes on Brae as she closed the final distance between us. She spared Seth a glance as they passed, showing no signs of emotion to his presence, before turning back to me.

Now that she was closer, I took a moment to observe the small changes in her. Her hair was shorter, bleached lighter from the sun. Her skin was tanned all over, perfectly golden against the white sundress she wore. She was as beautiful as ever, and even now I couldn't help but feel a little less pretty standing next to her. Old habits died hard.

It was Brae who broke the silence first.

"Hey."

I almost cried with elation when she spoke to me. "Hi."

"Can I sit?" she asked, tentatively. It was only then that I realized she thought I would say no. That she might actually be as nervous about this as I was.

Unable to form words, I nodded before watching her lower herself into the seat Seth had vacated.

We stared at each other for a while. Slowly taking stock of the person we knew better than ourselves. I wondered if I looked as different to her as she did to me. Little things, the kind of changes you wouldn't normally notice unless you spent time apart.

After a few moments, she turned to look over her shoulder toward the boys, who were talking comfortably by the counter a few yards away. It was shocking to me how boys could just move past drama so easily with nothing more than a clap on the back and a handshake, while girls always seemed to struggle to find the words to express how they felt. Maybe that was because girls always felt the need to use so many words, while boys had the gift of unspoken understanding.

"So. You two are together now, I guess?" she said, breaking the silence. There was no bitterness, no blame in her tone. Merely a question.

"Yes."

She nodded before turning back to me. "You look good together."

"Do you mean that? Or are you—"

"I mean it," she interrupted. "Seriously, Hannah. You guys are perfect together. I guess I always kind of knew that. I think that's why it hurt so much when I found out he liked you. Because even I always thought you were the better fit."

The sincerity and honesty in her voice broke a dam inside me, weeks of missing my best friend and apologies came crashing forward.

"Brae, I am so sorry for everything. I never meant to hurt you or for any of this to happen. You're my best friend and I would never intentionally do something to hurt you or to make you think that you don't mean everything to me."

"I know." She nodded, swallowing back her own emotions. "Hannah, I'm so sorry for how I acted. I was just so shocked when I found you guys, I freaked out. I had already wondered if he had broken up with me for you, only because I knew how perfect you guys would be together and figured eventually he would realize it too. My anger was never really at you, though, and I know you didn't mean for me to find out like that. I just wish you had told me sooner."

"I was scared to," I admitted. "I didn't want you to hate me."

"I could never hate you," she said quickly. "I might be mad at you, but I could never hate you. Besides, I want you to be happy." She paused, tilting her head. "Does he make you happy?"

I considered the weighted question but knew it was not asked out of malice.

"Yes."

Brae smiled. "Then that's all I could ask for."

I burst into tears at the same time she did, the two of us jumping out of our seats and into each other's arms. We cried and hugged, rocking each other back and forth while Liam and Seth watched us with curious, bewildered expressions. It had been so long since I had hugged her, I relished every second in the familiarity of her embrace.

"Thanks for the birthday present, by the way," she said against my hair. "We were planning on using the coupons today actually," she added with a laugh.

Pulling back, I sniffed indelicately. "I'm sorry I didn't come to the party. I just didn't think you would want me there and didn't want to ruin it."

"I did want you there," she admitted. "But I understand why you didn't." She laughed as she brushed a lock of hair behind her ear. "I ate the whole freaking bag of Twizzlers in a week."

I snorted at her with a roll of my eyes. "You always were the stress eater."

"Rude," she laughed, pushing my shoulder.

We laughed with relief, taking in the sight of each other like we had been starved of it. No matter what we went through, or what happened, she would always be my best friend. Her absence from my life had been tangible, and even though we both played a role in reaching such a low point, I couldn't deny the liberation of finally finding our footing again.

"I'm sorry," I said once more, feeling the need to make sure she heard it.

She smiled. "Good thing we have a rule to always forgive each other, huh?"

I chuckled before reaching out and pulling her back into my arms. "Definitely."

EPILOGUE

_____

* One Year Later *

Every nerve was alive as I followed the gravel path, my senses heightened, eyes trained on the trees that lined either side of the narrow walkway. Taking a deep breath of the warm, summer air, I concentrated on the gentle crunch of stone beneath my feet and the soft sound of chatter coming from all around us. The sun was setting to the west, casting a soft, muted hue across the grass. Through the trees, I saw the faint glow of the sun coloring the clouds in beautiful shades of orange, blue, and red. It was the perfect hour to arrive here, and by the crowds that were gathering, it would seem that many others had the same idea.

Glancing to my right, I found Brae, with the same expression of wide-eyed awe, mesmerized by the sights and sounds of the city around us. The skin around her eyes was colored a faint bluish purple, evidence of her exhaustion, and I knew I looked the same. We had arrived that morning after an almost physically painful overnight flight, but from our first steps onto the Paris streets, neither of us felt our fatigue any longer.

All we felt was contentment, excitement, and pride.

We had made it. To Paris, but also through one of the hardest things I think our friendship would ever have to endure. Neither of us ever expected a boy to come between us. That was something that happened on television as a popular trope of love triangles or on reality shows for ratings. But never in real life, and definitely not to us. If you could have asked us two years ago, we would have told you it was impossible.

But, as it would turn out, nothing was impossible.

The weeks that followed our first official run-in after our fallout were a little awkward, a little tense, but also like a wave of relief had washed over me. After struggling against my happiness with Seth but the pain of losing Brae, I didn't know what to feel. As it would turn out, she felt the same; happy with Liam, but missing me. Despite the words said and the hurt we caused each other, we were determined to work through it. We all had to begin again, rebuilding over the foundations of what we broke by following our hearts.

It took some time, but Brae and Seth finally reached a place where they could be happy for each other. So much so that Brae even gave Seth her blessing, mixed in with a firm warning that if he ever broke my heart, he would have to answer to her. He took it all in stride, laughing like it was a joke and friendly teasing, but I knew full well she meant every word.

Liam, as it would seem, was Brae's perfect match. He indulged her often, but unlike those that came before him, he didn't let her have her way all the time. And, to everyone's surprise, it only seemed to make Brae fall for him harder. Having someone strong at her side, who balanced her impulses much like I did, turned out to be exactly what she needed in a partner.

For Seth and I, finally being able to be together after all this time felt almost too good to be true. Like something straight from the pages of a romance novel; star-crossed lovers finally finding their way together was more of fiction than reality. Our first summer together was the most romantic time of my life as I learned to love him for everything he was and not just the parts I admired from a distance. Seth liked to remind me of our Romeo and Juliet beginnings and that our love would not end tragically, simply because of clear communication, a little determination, and his willingness to scale the wall outside my window.

Braelyn, for the first time in her life, was living for herself rather than letting social status and reputation dictate her every move. It was as if her breakup with Seth changed her, as she no longer worried about rumors or what other people thought. She still held the highest social standing of the senior class, but she didn't wear it like a shield, focusing on it incessantly to the brink of obsession. Her mother was still difficult, the voice in Brae's ear to always look perfect, be perfect, for fear of a fall from grace. But for the first time in her life, Brae made her decisions for herself rather than for what others would think of her.

For me, I finally learned what it meant to speak up for myself, to stand up for what I wanted, and to be my own person. For years, I was focused only on what others wanted and how I could make sure everyone else was happy, even if it meant my own desires came second. By admitting how I felt for Seth, by finally speaking out and being honest to both him and Brae, I was able to break the chains that held me down. I was still a work in progress as far as standing up for myself was concerned, but I was growing. And that was all that really mattered.

Breaking through the trees, Brae and I stepped into a clearing of expansive grass and lamp posts. Immediately, our attention was drawn to our left, to the iconic structure dominating the Champs de Mars. Goosebumps rose along my skin at the sight, a smile breaking out across my face that made my cheeks hurt.

Wandering toward a small fountain, the ground sloped toward its base, we spread out the blanket I had tucked under my arm before setting down the cheese, bread, and strawberries we had picked up at a market by our hotel. Finally settled, we leaned back and watched the sights before us with quiet reverie.

Gently, Brae slid her hand into mine.

"We actually made it here," she mused, staring at the Eiffel Tower with the same sense of awe as I felt. "It feels so weird to *actually* be here. I mean, we've been talking about this for so long, I think part of me never thought we would make it. I can't wait to do everything we planned. The Louvre, the pastries, the Champs-Élysées."

I nodded, turning to her with a grin. "Even meeting a sexy French stranger?" I teased.

To this, she laughed. "Nah. I don't need grand romantic gestures anymore. Besides, this is *our* trip, and no boys are going to come between us."

ACKNOWLEDGMENTS

What started as nothing more than a title during a long commute home from work, has officially become a book, and it never could have gotten here without an army of incredible people.

Thank you to my husband, Craig, for supporting me in everything I do. Whether it is my goals in the arts, academia, or simply the challenges of life, you are always there to hold my hand and have my back, and I know I wouldn't be here without you. I love you.

To my mother, Alice, whom this book is dedicated to, you encouraged me my whole life to chase after impossible dreams, and I am achieving them because of you. You gave me opportunities and adventures I will cherish for a lifetime and are truly my best friend. Now, you can not only say "I'm the mother of an author" but "I have a book dedicated to me." And to my stepdad, John, for your unfailing support, optimism and your never-ending patience. We are all Team John!

Elana Gibson, my incredible editor, who held my hand and calmed my fears throughout not one, but two books. Your insight, expertise, and passion for my work gave me the courage and confidence to keep going even when it felt impossible. Thank you!

To the entire CamCat Books team: Sue, Helga, Gabe, Nicole, Maryann, Laura, Abigail, Bill, Meredith, and anyone I may have forgotten, thank you for taking a chance on yet another of my stories and for helping me achieve my dreams. And to my amazing copyeditor, Bridget McFadden, thank you for being my grammar and punctuation police!

Through my debut journey in 2023 I was fortune enough to be included with some truly incredible authors launching our stories into the world that year. The support, encouragement, advice, and love we share extends beyond debut year, and I am so fortunate to have entered this crazy journey with you all! Lauren Thoman, Mia Tsai, Edward Underhill, Jenna Miller, JR Dawson, Neely Alexander, Federico Erebia, Justine Pucella Winans, Elisa Leahy, Al Hess, RaeChell Garrett, EM Anderson,

Robin Alvarez, Jackie Khalilieh, Khadijah VanBrakle, Hannah Fergesen, and so many more, #2023debuts for life!

I have been incredibly fortunate to have some of the most supportive friends in the world, who kept me going when this journey felt too difficult. Morgan Shamy, my official book sister and an eternal publishing optimist, you are a talented, kind, beautiful soul, and I am so thankful to have you as a friend. To the GTGH crew, Erin, Sherry, and Helen, thank you for the laughs, the tears, and the family we've formed across the globe. Katie, Lynn, Maui, Brenda, Elaine, Bailee, Iliana, Nic, Nat, and so many others . . . THANK YOU!

Lastly, thank you to the readers, those who love stories and seek adventures in the pages. Here's to many more to come!

ABOUT THE AUTHOR

————

Kristi McManus is a registered nurse, photographer, and writer. She has always been drawn to writing since the age of 10 when she was tasked with rewriting a fairy tale. After selecting "Little Red Riding Hood" and retelling the story from the point of view of the wolf as a misunderstood hero, she fell in love with storytelling.

Finding her passion again in adulthood, she has dabbled in adult, young adult, romance, fantasy, and non-fiction and was a featured and #1 ranked author on Wattpad. *Our Vengeful Souls*, her debut young adult fantasy villain origin tale, was published in summer 2023.

Kristi enjoys any form of creativity, runs a small photography business, loves travel, and is slowly checking items off her bucket list. You can find her on Twitter and Instagram at @kristimcmanus or check out her website at kristimcmanus.ca.

If you liked Kristi McManus's

HOW TO GET OVER YOUR (BEST FRIEND'S) EX,

you'll enjoy
Lindsay K. Bandy's

INEVITABLE FATE

CHAPTER ONE

———

If life was a highway, Evan Kiernan's consisted of riding shotgun while his mother inched along in the right lane of I-95, looking for an exit so his little sister could pee.

This time, they were headed to Manhattan. It should have only been a two and a half hour drive from Lancaster, Pennsylvania, but in Evan's experience, what *should be* rarely translated to reality. For example, kids *should* know who their fathers are. Diamond rings (plural) *should* lead to weddings (preferably singular), instead of pawn shops and moving trucks (plural). Five-year-olds *should* have a greater bladder capacity, and seventeen-year-olds *should* still be in high school—not riding shotgun while their mothers drive them to freshman move-in day at NYU.

But maybe, for once, Evan Kiernan was about to be exactly where he should be. According to his mother, the Promising Young Artist program was his destiny, as if the sparkle-winged gods of the arts had arranged for his early college acceptance. Really, it was her, conspiring with his art teacher, Mr. Burns, to fill out the application behind his back. Evan had been sure he had no shot in hell at getting into the elite program, which accepted one upcoming senior. *One.* But somehow, against all odds, they'd chosen him. He was still convinced it was some sort of mistake, due to his mother's exaggerated belief that her son was exceptional and Mr. Burns' flair for the dramatic.

But the written application wasn't the main criteria. His portfolio had gotten him into the program, and he couldn't deny being proud of that, even if he wasn't sure he was really Greenwich Village material. And as Hailey kicked the back of his seat in time with *Look What You Made Me Do* on the radio and wailed about needing to pee for the thousandth time, he couldn't deny that it would be amazing to have a little time to himself for once.

"Rest stop ahead!" his mom exclaimed, removing her hands from the steering wheel to applaud as she read the sign. "One more mile, okay, Hails? Envision the desert. *Be* the camel, baby." She brought her thumbs and forefingers together as if meditating before taking hold of the wheel again.

Evan glanced at the speedometer. They were crawling along at six miles per hour. He ran a hand through the dark curls flopping into his eyes, then pressed his palm against the freshly trimmed sides, trying to ignore the small feet pounding his back. The song switched to *God is a Woman*, and when his mother started singing along with Ariana Grande, he cringed and tried to go somewhere else—anywhere else—in his mind. He could have envisioned the desert, or been the camel, but instead, he went back to Advanced Drawing class.

To the day he drew *her*.

The drawing that changed everything.

It was the first day at Pennwood High School. They'd just moved out of their mother's ex-fiancée Dave's house and into a little Cape Cod with peeling white paint and a picket fence missing a few teeth.

That morning, he'd pulled rumpled jeans and a black-and-red flannel shirt from the box at the foot of his bed, wishing for another ten years of sleep. Hailey had woken him multiple times through the night, scared and disoriented in her new room. His mom was downstairs already, in her bathrobe and slippers, cooking the traditional fresh-start breakfast/peace offering. He wondered, sometimes, if she'd chosen the realty profession just to have the inside scoop on immediately available rental properties.

"You want me to iron your shirt?" she'd asked over her shoulder while flipping a pancake.

"Nah." He gave her a sideways hug with one arm and reached for the coffee pot with the other.

She rubbed her cheek where his had brushed against it. "You should shave."

"I can't find the razors," he said, even though he hadn't really looked. "It's fine."

"Come on." She cracked an egg into sizzling butter. "Don't you want to make a good first impression?" She said it a little too brightly, and even without his contacts in, he could see from the puffiness of her eyes that she'd been crying already this morning. He wanted to throttle Dave.

First impressions had lost their charm years ago, but transferring to Pennwood had been easy enough. After reviewing his portfolio the previous week, the head of the art department had agreed to place him in Advanced Drawing, Ceramics, and Advanced Painting Techniques.

"Honestly," Mr. Burns had said during Evan's registration appointment, glancing between his sketchbook and his mother. "He's probably more advanced than the staff here. Have you considered art school?"

"He's always been exceptional," his mom had gushed, while Evan looked at his shoes. She'd insisted he be tested for the gifted program in kindergarten, and ever since, she'd been using that word. *Exceptional.* She might as well have called him an alien. Exceptional was just another word for different. He'd read somewhere that all great artists and writers feel that they experience the world fundamentally differently from everyone else, and he assumed that's why so many great artists became alcoholics and vagrants and mental patients. But Evan liked Mr. Burns, whose easy smile didn't seem to be covering up psychotic tendencies. And best of all, he was gay, which meant his mom wouldn't be trying to line up any dates with another one of his art teachers.

His first assignment in Advanced Drawing class was to draw a face entirely from memory, so Evan closed his eyes and tried to picture Hailey. He couldn't believe how hard it was to conjure up a detailed image of his own sister's face. She had brown eyes like his, but how far apart were they in relation to the corners of her mouth? Her nose was . . . kid-sized, but what was the exact shape? Glancing around at his classmates' work, they seemed to be having the same problem, laughing at each other's attempts to draw friends or teachers from other classes. People they recognized, but who were all strangers to him.

Mr. Burns went behind his desk to pop a CD into an ancient-looking stereo system, and suddenly the deep thrum of electronic trance music transformed the atmosphere of the room. The rhythm became hypnotic as the beats per minute steadily increased, and the notes blurred, like a dream. Evan stared at the backs of his eyelids, feeling like he was lost in some sort of European dance club. He tipped his chin toward the ceiling, and flashes of red flared through the darkness. Splotchy afterimages danced like flames, like the time they went camping with Dave and Hailey wouldn't quit shining a flashlight in his face and gave him a migraine.

But then slowly, like a Polaroid picture, a pair of eyes began to develop. Not brown and familiar. Not his mom's or his sister's or anyone's from his old school. These eyes were a startling jade green, peering at him around a huge, heavy black door.

A girl.

Her nose and the apples of her cheeks were sprinkled with freckles, and her mouth was open in a tiny gasp of surprise, revealing a small space between her two front teeth. She was frozen in this expression, as if he'd knocked on her door and snapped a photograph as she opened it, shocked to find a stranger there.

He was afraid that if he opened his eyes, he'd lose the image, so he fumbled for a pencil and began drawing furiously without looking at the paper. Who was she? Why was she opening the door? Would she invite him in? He didn't want to be a stranger to this girl.

But as soon as he finished the last wavy strand of her soft, black hair, it was as if the door closed.

The sound of murmuring and stools scraping the floor brought him back. When he opened his eyes, the whole class was gathered around his table, staring in silence.

It was only pencil, but the luminosity of the eyes was apparent even without color. He'd captured the girl's surprise, and there was something so perfectly adorable about it.

"Who is she?" someone whispered.

Evan opened his mouth, then closed it again. He couldn't tell an entire classroom full of seniors that he had no idea who she was. Not on his first day at a new school. Probably not ever.

"Just . . . a girl I used to know," he said with a shrug, and looked into her pencil-drawn eyes again, overcome with a sense of wonder.

She was beautiful, but not in a magazine cover way.

She was beautiful because she was so . . . so . . . real.

And that, he knew, was ridiculous, because she was absolutely not real. He was sure he'd never seen that girl before in his life.

He would have remembered.

Ten months later, here he was, pulling into a rest stop in New Jersey with his mom and sister on his way to NYU because of her. *The Green-Eyed Girl*, painted life-sized in oil, became the centerpiece of his portfolio. The piece that earned the attention of his program mentor, Dr. Vanessa Mortakis.

Absolutely luminous, she'd called it in the acceptance letter. *Intensely realistic and gorgeously sensitive. I can't wait to work with you in New York.*

When Dr. Mortakis strode into the admissions office later that afternoon, Evan exchanged a surprised glance with his mom: Hourglass figure in a tight black dress, glossy ebony hair to her waist, and blood-red heels that defined her calves beyond professional levels. None of that had shown up in her headshot.

"Evan Kiernan!" she exclaimed warmly, as if greeting an old friend. "Welcome to NYU!"

"Thank you so much." He shook her cool, slender hand, and her delicate bracelets jangled. "This is my mom, Melissa. And my sister, Hailey."

"You must be so proud," Dr. Mortakis said, clasping hands with Evan's mother, then bending down to shake with Hailey, too. "And you must be really proud of your big brother."

Hailey bounced up on her toes and nodded, and Evan felt a twinge in his chest. Ever since the acceptance letter arrived, his mom had been waving off his concerns about the cost of after-school care for Hailey and who would drive her to ballet or tuck her in when their mom had to work late. *You're her brother, not her dad*, she kept insisting. *It's your job to grow up and live your life. It's my job to take care of the two of you. Okay?*

"You are cute as button!" Dr. Mortakis exclaimed, booping Hailey's nose, and she giggled. Clearly, the professor hadn't been along for the car ride.

"He's so good with her," his mom bragged as they took their seats in the admissions office. "He even illustrates little stories for her."

Dr. Mortakis' eyes brightened. "Really? Well, we have an excellent illustration department. That could be a great option for you."

MORE FANTASTICAL READS FROM CAMCAT BOOKS

CamCat Books

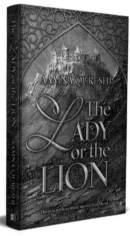

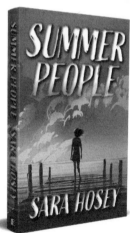

Available now, wherever books are sold.

CamCat
Books

VISIT US ONLINE FOR MORE BOOKS TO LIVE IN:
CAMCATBOOKS.COM

SIGN UP FOR CAMCAT'S FICTION NEWSLETTER FOR
COVER REVEALS, EBOOK DEALS, AND MORE EXCLUSIVE CONTENT.